Oh, Say Can YOU SEE

Contents

For the dreamers of 250 years ago.
And to the dreamers still ahead.
May we carry that same courage.

Stars & Stripes
Tournament Rosters

Dear Reader,

Welcome to our *Stars, Stripes, and Hockey Nights* series created in celebration of America's 250th birthday. This world has been such a joy to build, and this story an absolute thrill to write. Thank you for being here and stepping onto to the ice with us. Below is the complete roster for each team. For a full cast of characters featured in my book, be sure to flip to the back.

Enjoy the game,

J.P.

Stars & Stripes Tournament Rosters

West Stars				East Stripes			
#2	F	Rohan Kirkat	MON	#1	G	Noah Wilcott	NY
#6	C	Dante Leinecker	SEA	#2	D	Baptiste Marchand	NY
#7	C	*A Wyatt Hartman	UTA	#4	C	*C Taz Houlihan	BOS
#9	RW	Holden Prescott	MIN	#5	D	Carson Seeley	PHI
#11	LW	Jeremiah Precio	IRV	#8	LW	James Adler	NY
#12	LW	Luke Ryder	MIN	#11	C	Chase Sullivan	CHA
#14	D	Xavier Schwann	DEN	#13	D	Diego Alvarez	TB
#16	LW	Kingston Brewer	DEN	#17	RW	Jackson Reeves	BRV
#17	F	Mario Sanchez	SEA	#19	C	*A Caleb Hawthorne	NY
#21	LW	Erik Schultz	UTA	#21	LW	Adam Lombardi	DET
#22	D	*C Tyson Lane	MIN	#27	F	Casimir Citronov	MIA
#23	G	Joel Kitcher	DAL	#28	RW	Maxime Beaumont	NY
#25	D	Dashiell DiFranco	UTA	#29	LW	Camden Floquette	MIA
#26	D	Bryce Chambers	DEN	#31	G	Blake Davis	BOS
#27	C	Micah Lemon	NEB	#32	LW	*A Jayce Brady	TB
#29	G	Josh Henson	UTA	#33	C	Liam Maddox	BOS
#31	C	*A Levi Nyberg	ANA	#34	F	Christian Lopez	MIA
#37	RW	Neal Sanderson	NEB	#35	RW	Whittaker Hayes	DET
#43	RW	Colt Bradley	DAL	#44	D	Aaron Miles	NY
#47	RW	Jake Twiles	NEB	#47	RW	Declan Nash	BRV
#53	D	Sean Abercorn	MON	#64	D	Tore Aaberg	PIT
#58	D	Ted Powell	NEB	#70	D	Otto Stagmeier	NJ
#77	D	Stone Reilly	MIN	#72	G	Josef Svenson	BOS
#86	D	Paxton Blackburn	NOL	#94	D	Nick McDonough	PIT
#88	G	Jason Dexter	DEN	#97	D	Burke Masters	DET

*F=Forward C=Center LW=Left Wing RW=Right Wing D=Defense G=Goaltender *C=Captain *A=Alternate Captain*

Stars, Stripes, and Hockey Nights: A sweet hockey romantic comedy series where hockey isn't just a game—it's an American tradition. This summer, celebrate our nation's 250th birthday with the swooniest hockey all-stars as they take the ice in a festive exhibition tournament.

When USA's top NHL stars arrive in Washington, DC, they're competing for more than a championship title. Between face-offs and slap shots, these all-American heroes find themselves taking their biggest risk yet—falling in love. Expect prank wars, locker room banter, fireworks—on and off the ice—and sparks that light up more than the scoreboard.

Each book in this closed door romcom series is a complete standalone, featuring a different hockey hero taking his shot at forever. Because love isn't just won in the arena—it's written in the stars and stripes of the heart.

Let the fireworks begin!

Blurb

She has always been my always, but I'm still her someday.

Tyson Lane

Lottie's the only woman I've ever seen.

My best friend's little sister, a.k.a. the senator's daughter, who is forbidden to date hockey players because it will destroy her mom's perfect image.

Lottie, the one girl I wasn't supposed to fall for, but, whoops, I did, a long time ago.

I almost kissed her once, but she made it clear she wasn't interested and moving to DC forever.

For five long years, I tried to get over her. Every. Day.

Imagine my surprise when I'm called to play for a hockey tournament to celebrate our nation's birthday, and I find out I'm spending my summer in DC—right where she is.

It doesn't take long for me to see I still have a serious case of loving Lottie. Something else hasn't changed. Her mother still hates me and devises a plan to keep us apart. But my country hasn't picked me to wear a jersey for no reason. If an entire nation can trust me to fight for victory, I must believe in myself.

Between the pressure of games and the late-night fireworks—I'm not talking about the ones in the sky—I've decided I'm not backing down.

Not on the ice.

And not with Lottie.

Lottie Halloway

My mother says Ty will ruin my future. My heart says he's the only future I want, and someday we'll find a way to be together.

Five years ago, I chose the easy path. I pretended he didn't matter, hoping that if I ignored the sparks long enough, the fire would burn out.

Now Ty's in DC for our nation's birthday, and it doesn't take long to find out the feelings I buried are more explosive than ever.

My mother still expects me to walk the line she drew for me. But I'm finally realizing that "someday" has a deadline. I have to choose: her expectations, or the man I can't afford to lose again.

Oh, Say Can You See is a brother's best friend, sweet hockey romcom. It's a complete standalone that's part of a multi-author shared world, Stars, Stripes & Hockey Nights.

One

Tyson Lane

July 3, 2021

IF ANYONE ASKS, YOU *can* die from shock.

A breath whooshes out of me as my jaw tightens before I can stop it. Ramming against my chest, my heart ceases pumping as my body goes frozen.

It's clearly rigor mortis kicking in.

I'm on the brink of death, teetering between two worlds. I grab my throat as my eyes bug out of my head, and my mind erases everyone in the room...but her. Even though she's clear across the room, a spotlight beams hot on my beautiful queen.

Sitting on a barstool—one she definitely shouldn't be sit-ting on—is my best friend's little sister, otherwise known as the love-of-my-life-who-doesn't-know-it-yet. With an angel of a face framed by high cheekbones and arched eyebrows, she could pass for twenty-five, but that's not the point. She's still weeks from being twenty-one. I know that for a fact because I've had her birthday, July twenty-ninth, memorized for ten years. Her legs are crossed like she's been sitting on barstools for years, but that's not the worst of it.

The worst: She's leaning toward some guy in a polka-dot bow tie.

My ribs are kicked.

Seriously?

Who wears a bow tie to a lake bar?

Hardly a slice of air remains between their bodies as he wraps his sleazy arm around her. Tightening my hands into fists, I force a shallow breath through my throat. He doesn't know he's risking his life by standing too close to her in front of me. I glare at Ham—short for Hamilton. Don't ask. His parents are in politics. I won't create a scene, but surely Ham will put a stop to that creep touching his sister.

Ham hasn't noticed Lottie yet, but I'm struggling to keep pace with him as he strides right past her toward the pool tables in the dimly lit back room. Lottie with Mr. Polka-Dot Bow Tie knocks something loose in my chest, and I can't walk straight. I drag my eyes away, pretending to study the pool tables. "She's not even twenty-one," I leak out, mostly to myself.

Ham frowns as his overgrown tawny mop of hair hangs long on his forehead, apparently blocking him from seeing this breaking news. "Who are you talking about?"

I jerk my chin toward the bar but do nothing to hide the snarl that curls my lip. His smile fades the second he sees Lottie. "Oh, no way. How'd she get in here?"

"I'm guessing with a fake ID." I fix my gaze onto the pool table, hoping to appear casual as I ask, "Who's the guy? He probably got it for her."

"Did I forget to tell you? That's Brett." Ham groans as his eyes bounce from him back to Lottie. "He's the new grad my mom hired for her campaign. I guess he doesn't have any family or friends or a life or whatever. Since my mom is a control freak who believes in working her staff to death, she invited him to Mapleton for the holiday to help with the parade and fundraising events. Thankfully, he got a room at the resort and is not staying at our house, or I'd lose it."

Still trying to play it cool, I force a good-natured laugh. My throat is so tight that I end up choking and have to cough to catch my breath. "So Brett? And he's in politics. I guess that explains the bow tie."

"Not sure." We hang back for a second, staking them out. Ham's eyes narrow on the guy. Mine are probably doing the same. My mind is reeling faster than my heart is pounding.

The Fourth of July is our thing.

Mine and Lottie's.

It's not written in stone, but close enough. We literally carved it in the oak tree trunk behind her family's lake home. It's still there. Well, at least I think it's still there. I haven't exactly checked. Now that I think about it, I have half a notion to grab her hand, rip her away from that barstool—where Mr. Bow Tie is hanging all over her—and drive her back to the rotten stump so she can read what we carved all those years ago.

Always July.

That's what it says.

That's been our thing…to spend every July here since we were in grade school. Yet, even though it's our thing, here she is with Mr. Bow Tie—who, may I add, has the lankiest, scrawniest arms. I don't doubt for a second that she could take him in an arm-wrestling match.

And the worst part is, nobody warned me. Had I known she was bringing a date to *our sacred event*, I'd have stayed far away. Ham grabs a pool cue. "Let's shoot a game."

I nod, though my focus keeps drifting. Every laugh from her direction cuts through the music like a blade. We don't speak as Ham sets up the table and takes the first shot. Two shots into the game Lottie's voice rises. I know all her inflections. She's clearly annoyed when she blurts, "Maybe just give me a second."

In unison, Ham and I glance over. The guy's literally crowding her with one hand braced on the bar and the other on the back of her stool. When he doesn't budge, I do. My cue hits the table, and I stalk across the room before Ham can blink. "Hey there, Bow

Tie." I step up behind them. "You heard her. I think you might need to take a step back."

The guy scans me, sizing me up. His dark eyes blaze as he huffs, "We're just talking."

"Ty." Lottie's eyes flash when she recognizes me. "It's fine. I don't need your help."

"Are you sure about that?" My voice comes out rasping, how it always sounds when I'm fueled by adrenaline. "You know you shouldn't even be in here."

Ham marches up on her other side, and his hand lands on Lottie's shoulder. "Ty's right. Mom will kill you if you get caught underage at a bar. You know what that will do to her approval rating. Let's go. It's late, and we have to be presentable for her campaign parade float tomorrow, remember?"

"I'm not ready to leave." Stubborn as ever, Lottie lifts her chin.

"Fine." Ham opens his mouth as if he wants to argue, but instead he sighs. "Learn the hard way." He turns to me. "I'm not sticking around until she gets caught. The press will blame me for contributing. I'm leaving. You ready?"

I start to say yes.

I should go.

He's right.

Though Ty and I are a legal twenty-two, we aren't drinking. We came here only for the free pool, but the press hounds his family over every little thing they do. If Lottie gets busted for being in the bar underage, somehow we'll get blamed for it. I glance at the exit, but Lottie laughs at something Bow Tie whispers in her ear, and it yanks me back. Everything in my chest burns because something isn't right about this guy. He's clearly not looking out for her best interests when he brought her here, since she's underage. Playing it cool, I slide my feet toward the pool table and say, "Nah, I'll stay to pocket all these balls."

Ham gives me a look I can't read. I've never told him I have feelings for Lottie. Sometimes I think he has to know. I'm not exactly the coolest guy at hiding these things. "Okay," he mutters. "I'll grab an Uber and leave you the Land Rover in case Lottie needs a ride too."

My eyes bounce from him to Lottie, where I can't help but let them linger. "Yeah, I won't be too long."

He digs in the pocket of his cargo shorts, removes a leather key fob to the vehicle they share when they're in Mapleton and tosses it underhand. I snatch it out of the air one-handed as he turns and leaves. I get what he's doing. He manages security for his mom, and he never switches out of that mode. He's got a lot at stake if he gets in trouble, and he trusts me to take care of things.

I pick up my cue again, pretending to care about it, but my focus never leaves the bar. My gut was right about this guy, because only one song later, Bow Tie crowds Lottie again. Strain stamps her face as she leans away from him. My ear lasers in on what she's saying, but she's too far away from me, and the music is too loud. I settle for reading her lips, which is something I've become an expert in over the years. Her lips. Not in the way I would like to be an expert, but I can read her words. I don't miss a syllable as she grabs her phone and says, "I'm calling a ride."

That's it.

I toss the cue down for good and stride over. "What's this? I heard you need a ride?"

"Ty? I thought you left with Ham." With hesitation her gaze flicks from Bow Tie to me. Then she nods. "Yeah. Sure."

Stepping in between them, I bask in the opportunity to give Bow Tie a gentle nudge backward with my elbow to allow Lottie space to slide off her barstool. Not waiting for me, she quietly slips through the crowd and heads toward the door with her shoulders back. I'm right on her heels as the door closes behind us.

Outside, the air is sticky and warm, and we don't talk. Walking straight to the Land Rover, she fiddles with the bracelet on her wrist as I open the passenger door and stand back while she gets in. "You know I wasn't drinking," she says softly. "I wouldn't be that stupid."

"That's your business." I shut the door and run around to the driver's side and get in. I start the engine and remain quiet as I back out.

"I'm sorry, but you don't have to babysit me, you know," she mutters under her breath.

"I know," I say casually as my chest still burns with the visual of her with that guy. I pull forward and steer out of the parking lot. I'm not surprised the first thing she says is an apology. Sure, she should not be in the bar. Everything tells me it wasn't her idea. Due to her high-profile family, she and her brother are both meticulous rule followers. I wouldn't be surprised if she told Bow Tie not to even go there, but aside from being a rule follower, she's also a people pleaser who has trouble drawing the line. "You know, you say sorry too much."

That earns me a joyless scowl, which I use as an excuse to stare at her and index all the lines in her face. Not many. Just the disapproving one pinned between her brows. "What does that mean?"

I raise a shoulder and hold it there, pondering how much I want to say. After a few minutes of silence, I resign to the fact that it's better not to say anything. Her mother bred her to believe she's always the problem. If she's not apologizing for something someone else did, she's trapped in her alternate stage of existence of overthinking. She wasn't like that when I met her. Back then, she was bright-eyed and talkative. That changed when her mom got elected to the Senate, and every detail of her life became public knowledge.

Their anything-but-modest house is only a quarter mile down the road in the little town we grew up in. It's a modern two-story home, and one of the nicest in all of Mapleton, with several acres of wild grasses and the best deck-view of the lake. When we pull in, I drive onto the grass, leaving the driveway clear for her parents to back out. Ahead of us, the water stretches out, with the house dark, except for the porch light, indicating everyone's gone to bed. After killing the engine, I wrap one hand around the steering wheel and squeeze, staring straight ahead.

Neither of us moves. The engine ticks as it cools. "So, ah ... I hope I didn't ruin your date, but he looked like a tool."

"Seriously, what would you even know about him?" She sighs, her gaze following mine to the still water. "You looked at him for all of five seconds."

"That's all I need." This is infuriating, and I resist the urge to grind my molars—playing hockey defense my entire life has left my dental health at enough risk. "Trust me, he's not the one, Lottie. A guy in a bar in a bow tie is only capable of loving himself."

"He was dressed like a gentleman," she scoffs. It's not lost on me that she pulls her feet up on the seat and wraps her arms around her legs, like she's content sitting here for hours. We should go inside, but this is what we do. When the whole world sleeps, we find a way to each other, and we talk about anything and everything. For hours. I don't remember a time when we didn't connect this way.

It's why, in my heart, I know she's mine.

Maybe not yet, but someday. I feel it in every fiber of my soul. So much so that the thought of seeing her in a bar, trying to connect with Bow Tie, makes my chest physically ache. "That wasn't giving off gentleman." I maintain an even voice. "That was a sleazeball, and you need to be more careful about who you allow to take you out."

"Are you my dad now?" She rolls her eyes but still makes no move to leave the car. "Even Ham doesn't care this much, and he's my brother." Her voice trails off, and her lashes flutter gently, like she's struggling.

"That's right. He is your brother," I say softly, studying her side profile for any reaction. "But I'm your ... friend." I stumble over the last word; it doesn't convey the feelings I have for her. There isn't a word to describe the weird limbo of emotions I've been in with her.

Her jaw twitches, tipping me off that she is, in fact, struggling, and she maintains her straightforward stare fixed on the lake. "Right, you're my friend."

"Aren't I?" I level my gaze on her eyes, challenging her.

She accepts my challenge, turning her head to me. "You tell me, Ty."

My head jolts back in shock. *How dare she even ask?* We've been friends since she was nothing but knees and elbows. Even though these last few years the chemistry between us has been palpable, I've never said anything to indicate my feelings toward her. We are friends. That's what we are because she's always kept me at arm's length, insisting she didn't want to date anyone. Seeing her tonight with a date clearly means she changed her rule about dating. I guess I changed my rule about grinding my molars, because it's all I can do in the moment not to belt out my true feelings. It's complicated because we live in different states, and our synchronization, which used to be so easy, is always off now. Even with all the recent disconnect, the one thing that's always stayed the same is July, together here. It's an unspoken thing, where we come together and just vibe. Well, until this year, when she ruined it by bringing Bow Tie.

Dropping my gaze to my lap, I take a deep breath. This night needs a redo. More than anything, I look forward to this weekend all year. "Hey, I didn't mean to ruin your date or anything. I was hoping we could hang out like we always do over the Fourth. If I'd known you were bringing a date, I would have made other plans."

"Don't." Her voice is so soft it's hard to hear. "I want to hang out too, but it's not like you own me." Dropping her tone into a whisper, she adds, "Plus, I might have gotten nervous to see you this year."

The skin between my brows pulls tight—I am thoroughly confused, so much so I bleep out a chuckle. "Nervous for what?"

"I don't know." She raises her hand, tucking a long strand of hair behind her ear, giving me a front-row seat to her side profile. Stun. Ning. Yes, it's two words for stunning because one isn't enough to describe the absolute natural beauty she is with those pouty lips. I bite my lip, and she goes on, "You've changed so much since you started playing pro hockey. Like you're literally famous."

"I'm not famous." I shake my head. "And even if I was, it wouldn't change, you know, me being your ... friend."

"I guess I just wasn't sure. It's been weird. It was like whenever one of us called the other, we missed it, and it's been a year of phone tag."

"Yeah." I nod dramatically, because I hated that too. She's right about this year. No matter how many times we tried to talk, we always ended up missing each other. It was actually comical. Our timing was wrong. "What was up with that?"

"I don't know, but it was the worst." She's quiet as her gaze drifts down, where she finds a string at the hem of her shirt and flicks it with her thumb. In an even voice she adds, "I'm proud of you though. Not just about hockey, but you seem to be doing really well."

I continue studying her side profile as her bottom lip rolls under her top lip. I can't help but think that nothing feels wrong now. It's funny how you can go months without seeing someone, but the second you're with them again, it feels like no time has passed. That's how it feels with Lottie.

I forgot about Bow Tie already.

Well, come on—realistically, I will probably never let her live that one down.

"I missed you," she says softly but keeps her gaze level on her hem. She has to know the games she plays and what she does to me. I'm so over not being honest about my feelings. Frankly, tonight was a huge eye-opener for me. For years she always swore off dating, citing no need for that drama, but seeing her date right in front of me is a nightmare I don't care to experience again. I'm not waiting for Bow Tie to return and steal her from me.

"Same." I swallow and raise one side of my lips into a grin.

"Well, I think we were both stupid tonight. You ruined my date, but I think you were right, it was stupid for me to be there. Just please don't butt in like that again." Her tone is flat, as if warning me, but she slowly cuts a glance level with mine, and it quickly undoes me.

"I've done a lot of stupid things in my life but, Lottie, getting you away from Bow Tie wasn't one of them." The space between us tightens.

"There's no way you can know that," she snaps, glaring at me. "And besides, even if you did know, why do you care who I go out with?"

"I care because I know how guys are, and because I c-care about you." I trip over my words, then I abruptly stop, letting my statement hang there. I pray she hears it the way it's meant to be heard. Not that I care about her in the sense that she's my friend's little sister, but in the sense that whenever she's near, it's impossible for me to function. After a moment of the thickest silence I've ever felt, her eyes leave mine, dipping down to an unmissable angle that zeroes in on my lips.

And I'm dead.

I'm no longer thinking with my head, as a magnetism takes over, and before I know what's happening I lean in. Sitting next to each other, we were already close—but now we are so close her breath brushes mine. I've dreamed of so many versions of this moment, waiting for the nerve to finally make a move. It's nothing like my dreams. I'm far from relaxed. My pulse quickens as the oxygen drains from my lungs. She's not moving, and I freeze, giving her one more chance to resist—and that pause ends up being the death of me.

It's long enough for her to gasp, and her hand slides to the door handle as she breathes out, "Goodnight, Ty."

She slips out of the vehicle before I can make an audible reply.

"Night, Lottie," I say, loud enough for her to hear, though she doesn't respond. I stare after her as she slams the car door and hurries up the walk, alone, not waiting for me—clearly a warning to keep my distance.

I get it.

Maybe I get it?

I can't say she's not interested, because I can feel the tension when we're together, but it's complicated.

I hate that it's complicated.

Shaking my head, I yank on the door handle and follow her lead, even though she's already passing through the front door, clearly racing away from me. I don't know how much longer I can keep pretending she's just my best friend's little sister.

I don't know how to explain what she means to me.

It's just ...

She's meant to be mine.

When I was little, along with all the toys I wanted, I put her on my Christmas list every year. I didn't make it obvious, because my mom would see it, and she'd be all weird. I developed a code that only Santa would know, because he reads minds like that. It was a tree stump with the words "Always July" carved in it. My mom thought I just hated winter, and I was asking for summer year-round. It was the perfect code. Obviously, I don't believe Santa can help me with this anymore. My heart throbs in my chest, so hard I don't doubt it's bruising.

She's always been the queen of my heart.

Lottie deserves so much better than Bow Tie. She actually deserves someone so much better than *me*. Her mom has made that clear many times over the years, and maybe that's part of the reason she keeps her distance from me. It has to be. I'm not sure why Senator Halloway has it out for me. Sure, I'm welcome in their home, but there is always a clear boundary with Lottie; I'm Ham's friend, and that's where it stops. I'm not good enough to date her daughter. "Lottie is a political princess who doesn't date hockey players." She actually said that once out loud at the dinner table when they were talking about who was taking Lottie to prom. Ham suggested going with me as a friend since she didn't have a date. Her mom's disapproval is clearly one of the main reasons I've never gone for it, but if she's going to waste her time with losers like Bow Tie …

She needs to know she's better than him. She's honestly too good for most guys. She's so pure and sweet. The thought of anyone touching her makes my blood boil. I roll my hands into the tightest fists. I'm not going to beg. That's not my style, but she's clearly holding back, because she sees something in me that's not good enough too. Maybe her mom has convinced her? My stomach wrenches at the thought.

Something changed this last year; she's not who she used to be.

Lottie puts up a guard, but it's not a good one because she dropped it a little when we were in the car. I saw the way she looked at me for just a moment. I know deep down she has to want this too. She's just fighting it because for some reason she doesn't think I'm good enough. *Yet.*

That's it. I thrust my jaw forward and clench it, resisting the urge to whoop out loud. Raising my gaze to the heavens, calling God to be my witness, I vow, "I'm going to be good enough. I'll become the best man—one she will notice. One her mom can't ignore. One who has earned the respect of everyone. One who makes me worthy of loving...a queen."

Two

Lottie Halloway

D

AYLIGHT BURSTS THROUGH THE picture window, heating the side of my face like it's trying to burn away every secret from last night. I blink awake, discovering I'm lying on the den couch. Apparently, I face-planted here instead of going to my room. Groaning, I remember last night all too well. My mom forced me to take her new campaign manager out to dinner, to entertain him while he's here.

Everything was fine-ish until Ty came blazing over like a hot July storm cloud—emphasis on the hot part. I wasn't doing anything wrong, but his presence took me by surprise. I hadn't expected to be chastised by him. He was way too protective of me. Even when he wasn't talking to me, I felt his watchful gaze from the pool tables. It did something to me. Heat washes over my cheeks, and I have to fan myself just from the memory.

Pulling myself to a seated position, I rub a palm over my forehead. My head isn't pounding, but my thoughts are, as I instantly get a tangled replay of Ty's face in the car.

With one side of his face bathed in dark shadows, he had this whole dark-vibe thing that made him look insanely handsome—like a bad boy we both know he could never be. When he leaned in, eyes wild, to kiss me, I just gasped. We've been alone hundreds of times over the years, but he's never made a single pass at me before.

Not. One. Single. Time.

Not that I didn't want him to.

Or not that I hadn't imagined it.

Man, I've dreamed of that moment so many times.

I wasn't prepared for the change in his demeanor. Rubbing my hand on my forehead, I replay that gasp and how inexperienced I must have looked. I didn't even know I made any sound until I saw the look of disappointment in his eyes, like I'd pushed a knife into his chest. After that, I didn't know what to do.

So I fled.

So childish.

I shake my head as I push all the memories out. Last night was just an all-around, too-much-to-even-think-about night because...because my heart just can't go there.

Voices drift in from the kitchen. Ham's hoarse morning voice and Ty's lower one that always winds my stomach into twisting knots. It's no different this morning.

And someone else's. A woman I can't make out. What time is it? I glance around the room, even though I know there's no clock. Then, like I suddenly remember I have a phone, my gaze drops to the floor where it landed last night. I grapple for it and check the time. I don't miss the five unread text messages from Brett when I see it's after nine. Wow. I skip the messages from Brett. For now.

Or maybe forever.

I mean, what am I going to say to him? "So, about last night... you were sort of a creep, so ah, yeah, let's pretend that never happened." Oh, wait—we work together, so I still have to see him...every day. Doh!

I scrub a hand through my hair, hating I slept down here. With an open floor plan and the kitchen as the hub of all the rooms, I have to walk past everyone to get to my room. I can't hide forever, so I pad down the hall and slip into the half bath near the kitchen for a quick refresh. Just as I feared, I look a mess. I never even washed my face last night. Double-wear mascara has blackened all around my eyes, like I'm experimenting with some new gothic makeup. I splash water on my face and dab as best I can, but until I get makeup remover from my bag upstairs, it's pretty pointless. Giving up, I pat my face dry with the hand towel and head to the kitchen.

The smell of freshly brewed coffee and pancakes greets me. Ham is at the stove, of course—always the one concerned about filling his stomach. Already dressed for work, he's wearing dark pants and a black T-shirt. My parents aren't here, but that doesn't surprise me; I'm sure they had to get to the Fourth of July parade lineup early. Ty is at the round table with Maddie Malone, our mutual friend, who's in town for a horse event and staying in the guest room. Though they are sitting next to each other, I know Ty's not interested in her, because she's an ex-girlfriend of Taz, his hockey friend. Nonetheless, their cozy laughter irks me in a way it wouldn't have yesterday.

Maybe it wouldn't have bothered me yesterday.

Ty nonchalantly glances over his shoulder as I pass behind them. I try not to notice the deep smell of oak from his aftershave wafting off him. He's not one to overspray himself, but he's clearly just showered. The ends of his hair are damp by his ears, and he's wearing a fresh T-shirt and basketball shorts.

"Well, Lottie Dah, look who finally woke up from her traumatic night." My intestines loop as he deploys the nickname he's had for me for years, and his voice is soft enough for me to feel the secret message he's sending. Sure, he doesn't come out and say it, but I know his word choice alludes to what happened in the car.

"Hey, hello, ignore the hair." Forcing a joke to lighten the mood, I avoid his eyes and go straight for the full coffeepot on the counter.

Maddie turns toward me, looking fully awake as horse people who have been up since the break of dawn are prone to do. She's also wearing the cutest denim dress that sits above her knee, a contrast to my hot-mess couture. "What did you do last night?"

She's unaware of the situation, and I shoot her a look to drop it. Ham tilts his head, studying me in that big-brother way, assuming I've done something stupid. "Wait, what time did Brett bring you home?"

Before I can answer, Ty does it for me, still chewing on his pancake. "I brought her home right at midnight."

My heart stumbles as my mind instantly replays that awkward lean in. Or maybe I never stopped remembering it. It's been there all night. Am I going to remember that forever?

Possibly.

Especially since it's something I've dreamed about for years. I wanted to kiss him so badly my stomach hurt. Something about the timing of it made me not know how to act. I had literally just come from a date with Brett. It felt so rushed, like we missed a step. Maybe he thought we would casually hook up. I'm not that girl. Yeah, I've dreamed of kissing Ty so many times, but when I do, I'm NOT giving him back into the world of hockey fan girls swooning over him. He's going to have to lock it down better than that.

Ham's brow shoots up, interrupting my thoughts. "Please don't tell me something bad happened with Brett."

I groan as I grab a mug from the cupboard and fill it with the aromatic dark roast coffee. "Nothing happened. Brett was fine. I was ready to go, and it made sense to ride with Ty since we were going to the same place."

"Brett probably didn't even care if you made it home safely," Ty mumbles softly as he serves himself another pancake from the stack at the center of the table. Even though he's engaging in the conversation, his shoulders tighten, like he doesn't love hearing about Brett. Or maybe because last night sits heavy on him too.

I open the stainless-steel fridge to retrieve my favorite cinnamon dulce creamer. After dumping a generous amount into my mug, I return the creamer to the fridge. Then, because I don't want to appear as if I'm avoiding Ty, I force myself to slide onto a chair at the table, leaving an empty one between Ty and me.

I can't make this up, but it's like the whole right side of my body heats from his nearness. So much so that I lean away, bracing an elbow on the table as I do everything I can to avoid feeling his presence. It's no use. Not only is the memory of last night burned into my brain, but apparently his nearness now burns me too.

Maddie looks at me with that bestie look that says, "Girl I expect the full story ASAP!" I groan inwardly to not draw any more attention to myself. I'm not ready to voice what I'm thinking about.

Ham finishes frying the last of the pancakes and brings another full stack to the table, pulling up the chair next to me. "So, are you done with Brett?"

"What do you mean *done*? I wasn't ever *starting* him. Mom pressured me into going because he came all the way to Mapleton to help her, and he doesn't know anyone. She wanted me to make sure he had fun. Plus, why do you care?" I give him a side-eye. "It's not a big deal that we hung out. I sort of see him every day."

"Of course you do," Ham mutters through a full mouth of pancake. "Maybe that's all the more reason to avoid dating him."

Ty's jaw flexes. It's just once, but I catch how he locks it tight.

I shouldn't notice. Like I shouldn't notice the subtle ways Ty tenses up when I talk about any guy, even if it's just a guy I'm friends with … but I notice everything about him. If I'm honest with myself, I'd say I have similar reactions when I hear about him with another woman. It's seriously the most messed-up situation. Every summer since I was sixteen, I wondered if this would be the summer we finally cracked and dropped this invisible guardrail between us, but if anything, we've only drifted further away.

Maddie helps herself to a pancake before leaning toward me. "If anything untoward happened, I'll finish him. Just say the word."

As I picture her horse tossing Brett off his back and down a long, jagged cliff, I shrug, unable to stop my voice from rising. "Nothing happened. Everything was *fine*." I force the f in *fine* so hard my jaw drops open. Everyone's gaze locks on me, a little stunned by my mini outburst.

A cracking beat passes as everyone exchanges indiscreet looks. Ty sets down his fork and finally looks directly at me, and I swear I feel my hair expand at least another inch. Self-conscious, I run a palm over it. The unusual sharpness in his deep espresso-colored eyes takes me by surprise. And now, for the third—or is it the fourth—time I'm back in the car, his face inches from mine. My brain throbs with the memory of how close I came to leaning in.

Or maybe it's throbbing because I didn't lean in.

All I've wanted for years is for him to see me.

I just know my heart wouldn't have wanted to stop at one stolen kiss. I want it all. I want to be the girl he calls when something good happens. And something bad. I want to be the person who has inside jokes with him, and we make our holiday plans together.

I wasn't going to be a hookup.

I hope he doesn't think I'm into that.

I hope he's not into that.

I bite my lip, noticing that each year Ty gets a little more impossibly gorgeous than the last. It's absolutely maddening. And now it's awkward at the breakfast table, which is precisely the main reason why I can't cross that line with him. He's been my brother's best friend forever, and he's practically part of my family.

I raise the brim of my mug to my lips and sip, avoiding looking at Ty and Ham. It's hard to explain what it's like to have them around. Not only are they protective of me, but in some ways, I feel like they don't ever want me to live my life. Seriously, I went out last night, and they made it sound like I was robbing the bar—with explosives.

Maddie kicks me under the table, mouthing, "*TELL. ME. LATER.*"

My brow furrows as I mouth back, "*NOTHING. TO. TELL!*"

"Did you hear Dad resigned his position at the college, and he's officially moving full time to DC?" Ham leans forward with both elbows on the table. "He's retiring."

"I knew he was thinking about it, but I didn't realize he was doing it so soon." Unaffected, my tone stays neutral. It's been the plan for a long time to have him stay in Washington, DC with my mom as her career keeps exploding, and he already helps her enough. There's always a need to have the perfect trophy husband around.

"Wait. What?" Ty's gaze locks on Ham. "For real? Your parents are moving there full time?"

"I guess." Ham nods as he swallows his pancake and continues, "We're never here anymore. I don't know what they'll do with this house. Dad never really said. Maybe they will sell it. Mom only comes back here to show her face to the voters, but she also has a condo in Montpelier. Plus, it's surprising, but my dad enjoys puttering around the place in DC. Since my mom is a second-generation senator, her family has been collecting acreage around the main house for decades, and it's basically turned into a hobby farm. Dad's doing all kinds of things, even boarding horses in this new barn."

"It's always been a lovely spot," Maddie says with a faraway look in her eyes that tells me she's remembering a certain trail ride with Taz three years ago, back when they were dating and visited us there.

"Right," I agree, because it's the truth. My mom travels home to "make appearances" in Mapleton, where I grew up. She needs to engage the voters, but we've mostly been living in DC. The family compound has several houses to fit us all, and my work is there.

Ever since I graduated from high school, all my friends have gone different ways. Ty doesn't even live in Mapleton anymore, as he is living his best hockey career. He only returns around holidays to visit his family. "I would think he would sell it or maybe rent it out," I add. "There isn't a good enough reason to hold on to it."

Ty shoots me a look that lands straight in my gut. I know what he's thinking. We've spent every Fourth of July since we were kids in this house on the lake. It has to be a blow to him.

With an encouraging smile, Maddie breaks my thoughts, "You'll make new memories in DC, and I'll come visit you there."

"Yeah. I won't miss it here," Ham says before popping the last bite of pancake in his mouth.

"Wow, so this might be our last summer here." Ty's words are spaced, piecing them together in the slowest manner.

"Maybe," Ham says in a low tone, like he just figured that out too. "But you know you're always welcome to visit us in DC." He stands, grabs his empty plate, and takes it to the sink. "All right, who's riding with me to the parade lineup? We'd better get moving."

The air feels too heavy to leave the conversation like this, and I hesitate. Ty pauses at the exact same time. His eyes dart to me first, then back to Ham. Ham notices neither as he stretches his hands over his head and quickly speaks through his exhale. "Be in the Land Rover in fifteen minutes." He grabs his phone off the counter and heads upstairs.

Maddie pushes back her chair, grabbing her empty plate and slides it into the open dishwasher. "Well, that's my cue." She looks at Ty and then adds, "See you guys later." She heads out the door, letting a breeze of morning lake air drift into the room. As soon as she shuts the door, I'm all too aware it's just Ty and me.

I get up, keeping my gaze low. He clears his throat and starts in a low voice, "About last night—"

"Nope," I blurt as a flash of heat rises in my chest. "We're not doing that."

His eyebrows lift. "Doing what?"

"Talking about it." My words are oddly harsh, so I soften my tone. "There's nothing to talk about."

"Okay." His throat bobs, marking a swallow. "We don't have to talk about it." He doesn't look away, and since there's some sort of magnetic charge in the air, my gaze stays locked on him.

Who am I kidding? I couldn't look away if I tried. The air is literally dripping in tension. It's so hard to explain our relationship, because as much as I say he's just Ham's best friend, we have our own friendship. Things got complicated because he's always on the road. Then add into the mix that my family is always in DC. We said we'd keep in touch, but it's been tough. I'd catch snippets of the sport's coverage. I can't explain it, but it steals the air from my lungs to see all those girls fawning over him. Sure, I'm happy he's doing well, but it's hard not to assume he's changed.

It's hard not to wonder about all the girls.

I'd like to pretend he's still the shy boy who blushes when I compliment him. I can't fathom him dating those girls, or worse, having casual hookups. Vomit forms at the base of my throat at the mere thought. Not to mention the microscope I've been living under since my mom joined the Senate. I don't want him in that drama.

He shakes his head; his tone fills with what I can only describe as disappointment. "I can't believe you guys are thinking about selling the lake house. I always thought you'd return someday, once your mom was done with government." His inflection evens into something more nostalgic. "Remember what we carved into that stump? Always July."

I smile despite myself. "Hum, yeah, because you spelled *always* with an O and an extra L. It literally says 'ollways.'"

"That's how it sounds!" He chuckles and jabs an index finger in my direction. "Plus, you agreed with me."

"I was like ten and, remember, I was in an experimental spelling program that focused on sight words, and I never learned phonics! You had to be like, what, in middle school?"

"I was twelve." He laughs, throwing his head back. "Yeah, maybe you were that young, but you fooled me." I swallow as his jaw twitches, tipping me off that there's some double meaning there. As much as I miss the way it used to be between us, I can't live in the past. I have to face the fact that we grew up. Our lives moved on. Just like we are more than likely selling our family lake home—it doesn't make sense to keep it anymore. Some things just make sense to let go.

Even if it's hard.

Even if it's excruciating.

I make the mistake of leveling my gaze with his, and I quickly lose myself in the spirals. Brown eyes as thick as a mystery novel. Ever-changing, full of surprises, and now they fire all the hues of caramel at me. "I should go." I shift the weight from one leg to the other until I am leaning toward the exit. "Ham's waiting."

He pushes back his chair and stands, taking a step toward me. He's close enough I feel the brush of his arm as he walks behind me. "Yeah," he murmurs. "Guess you should."

"You're not coming to the parade?"

"Nah, you know your mom doesn't welcome me to that stuff. Since this may be the last time we'll be here, I think I'll go fishing." His lips purse before his head jerks toward the screen door that leads to the back deck. "You know, say goodbye to the place my way. But I'll catch up with you guys later."

"Later." I surprise myself how defensive my echo sounds. "Aren't you flying back to Minnesota tonight?"

"Oh, yeah." There's a flicker of disappointment in his eyes. "I guess I am. So, I'll, ah, maybe see you ..." His voice drops off as he forces a chuckle, then says, "I was going to say next July, but if you're not coming back here, I'm not sure when I'll see you."

"Right." Stunned at the sudden realization this is a *real* good-bye; it's never been harder for me to force even one tiny word through my lips. I wait for him to take the first step away from this conversation. My heart slams against my rib cage like it wants to break free. It never dawned on me I would ever have to say goodbye to Ty—like a final, *final* goodbye. "I'm sure we'll run into each other sometime. If you ever make it to DC, be sure to call."

"Sure. You bet." It might be my imagination, but his voice cracks, and he doesn't move away.

And I don't either.

I need to ask why things got so complicated. I wish I didn't have this stupid parade. There's nothing I want more than to head down to the docks and waste the day away with him like we used to.

That's not my life anymore.

I have to work. Not just because it's my mom, but it's my job as her assistant. "Well, I guess goodbye." I flash my palm and slowly start to pivot.

"Wait, one question before we do this goodbye thing." His voice cracks, and he doesn't pause long enough for me to ask what. "Do you ever wonder what would have happened if we never had to move apart?"

"I—" My teeth crash down, holding my lip back, and I freeze like I did last night. This is it! Our chance to finally break past the guardrail. *Please don't gasp again. Say something—*

"Seriously!" Ham's voice blasts from the doorway. "How are you still standing there, Lottie? I was outside waiting for you. We need to leave now."

My heart squeezes. It's always been faster than my words, beating me to every reaction. I mean, what am I really going to say to Ty's question? Ham's standing there, and he's right—I need to leave. My mom needs me, and I need to end this conversation.

What do I even say?

My eyes snap to Ham, whose hand rests sharply on his hip. Then back to Ty. His eyes have darkened, almost as if pleading with me to not drop the conversation.

I don't have any words that can match what my heart is doing in my chest.

So, I turn on my heels and call over my shoulder to Ham, "Just one second. I need a minute to change." Then I rush toward the stairs with tears brimming in my eyes. I wish I could tell Ty how I feel, but it will only make things worse. He's living his dream. I'm moving to DC full time. It doesn't make sense to hold on to something that can't ever be.

Three

Tyson

Five Years Later

THE WEIGHT BAR SHAKES as I inhale and lower it to my chest. My muscles loathe Monday mornings as much as I do. The only good thing about today is the last of the snow is gone. On my drive to our practice facility, I saw nothing but sweet, sweet grass. Mostly dead grass, but it was dry. That's all I care about. Seriously, Minnesota winters are no joke. I exhale and raise the bar, racking it. I should do another set, but my eyes drift to the overhead TV that one of the guys has switched to the national news. My breath catches in an instant.

Standing in the center of the screen is Lottie. It doesn't surprise me one bit she's right next to her mom, shaking hands with several important looking people. Knowing nothing about politics, I therefore have no idea what they are doing, but I beam at the TV. Dressed in a patriotically colored blazer, with her long blond hair tied in a bun, she looks untouchable. I haven't seen her in five years, and my chest swells with pride. She's living out her dreams, helping her mom save the world. I don't doubt there's anything she won't accomplish. I truly want her to have everything she desires in life. The camera zooms out.

What do you know?

Bow Tie lurks off to the side, his sleazy smirk locked on Lottie. And my gut plummets to my knees. Has he seriously been working next to her for the last five years? Before I can fully spiral, my phone buzzes, saving me. Swiping it off the mat, I take one look and hike an eyebrow. Uknown number. Probably scammers. I almost end the call, but something makes me stop. Warily, I swipe. "Hello?"

"Hello, is this Tyson Lane?"

"It is?" My reply comes out like a question, since the voice is unrecognizable. I'm half expecting him to try to sell me something.

"Tyson, this is Coach Badaszek, the head coach for the US Stars team. Are you sitting down?"

"Aw, I'm lying on my weight bench, which is even better." A knot swells in my gut. I know exactly what team he's talking about. The rumors about this tournament have been circulating for months. It's one of two national all star teams the league is building for an exhibition tournament celebrating America's two-hundred and fiftieth birthday this summer. As far as I know, no one has been given any privileged information about the game details. My guess is they take the Olympians, which I'm not. So, my brows bend down as I ask, "What can I help you with, Coach?"

"Tyson—" He exhales like he's been holding this in. "You've officially made the roster for the Stars team."

My brain blanks. All that's left is white space. I hear what he's saying, but it doesn't make sense. "Wait. What? How?"

"You're an amazing player. Yes, it was your first year in the NHL but the fans love you, everyone loves you. This last year was mind-blowing. You shut down two breakaways in that double-OT game against Florida. You led all rookie defensemen in blocks. You earned it."

I open my mouth to speak, nothing comes out. Instead, I curl up to a seated position and stare as the room tilts for a second. Finally, I manage, "I—I don't know what to say."

"Say you accept." Coach chuckles.

"Absolutely, yes, I accept." My voice cracks, which is uncharacteristic of me. My chest inflates, giving me the chance to finally take a deep breath. "Thank you, sir."

A beat passes before he says, "Also, you're captain."

So much for finally catching a decent breath, as I choke on his words. "I'm what?"

"I went with my gut on this one. If it's all right with you, you'll be wearing the C."

Someone injected electricity straight into my ribs. My eyelids work though. Blinking in rapid succession, it's like I'm trying to flip some switch on and off to see if it resets this conversation. Sure, I worked my tail off. It's all part of my plan to be better for...that woman whose name chokes me up. I just want her to see me. Well, that's not true. I need her to do more than see me. I need her to think I'm good enough for her to see herself *with me*. Even through the best year of my career, never in my wildest dreams did I imagine anything like this happening.

Coach keeps talking, oblivious to all the ways my attention is malfunctioning, and I struggle to keep up with the details. "You'll be flying out to DC this month, where the PR team has some early media planned. We need you to be a heavy hype machine to build up all the fanfare. I hope you're ready."

DC.

My heart stutters. There's no way I can hear that word without Lottie's face instantly slamming into my brain. Five long years ago, we said goodbye to our long-held tradition of Julys, and what do you know—it looks like fate is forcing a reunion. That has to mean something, right? Some kind of cosmic shove.

"Does all that sound okay?" Coach's voice cuts through my thoughts, and I startle, realizing I hadn't exactly caught any of the last details. I can't admit that though.

"Sure," I rush out. "Maybe just to be safe, would you send me an itinerary?"

"Absolutely. I'll have my assistant copy you on everything." His tone is surprisingly warm, not intimidating in the way most coaches are to me. A twitch in my gut tells me that's a good sign. Everything is happening for a reason. Curling my bottom lip under my top one, I can't help but think I already know what this is really all about. "Thank you, sir."

"You bet. See you in DC." He ends the call, and I drop my phone to my lap.

A tsunami of emotions slams into my chest. Sure, I'm going to play hockey. That's huge enough on its own, but this feels like fate telling me to get Lottie—my queen—away from Bow Tie before it's too late.

Picking up my phone to text her, I cut a bombastic side-eye to the TV. On cue, my stomach knots so tight it sends a wave of nausea through me as my mind flashes back. Lottie lives this Pinterest-perfect world of speeches punctuated to perfection and relationships statistically cultivated. Every detail of her life starts in Harvard-educated planning committees.

It's the kind of world I don't belong in.

Surprisingly, Bow Tie fits in perfectly.

Nope. I shake my head and set my phone back down. I'm not calling her. She's clearly with Bow Tie at this very moment. I'll be a third wheel, but my excitement is overflowing. I have to tell someone. I blow out my breath and open another contact: Taz. My friend, also in the NHL, and the only person who would be both jealous and understanding of this accomplishment.

He picks up on the first ring. "Bro, you better be calling to tell me what I think you're calling to tell me."

I laugh. His voice is so pumped up, I can't fathom he already knows. Does he know? "There's no way you know."

"I bet I do," he booms so loudly, I have to pull the phone away from my ear. "Because I'm on the roster for the East!"

I freeze, knowing this means we are rivals. Hearing his smirk through the phone, I add, "You'd better bring it, Rookie."

"Oh, yeah." My voice drops as it all sinks in at the slowest speed imaginable. Though we played together when we were younger, Taz beat me to the NHL, and he never misses an opportunity to remind me of that fact. His laughter fuels me, and I dare to confess the next part. I might as well get it over with—he's going to find out anyway. "The craziest thing is they made me captain."

"Nice?" The C comes out like a happy kiss. "You're a natural leader," he says, "but I'm going to look better in my C than you ever could."

"Please," I snicker, as this conversation keeps getting better. This can't be happening. "That must be a mistake. There's no way you got that letter. You don't even know how to put your jersey on the right way."

Chuckling through his words, he says, "You'll be the one struggling to get your jersey on once I get ahold of it."

It feels good to know one of my best hockey friends is going to DC with me. "Congrats, Houli. Seriously." I grin so hard my cheeks hurt. Taz was one of the first real friends I made when we played outside Boston together before I went to the AHL. That was so long ago. "Dude, if I have to play against anyone, it's an honor that it's you."

"Right back at you." His tone picks up urgency. "Hey, sorry to cut you off, but I need to run, but see you in DC, Captain."

"Same." I hang up and sit still, breathing in the insane reality that somehow this is my life. All the hard work is paying off.

Against my better judgment, I can't help but look back at my phone. I don't need to scroll to find her number—I've memorized it. My thumb hovers over the keypad, but I can't do it. I set the phone face down. It doesn't matter. It doesn't remove her from my head.

DC might have called me first.

But it doesn't surprise me that *Lottie's calling louder.*

Four

Lottie

I press the phone between my ear and shoulder while scrolling through three calendars on my desktop screen. Although the phone is always busy, today proves to be another level of inundation as people keep demanding interviews. My mom has a personal calendar and another for work. Then I cross-reference those with what I have available on my calendar, since I'm her executive assistant. Though I don't know why I bother with my calendar at this point. I have no life beyond her work. Aside from a rare dental cleaning, my schedule is pretty much her schedule.

"Yes, ma'am, I can schedule an interview on Monday at one." I click the speaker icon and set the phone next to me. I type so fast my fingers blur. If I had one superpower, typing would be it. I love the *clicky-clicks* of the keys. "Yes, Senator Halloway looks forward to meeting you. Thank you for calling."

I end the call and shove a handful of plain M&Ms in my mouth from the bag I have stashed by my monitor right as my mom strides past my doorway. Her Jimmy Choo heels click with purpose as she rushes down the hall between two staffers. She doesn't even glance into my office to say hello.

She never does.

Mom assumes I've got everything under control. For the most part, I do. I'm excellent at smiling through the drama. I'm the senator's daughter, the one who absolutely must uphold a "perfect image," as Mom puts it. Which means, not dating anyone she doesn't approve of, which is about 99.99 percent of the population. That brings me back to the main reason my calendar is forever empty of personal events.

Well, that and the guy I want to date is halfway across the United States...

Leaving her calendars open, I dramatically close my tab, because really, there's no point in leaving it open. I shift my focus to the little window next to my cubicle, my mind restless. There might as well be bars on it to match my current mood. I know better than to let her know I'm daydreaming about another life while I'm at work. I've already been caught once doodling goats on government sticky notes. That resulted in a twenty-minute lecture.

"If you want to draw your goat things, do it on your own time," she hissed. "Not in a federal office."

What she didn't know was that I wasn't just drawing.

I like to call it my scheduled dissociating, and it's likely the single activity that allows me to stay sane.

I *want* a new life.

The problem is, I don't even know what that life looks like, because I've always done what my mom says is best—and my new life definitely doesn't involve listening to her. I'm not sure when it happened exactly, but somewhere in the last few years I've become disabled in my own thinking. I get so anxious when it comes to making decisions that I let her take control, which she loves. I hate it here, but I can't see a way out. Not when the public is so invested in my family's business. Until my mom gets out of politics, I'm sort of stuck here too. The closest thing I have to an escape is sneaking outside on my lunch breaks, where I race through the city park like I'm starving for air.

Maybe I am.

The horrible part is I always come back.

My watch buzzes. I check the text and groan.

Dad: Gate's busted again. Goats are loose.

Of course they are.

They hate their pen. *Just like me.* Maybe that's why I have so much patience with them.

With rolling grass, a picture-perfect red barn, and a flower garden my mom pretends she tends for photo ops, they much prefer roaming free over the hills.

I haven't given up on them yet.

They may be a tad feral, but I know they're still trainable. Toast is my sweet baby, and he only responds to my voice. I got lucky enough to bottle-feed him when he was little. Not that him losing his mama was lucky, but me getting to be his nanny was. Then there's Cinnamon, the only female and a real easy keeper. She's hardly any trouble. Well, unless the other two pressure her. She's not totally innocent.

Lastly, there's Crunch. Let's call him the instigator. Together they make the Cinnamon, Toast, Crunch trio. Yes, it sounds cute, but it turns out it's not. It's actually a giant, throbbing headache. But they are my headache and, oddly enough, I love them. I text back:

> **Tell Crunch if he keeps running away, I'm going to lose my job from leaving work so many times.**

Dad replies with a single photo of Crunch standing proudly in the middle of my mom's prized flower garden with a mouthful of something he shouldn't be eating. I snort-laugh loudly. Two seconds later, my mom pops her head in my doorway, and she snaps her fingers at me. "Lottie, decorum, please. Snorting is gross."

"It was a goat photo," I whisper with a small shoulder shrug. She's usually a control freak, but not this bad. She's never popped her head randomly into my office to snap at me.

"Decorum," she repeats as she wags her perfectly manicured nail at me.

Swallowing, I wait for her to leave, which doesn't take long. She never gives me more than a couple seconds of her time. The moment her heels click away, I sag back in my chair. My attention returns to my phone, where there's a notification from a news app. It's a clip of me and Mom shaking hands with the people she met yesterday—the heiresses of some drugstore chain who donated a lot of money to her campaign. Mom is happy. I look happy.

I tap on the photo and zoom in on my smile, which I can barely tell is fake. I appear mostly normal. Absolutely nothing like the girl who crawls under fences to drag a goat by its horns while lecturing it about manners.

Or the girl who daydreams about July.

And the man I shouldn't miss.

I close the notification before my heart gets an idea. Because I know what Mom would say. *You need to date Ivy League, not hockey league. He'll ruin the image we've built. Then he'll destroy your whole life, not to mention you'll be left broken-hearted and poor with no career.*

Swiveling in my chair, I make sure my back is toward the door in case someone walks by. They don't need to see my forlorn expression. This is a nice life for someone else. Sighing, I start plotting how I'm going to fix that fence when I get home. Nothing is safe with Crunch around. He needs a barricade. I push my lower lip out, deciding that might not be such a bad idea.

I'm pretty good at making those.

I already have one around my heart.

A shuffle in my doorway pulls my attention. I smile when I see it's not my mom. "Hey, Brett."

His knock on the doorframe hits the same time our eyes meet. "Your mom is sending me out for coffees. Want to walk with me?"

"Coffee sounds good." My reply is automatic as I search for an excuse. He's given me the creeps ever since our weird half date. Sure, it was years ago, but the memories still haunt me. My attention snaps back to my phone, and I pick it up like I'm offering evidence. "I better not. My goats got loose again. If I don't show up to help and at least fix the gate, my dad will find a reason to make them permanently disappear."

His lips curve into a teasing smile. "Oh, Crunch is at it again."

"I guess." I stand, slide my computer off my desk as I shut it, and stuff it into my computer bag. I take a moment to sling it over my shoulder. When he doesn't move even a toe out of my doorway, I figure something is up. "So, I'm headed in the opposite direction, but we can walk out together."

"Yeah, I'd like that." He's still staring at me. My eye twitches as I resist rolling my eyes, and we fall into step together, heading down the long hallway.

"How was working on the speeches committee today?" I ask after the silence gets cringe.

"Oh, you didn't hear?" His tone drops to an almost inaudible level, and I'm forced to glance at his mouth and resort to lipreading. "That wasn't the speech committee. That was PR cover-up."

"Cover-up for what?" Nervous bubbles fizzle in my gut. There always seems to be some reporter falsely accusing my mom of something, and I never get used to the feeling of being on guard.

"From yesterday …" His words trail off before he interrupts himself. "You seriously didn't hear about it? It's been all over social media."

My eyes bulge as I struggle to keep my voice concealed while we pass the last few offices in the hall. "I haven't heard a word. The phone has been ringing off the hook with requests for meetings…" It's my turn for the words to trail off as it suddenly makes sense. Something disastrous went down. Hence all the phone calls. I rush out, "What happened this time?"

Slowing his steps as we reach the exit, he pushes the door wide open, letting me pass first before following behind. As soon as it closes, he slides his phone screen toward me. "Why don't you just watch?"

The video from yesterday's donor meeting loads. It's the same photo I'd seen with my mom and me shaking hands with her new donors. I hadn't realized there was drama surrounding it. My chest tightens. *What if it's something I did?* That explains why my mom was snapping at me. My hand trembles as I tap the screen to press play. The logistics crew is running around the stage, taking down my mom's banner. I walk offstage. Instead of following me, my mom strides back to the podium and grabs her notes.

One of the crew members looks at her and says, "Hey, did you hear about the Mapleton hockey player who made the Stars roster?"

She dramatically throws her arms in the air like she's beyond exasperation. "Yes, I'm a senator, but I swear, if I have to pretend to care about hockey, I'm moving to Florida." Her lips barely move, like she's trying to mumble, but her mic is still clipped to her collar—and it picks up everything.

Oh, no!

She doesn't know her mic is hot. My hand flies to cover my mouth, suppressing a scream, and I keep watching in horror.

"They have hockey in Florida too." The crew member chuckles. "Anyway, just an FYI—it might be good PR for you to tweet your congratulations, since it looks like they'll be doing a lot of the same public events you are during Fourth of July week."

"Ugh, seriously? The last group of people I need to be seen associating with is hockey players. My daughter's goats have better discipline than half those guys—" The mic squeals and cuts out as someone from the crew must have finally realized it was on, but it's too late. My mom's eyes grow wide—cartoon-wide—and my jaw drops.

This is horrid!

And to think she was lecturing me about decorum earlier. No wonder she was paranoid. It all makes sense. Ever since Mapleton got its own AHL team, hockey has been huge there. And, sadly for Mom, a large portion of her voter base is hooked on it. My fingers float to my temple as I press them there, trying to ease the sudden headache. This is not the PR she needs going into one of the biggest holidays ever—the 250th birthday of our country—and we have a full itinerary of events for her to campaign at. "How bad was it?"

"Twelve points down." Brett's expression is grim.

"Yikes." My gut twists into a loopy knot, weighing heavily in my stomach. "What are you doing about it?"

"Well, that's where you might be able to help."

"Me?"

"Yeah. Turns out the player is your brother's friend. Remember—the one I met when we were in Mapleton? Tyson. We might need to pull him in for an event, so it looks like your mom supports him."

"Wait. What?" My brows knit together. Maybe Mom was right about me daydreaming too much? I haven't missed an hour of work, but apparently, I've missed a lot of details. "Tyson is playing hockey here? In DC?"

"Yeah, he's on the Stars team." Brett shrugs, then adds, "Do you think maybe he could help spin this?"

I hear his question, but my mind is racing in another direction.

Ty is coming here—to DC, where he knows I live.

And he didn't call me to tell me?

Does Ham know?

This seems so odd.

Unless Ty's avoiding me.

"So ... what exactly is this hockey tournament?" I get the question out, though my head spins with all the details I don't have.

"This year there is a special tournament to celebrate the 250th birthday of our country. The league built two all-American teams of the best players to face off right here in DC. There's a women's and a men's tournament, and it all starts on the fifth. The players are arriving any day now for media and practice."

"How did I not know this?" I force my face to stay neutral, but my heart sinks.

"You do spend an awful lot of time daydreaming." He shrugs again, adding a kind smile. "Anyway, back to my question. Do you think you can reach out to the guy and see if he'll help us? Maybe pose for a nice photo."

My heart slams so hard against my chest that I grab the step railing to steady myself. It's true, I've been avoiding the news a lot lately. If it's not something that lands directly on my desk to deal with, I don't bother with it. It's all overwhelming. Brett leans forward, as if to remind me he's waiting for an answer. "Hmm, that's an idea." I nod slowly, indicating I'm considering his request before I say, "I'll, ah, think about it and get back to you. I have goats to take care of." Before he can reply, I hurry off, speeding down the front steps with my heartbeat roaring in my ears.

I can't get over the fact that Ty is coming here, and he didn't text me.

And it will be July.

July is always our thing.

Or at least, it was.

That has to mean something.

He's not one to forget.

My throat tightens, and I swallow hard as the saddest thought floods my brain and my legs nearly buckle.

That must mean he chose not to care.

Five

Tyson

IT'S MY FIRST NIGHT in DC, and I'm staying at the Four Seasons. Since I'm here early, and the team promo stuff doesn't start until tomorrow, I reach out to Ham. Happy to hear from me, he invites me to his family's place to hang out. After more than an hour of riding in an Uber, I arrive at the long driveway that leads to the historic Halloway estate. Goosebumps dot my spine as the estate rises over the hill like something out of an old Southern novel. Huge white columns frame the sweeping porch. Eight long windows line the bottom floor, with eight shorter windows on the second story. Swallowing, I push down my nerves, because this feels like I've taken a turn and ended up in a previous century.

To my right, rustic cabins sprawl across rolling hills. From what I've heard, year-round caretakers live in these cabins, while others are for guests. With log siding and a pair of square windows framing the door, they certainly look cozy. Down to the left, a creek snakes along the property. It reminds me of a postcard, not a place where people I know actually live. With a variety of flowers in every color and size, it feels like a Martha Stewart magazine spread.

I'm not surprised to see two random goats trotting along the fence line like they own the place. They are about the same size, clearly from the same parents, with the exact same gray coat. I can't help but chuckle. Ham has told me enough stories to know they are basically tiny, horned terrorists.

I crack the window, taking in the fresh country air. With DC being such a bustling city, this place is a haven to treasure. Past the fields, the big barn comes into view. Calling it a barn feels wrong. The thing is nearly as large as some hockey arenas I've practiced in, with a gleaming white trim to offset the traditional red wood. This barn gives the impression that the horses probably get spa treatments. We drive around a gentle curve, and the main house dominates the windshield again. We pull in front of it, and I gulp, trying to act like my heart doesn't jolt a little harder.

I'm here to see Ham.

But, yeah. Sure.

I can't help being excited to see Lottie. I open the car door and drop one foot to the ground; I'm reaching for my phone when movement suddenly erupts to my left. The two goats I saw earlier charge out from behind a hedge like they've been summoned by their war leader.

"ABSOLUTELY NOT!" the driver yells, waving frantically at me. "Shut that door now!"

His reaction stuns me, and I stare as one goat rears up and plants its front hooves on the Uber driver's door, headbutting the window like he's trying to get even with the driver for yelling at him. The other goat goes straight for the side mirror, teeth clacking as it commits what I'm pretty sure is vehicular abuse.

"I said shut that door! I swore this address sounded familiar. I've been out here before, and those goats are monsters!" the driver shouts, scrambling to lock the doors. "Oh, that one bit my mirror!" His reaction is so extreme, I'm struggling not to laugh.

"I'm sorry," I offer, which feels wildly insufficient. One goat slides down the driver's door, screeching his hooves against the paint. I cringe as he immediately rams the door again.

This goat clearly has an aversion to Uber.

With my door still open and my leg half hanging out, the driver pulls forward a bit, but the goats follow. "That's it," he yells, pointing out the window at the goats staring him down. "Get out now, or I'm driving off with you hanging out the door. This address is now banned from Uber. I'm flagging it for abuse. We don't do goats. No more drop offs or pickups here. This place is dead to Uber!"

The goat at the mirror lets out a satisfied bleat. Does he understand what just went down? I manage to hop out of the car and kick the door shut before the driver floors it and fishtails out of the driveway. The goats take off after him, chasing the car like guard dogs. I stand there in the quiet aftermath, completely deadpan.

What was that?

After a moment, I collect myself and amble up the steps toward the white-columned porch. I'm here to see Ham, I tell myself again like I need some twelve-step program to get me through this mind trap.

I mean, Lottie's likely not even here. Never mind the white Land Rover in the drive that looks exactly like the one she drove in Mapleton. Does she really have the same car?

Keeping my eyes on the goats, who are now hanging back and watching the Uber speed down the dirt road, I step up to the perfect white door and knock once. If this were their Mapleton house, I'd walk right in after knocking, because that's what I've always done. But this doesn't feel like Mapleton at all. The door flies open. Instead of Ham, I get Lottie. Her hair's piled into a messy knot, with flecks of hay stuck in it like she's been rolling around in the barn.

My heart jolts.

I never thought about it before, but hay in her hair is hot.

Now, I'm imagining what it would feel like to roll in the hay with her— then I triple blink as my attention shifts to her hand, and I notice she's holding a large hammer. Playfully, I duck, throwing my hands in the air. "I'm innocent!"

"Ty." She blinks at me like she's unsure I'm real. "It's been a long time," she rushes out, and then quickly adds, "I mean, sorry. Hi. How are you?"

"Good. Uh, is Ham around?"

She raises an eyebrow. "Well, he's not here yet." She shifts the hammer to her other hand. "My mom's got drama at her office again, so she's staying late until the hecklers clear, and Ham stayed with her."

"So, it's just you." A warm flush creeps up my neck. It should be illegal how she does that. How does she actually change the temperature of my body?

"My dad's around," she adds like a warning.

Ba-dum ... Whomp!

A series of thumps rattles the porch. I don't need to turn my head to confirm the goats are back. Lottie exhales, her gaze following the thumps. "I came home early to fix the gate. As you can see, my goats got out again, and they only listen to me. My dad has given up trying to discipline them."

"Understandable." I give a side-eye in that direction. I don't know how much I should reveal about the humble way they greeted me. "Your goats are terrifying."

A soft burst of laughter slips from her lips, hitting me square in the sternum. It's crazy how I both forgot that sound and yet instantly recognize it.

"Oh, please. You just need to know how to talk to them," she says, nudging me forward with a wave of the hammer. "And come on. If you're here, you're helping."

I'm clearly not arguing with a woman wielding a hammer, and I follow her down the porch steps and around the side of the house.

I have no idea where we're going, but luckily, we don't walk more than a few steps before she calls, "Crunch, follow me."

When Crunch steps forward, I get a better look at him. I've never actually seen a goat that big. With the perfect shade of gray, he must be crossbred with a rhino. He locks eyes with me, and then, like we're in a horror movie, he charges at full speed.

My life flashes before my eyes. "Nope," I tell him, backing up and waving my hands frantically. "Remember you're a vegetarian, and I taste bad!"

Lottie snickers, trying not to laugh. "Don't worry. That's his he-likes-you trot. He's coming to say hi."

"No!" I repeat because that seems to be the only word that fits this encounter. "That's not what he's doing. That's not a trot." Having already seen him in action with the Uber, I've lost all trust for him and jump back. He's faster than me, and he rams my leg. I freeze as he sniffs my sneaker. For a fleeting moment, I hold my breath, waiting for the sharpness of his teeth.

Do goats have sharp teeth?

I mean, they must, because they eat everything.

Instead of biting me, he sniffs.

I suspect it's an act.

Sure enough, he clamps down on the front of my sneaker. "Stop!" I wave my hands in front of him, trying to get him to back off. "No!"

Lottie proves useless, doing nothing to get him off me. She laughs as he drags my foot like he's towing me into another dimension.

"Seriously, Lottie?" I shout while hopping on one foot, which I may add is an impressive skill as I don't wobble even once. Years of skating has given me exceptional balance.

"I'm sorry." She laughs through the tears forming in the corners of her eyes. "He's playing. I'm not sure why, but he really likes you."

"This is not how you act when you like someone!" I scream. "This is how you act when you're crazy!" The last thing I need to do is accidentally kick her goat, but my leg is tiring from hopping, and I tug back. The goat tows me forward, and it's taking all my strength to hold my ground. I plant my foot as hard as I can. Miraculously, Crunch lets go, and I face-plant into the dirt.

"Oh, wow." Lottie wipes her eyes, still giggling. "Okay. I'm done. I swear. No more laughing,"

I can't help but beam back at her—even if I'm being murdered by a goat. It's what she does to me. As Crunch moves closer to her, I let out a deep breath and I raise my gaze. Our eyes lock, and my heart twists. I've risked my life plenty, willingly diving in front of flying pucks every day as a defenseman. No amount of damage I take could ever stop my heart the way her eyes do. Sea-glass green from an otherworldly dimension that doesn't even exist on this planet.

"Sorry," she says softly as she strolls forward and lowers her hand to me.

An impulsive swallow hits my throat because she's always apologizing when it's not her mess. "It's fine." As much as I yearn to grab her hand, I can't show any weakness around her. I push myself off the ground and stand on my own. "I should have known better than to show up on his turf."

"Well, it's only his until I fix that gate." She waves the hammer at me again. Her smile falters slightly and becomes gentler. "So, I heard you made that USA team, or whatever it is. I'm really proud of you. It sounds like it's a huge deal."

Warmth spreads through my chest. She's one of the few people who has known me throughout my entire hockey career. She's seen all the sacrifices I've made. It means a lot to hear that from her. "Thanks." I clear my throat. "And I'm proud of you too. For, you know, making the news all the time doing all your impressive political stuff."

"You know I can't take any credit for that," she scoffs as she slides her foot forward. "That's me surviving my mom."

I walk a little slower than her, letting her lead the way. I don't miss the twitch in her lips when I say, "You survive it better than anyone."

"I guess." She slows her steps even more, keeping her gaze on the goat, who is actually behaving at the moment, just trotting alongside her. "But someone has to keep her from setting things on fire."

I smile. "Well, someone has to keep you from getting eaten alive by your goats."

She laughs as Ham's truck barrels up the driveway behind us, cutting off our conversation. She points to it with her hammer. "There's your friend."

"Yeah." I let out a breath, but all I can think is, I hate Ham's timing. "Look at that."

Ham's truck rolls to a stop at the end of the driveway. Before he even gets out, Lottie turns to look out over the pasture, ignoring me like we were never having a conversation.

Six

Lottie

RELIEF WASHES THROUGH ME for the tiniest second—until I see who's in the passenger seat.

My mother.

Of course.

Ham climbs out first, dark circles under his eyes, his feet dragging. Exhaustion radiates from him, which has become his default mode lately. Mom slides out after him, smoothing down her blazer. She lifts her chin like she's stepping onto a stage instead of our driveway. Some days I wonder what it would be like to have a normal mom, who doesn't expect everyone to adore her. "Lottie," she calls over to me.

Before I can respond, Mom's gaze snags on Tyson. Her eyes narrow, then flick to Ham like she's uncovered a conspiracy. "Oh, for heaven's sake, is this about what I said about hockey guys?" she demands.

"No," Ham groans. "I invited Ty to hang out."

Ty clears his throat, and I hold my breath. The awkwardness is so thick I turn my head, pretending to be interested in Crunch chewing a leaf.

Mom stomps her foot—actually stomps it—before turning her politician stare on Ty. "Well, I suppose I should apologize for what I said. My comment about hockey was ill-advised."

"It's fine, Senator Halloway." Ty gives a soft smile. "I barely heard anything about it." I pinch back a smile that's begging to slip out at him. There is no way he hasn't heard, but he's playing the game—kissing up to my mom like everyone else.

"It is *not* fine. Someone needs to be fired for leaving that mic hot," she mutters, stepping forward and sweeping past us. "Where was that mic when I just apologized? That would have boosted my likability numbers, but no, that never makes it to social media …"

I cover my forehead with my hand. "Mom, please stop talking."

She shoots me a glare, but then spins on her heel, striding toward the porch, muttering about how hockey is "too violent for her wholesome image …"

Ham's gaze drops to the hammer in my hand, and his jaw tightens. "No, Lottie. Stop whatever you are doing with that, and hand it over. Right now."

I flick my wrist in a playful gesture, swinging the hammer toward him with zero intention of handing it over. "I have to fix the gate before Dad eliminates my goats—"

"You almost broke your finger last time." Without waiting for me to give it to him, he plucks it from my grip and turns to Ty. "Come on. Let's fix the gate before we need to call an ambulance."

Without another word, they head down the hill together. Mom disappears inside, still muttering something about how "that hockey boy is sure cute but not good for branding."

I stand with my hand on my hip, warmth spreading up my neck.

It shouldn't bother me.

Ty is just a friend.

A friend who plays hockey—something my mom hates. But my gut tightens. I can't help wishing she could pretend to be nice to him.

He's a good... friend.

Breathing heavy, I head down the hill toward the guys. I didn't mean to pass my chore off to them. I'm capable of fixing a little wire. Ty glances up when he hears my footsteps, and his expression softens, and suddenly my knees become putty. "You okay?" he asks.

"Yeah, I'm used to my mom." I wave vaguely. What else is there to say? She's a full-time job, and Ham is right here, hearing everything too.

Ham takes all of three seconds to pound a nail in, securing the wire. Then he leans on the post to test it with his body weight. It holds. He turns to me. "It should be good for now." He hands the hammer back to me and grins. "Do you mind putting this back for me? I need to make sure the barn is cleaned out. I offered a stall to Maddie. Did you know that she got invited to the parade because she's an Olympic medalist?"

"I didn't know that." A smile tugs on my lips as I always enjoy my time with her. "That's amazing for her. It will be so fun to catch up. I don't think I've seen her in forever."

"Yeah, she's coming on the third with her RV, and I offered her a spot to park it since parking in the city is a mess. I want to make sure we are ready for her." With that, he turns on his heel and struts away.

Ty doesn't follow. If anything, he shifts his weight, planting his feet more firmly on the ground. He stays close to the fence, elbow leaning on the post. I mean to glance quickly, but when our eyes meet, they lock. There's a magnetism that keeps us entwined. He's always had the kindest eyes—I seriously could stare into them for hours. Yet all I hear is my mom's voice in my head: *a hockey guy is not good for your image!*

Something twists inside me. Because she doesn't *see* him. Not how sweet, patient, or unexpectedly good he is.

And I don't know why that makes me so angry.

"Hey," he says lightly, finally breaking eye contact, sweeping his gaze to the ground for a beat. "I saw your mom's name in the parade lineup. Are you helping her?"

"Of course. My mom's favorite past time is recruiting voters at the Fourth of July parade. I so miss the little parade in Mapleton.

This one's a whole other deal—so overwhelming." I tuck a stray strand of hair behind my ear. "What about you?"

He gives me his signature lazy grin, the one that surfaces after a full day in the sun. "Yeah. The team's doing a PR thing. The league gave us all five hockey sticks to sign and give out to fans. I guess since there are fifty players, the math adds perfectly up to 250. Each stick is numbered, and the media's going to be all over it."

"Wow. I bet you'll be popular." I pause, running my tongue over my bottom lip as the sun beams overhead. "I, ah, I'm sorry about my mom. For someone always scolding me about decorum, I don't get what she has against hockey—"

"It's fine," he cuts me off, waving his hand dismissively, but I won't stand for it.

"It's not fine." I raise my voice in a defensive tone. "It's your career, and you're amazing at it. There's nothing wrong with your job. Plus, you've been friends with Ham and me for years. She needs to be respectful."

Ty nods, which feels out of place—like a mistimed salute—as he goes quiet, turning his gaze from mine, as if it suddenly hurts to look at me. "What did I say," my voice goes softer; the air has shifted in a single second.

He shakes his head. "Just that word."

"Respectful?"

"Friend."

The single word lodges in my chest like a sharp edge. He tugs up one corner of his lips, then shrugs.

"Well, we aren't enemies," I blurt, my heart thumping against my ribs.

Our eyes lock again, and my insides completely freeze. "Lottie, we haven't spoken in five—"

"Lottie!" My mom's shrill cry from the front porch slices through the air. "I need help finding something to wear to the parade."

Scowling, totally annoyed she's intruding on my conversation, I yell back, "Just pick a suit!"

"Well, yes, of course I'm wearing a suit, but I need help ironing it."

I stare at her, counting to ten in my head so I don't explode. Somedays I wish she could hear herself. When I look back at Ty, he tips his head like he's wearing an imaginary hat. "Go ahead. I'll catch up with Ham. I'm here for a couple of weeks, and I'm sure I'll see you around." Without giving me a chance to reply, he hurries off, and I roll my eyes as I scurry back to the house to help my mom.

Ironing?

Seriously.

At what point do I put my foot down and say, *"This isn't part of my job."*? I guess that's one of the huge caveats to living with your boss—the tasks never end. I hustle through the front door, shoving it to slam behind me, and stomp up the old wooden stairs, sending a prelude of my mood echoing through the house. I only slow once I pass through her bedroom door, where she's already wearing her suit, spinning in front of the full-length mirror, admiring herself from every angle.

"Did you check the label to see if you can even iron that?" I force my voice to sound pleasant. "I would think it's dry-clean only."

"It was professionally laundered," she says, her tone more nasally than normal. "I just said that to get you away from that man."

"From Ty?" I tilt my head. That doesn't sound right—he's been around forever.

"Lottie," she says in that commanding tone, "we need to talk about my image."

Great. My favorite subject. "I know you care about it, and I do too, but seriously, we aren't in public. If I talk to Ty on the farm, nobody sees it." I dig way down deep in my belly for the strength not to sound defensive.

"This isn't about talking to Ty—although, I do have a plan for him to help me too. This is about you helping me more."

"How can I help you more?" I blurt. "I don't do anything for myself. I haven't even gone to so much as a book club, because apparently 'romance books' sends the wrong message for your Wholesome Values campaign. What else do you want? I literally can't give—"

"It's not about giving me more." She lifts a hand, slicing through my spiral like a guillotine. "It's about showing everyone a little something extra. You hide in the shadows, but you have the power to help me by stepping forward—take the press off me for a moment while it still remains all about me."

What is she even talking about. On what planet does that sentence even make sense? I blink. "Showing what?"

She turns to the side, continuing to admire her reflection in the mirror. "This hockey blunder isn't blowing over fast enough. We had hordes of hecklers at the office tonight. We need new news. Something that drowns out this whole hockey-comment-disaster situation." She waves a hand like the scandal is a fruit fly she can swat. "I've done some research. In moments like these, celebrities like to announce fake relationships to boost their image."

I gawk at her. "Mom. You're married. You can't be in a fake relationship."

"Yes, obviously *I* can't do it," she says, as if my observation is the unhelpful part of this conversation. "But certain politicians in need of a quick refresh often rely on their children. Think of Kate Middleton. Her kids are always stealing the spotlight in such a way that it makes her look even better."

My mouth falls open. "You're not British royalty! And I'm definitely not a cute five-year-old dancing outside Windsor Palace."

"No, you're not that cute, but it's all I have," she says, brushing it off. "Lottie." She gives me the political smile that signals she's absolutely done with my opinions. "All we need is something wholesome. A dreamy boyfriend for you is the perfect solution."

"A—what? Mom, who am I even supposed to pretend to date? I know, like, two people."

"Well, Brett is available. He graduated from Harvard Law," she says, and then adds under her breath, "and a very handsome dresser."

I physically cringe. "Brett? That's a hard no! I went on one date with him before, when you made me. Remember? He gave me the ick so hard I had to shower twice. He kept crowding me, and I don't think he had deodorant on."

"So, he's natural—" she says dismissively.

"Disgusting!" I interrupt.

She lifts her chin. "You and Brett are both integral parts of my political team, and the public will totally believe it. You know, relationships at work happen all the time. He's already on the payroll, so I won't be out anything extra. Plus, think of the photo ops—"

"Absolutely not!" I cross my arms over my chest and turn my back to her. She has lost her marbles.

"Fine!" she snaps back. "If you don't like Brett, you can find someone. He must be media ready and able to announce your relationship before the parade. I want new headlines for the big day, so I can start fresh. If you don't have someone ready, I'll have Brett step in—"

"You wouldn't!" I'm physically incapable of closing my mouth.

"Try me." Her eyebrow arches, and she tugs on her blazer lapel. "Oh, and stay away from hockey players. We need that drama to die down."

I open my mouth to argue, but it's no use. She's impossible. "Whatever," I mutter and storm out before I say something un-campaign-approved. The hallway feels suffocating, its framed family photos staring at me with forced smiles. I race downstairs, the echo of my steps ricocheting through the plantation-style foyer.

Of course, that's when I nearly run straight into Ty. He's on the bottom step, as if he's about to head upstairs. Hands shoved in his pockets; he looks like he belongs in every soft-boyfriend aesthetic mood board the internet has ever made. His brows pull together, concern swirling in his eyes. "Whoa, Lottie Dah. What's up with you?"

"Nope." I move to brush past him, but our elbows collide, and the mere friction from his body makes me pause.

Big mistake.

He doesn't let me pass and instead grabs my arm. "Lottie, what happened?"

I absolutely shouldn't talk to him.

My pulse is still sharp from the fight. The last person I want to witness my emotional combustion is Ty.

But it all comes out anyway.

"My mom is trying to use me for political PR," I blurt. "She wants me to fake date someone to distract from her hockey-comment disaster. If I don't pick someone, she's going to announce I'm dating *Brett*. I can't—I mean I genuinely *cannot* pretend to date him. It's hard enough working next to him, but if I give him a reason to get close, I don't trust that he won't push for more."

Tyson's lips twitch, and he steps closer, his voice low. "No, you aren't doing that."

"I know!" Relief floods me—at least one person in my life still seems sane—and my voice pitches higher. "I can't do that, but then what? I know nobody."

"I could help you."

I blink, taking a hot minute to register what he just offered. *Did he seriously volunteer to date me?* My heart squeezes as I hang on the softness in his gaze, while my stomach plummets at the memory of my mom's warning. "Ah, actually, even if you wanted to, you can't, because my mom said, 'no hockey guys.'"

"Seriously? That's messed up." He shrugs a shoulder. "Ah, I guess if it can't be me, I could probably help you find someone. I mean, I know people. Guys who are better than Brett," he adds quickly. "I can help you find someone. You know, to make sure he's not a creep."

My heart stumbles.

What is this even turning into?

First my mom pimping me out, and now Tyson offering to set me up.

That is fatal.

Upstairs footfalls echo down the hall. By the pacing, I know it's my mom coming after me. I can't argue with her anymore. My heart slams against my chest as I stare back at Ty. Working with him has to be better than fake-dating Brett. "If you think you can find someone before the parade, I'm in," I rush out, marking my agreement with a deep swallow.

Why does this feel like the worst deal ever?

Seven

Tyson

Oh, I didn't just do that!

My brain is bleeding!

That's surely the problem with why I just did that. Pressing a hand to my forehead, I apply pressure to the pain. I scurry out the front door, intent on leaving this conversation behind. That's what I get for needing to use the restroom. I had to go at the exact moment Lottie was barreling down the stairs, looking like she was about to cry. My heart pounds like I just finished running a mile instead of having a very stupid conversation I had no business being a part of.

I could help you find someone to date!

What the actual—

Who does that?

I know who does that.

A guy who doesn't have the nerve to ask the girl out himself.

What is wrong with me?

I scrub my hand over my face. It's my turn to nearly run into someone as I storm across the porch on my way to the pasture.

Perfect.

It's just what I need.

A witness to my unraveling.

Ham halts mid-step and squints at me. "Bruh, you look like you've seen a ghost."

"Yeah," I mutter. "I wish it was a ghost. I'd much rather be scared right now than mad at myself."

He falls into step beside me as I stride at top speed away from that house. "What's going on? Did my mom give you a hard time? She's been a mess lately."

"No, not your mother." I let out a very manly exhale. "Not directly anyway. More like your sister."

"Lottie?"

With my heart pounding in my chest, I keep moving, my stride purposeful, and I pull ahead of Ham. We barrel past the goat pen, where Crunch is actively chewing on the fence post we just fixed. Just like that I'm sweating through my shirt—and it's not from the heat. It's from the fact I'm about to confess to Ham I've volunteered to set up his sister.

I abruptly stop. He almost crashes into me. "Okay," I say, bracing myself. "I did something, and I need you to not punch me in the face."

He gives me a slow side-eye. "I can't agree to take punching off the table until I know what happened. What did you do to Lottie?"

"So, I know you're protective of her—"

"Just say it," he snaps, and his normally wide nostrils grow rounder.

I'm cooked.

I inhale and blurt everything out in one long breath, "Your mom came up with some garbage plan for Lottie to fake date for PR to get the media off her recent flub."

Ham groans instantly. "Of course she did. It's never her fault. She always wants someone else to fix things. Did Mom set her up with someone awful?"

"Well, she doesn't have anyone picked yet, but it sounds like she has her mind set on Brett."

"Brett?" He blanches. "Ew. That's a hard no. He's a creep."

"I know!"

A beat of crackling silence passes while I picture what it's going to look like when he punches me. He's not a hockey player. I doubt he's thrown a lot of punches. He probably doesn't have much more than a right hook. I can block that easy. When I take a peek at his hand, I find his palm flat against his side. Sweet, he hasn't even made a fist yet. I'm good. For now.

"So, what is it that you did?" he asks slowly as his eyes narrow on me. "You aren't going to fake date Lottie, are you?"

"No!" I say, feeling my whole life crumble. "That would be weird." My voice squawks. Suddenly, I'm grateful Lottie's mom had that "no hockey player" clause. That would make this conversation so much worse. "I couldn't do that. It's Lottie. She's like my sister, you know." I ramble as sweat pours down my lower back. "And I just—look, I couldn't stand there and watch her go into a full meltdown about being forced to date Brett. So I said I could set her up with someone. You know, vet a guy who's—well—a good guy and doesn't wear a bow tie."

Ham stares at me as a wall of judgment washes over his face. "You said what?"

"I said I could set her up."

"With who?"

Gulping, I rack my brain. All the guys I know are hockey players, except Ham, and well, hockey players are off-limits. "I'm not sure yet. I'll figure something out."

"You're setting up my sister with some dude you don't even know yet?"

"Yes. Apparently, I agreed to something like that."

He puts both hands on his hips like a disappointed gym teacher. "What is going on?"

"To be honest, I'm not really sure, I just couldn't let her go out with Brett. You know he's a creep."

"This is Lottie we're talking about." He points aggressively at the house. "She's been on, like, one date her whole life. She knows nothing about our species. Do you understand what you're getting her into?"

"I DIDN'T WANT TO!" I yell, then wince. "Okay, that sounds bad. I mean, look, it wasn't like a plan. I'm not exactly in the matchmaking business. I had this weird flashback of her at the bar with that jerk, Bow Tie. I couldn't let that happen to her again. At least this way, if I vet the dude, we can make sure he's not a creep." I drag my palms down my face. "Also," I add miserably, "I think she agreed to it."

Ham glares at me for a horrifyingly long moment. Then he sighs and rubs his jaw. "Be honest. Are you crushing on my sister?"

"No!" I lie, and, to change the subject, I add, "I also agree with your mom that the attention needs to get off how bad us hockey guys are, so it's like my good deed to help my team. Since my team is playing for this country, it was the patriotic thing to do."

He arches a brow, leaning in with a heated glare that feels more like a staring contest. I lose that contest in about three seconds. "Okay," I whisper, and then proceed to pour my heart out. "I'm extremely into her and have been for years. You can hate me, but that's just where I'm at. I won't do anything to act on these feelings, but there's no way I'm letting her run off into the sunset with some fake date. I've seen how these rom-coms play out. The fake dates always end up married. I'll set her up with someone who's a total dweeb and sabotage the whole situation. It'll be one fake date that doesn't get a happy ever after."

A wave of crimson washes over his face, not stopping until his ears are flaming red. "Are you nuts?"

"Maybe." I gulp again, as apparently this is my new fidget. "Are you mad?"

"Oh, I'm mad," he says, pointing at me with a sharp index finger. "But mostly because now I have to be involved in a fake relationship scheme, which is, like, my nightmare. And not just because it's Lottie. It's my mom, and she won't let it fail. You don't understand my mom. She has clearly seen all the rom-com movies too. She knows if this is played well, Lottie will fall in love. She wants this to be Lottie's *endgame*."

He just said the quiet part out loud. *Endgame* echoes through my body, making me go stiff, one limb at a time. A wave of dread slowly creeps through me. It's exactly what I was afraid of. "Not if I can help it." I wince and rush out, "Dude, I can't let Lottie get set up with some dreamboat who sweeps her off her feet. You have to help me!"

"All right, I'm in." Ham stretches his neck, cracking it like he's gearing up for war. "If you're going to do it, you're going to do it right. Don't make her look stupid, or it will screw this up. And if you think you're swooping in when she's all heartbroken, so you can take advantage of her"—he taps my chest with his index finger, causing me to take a step back—"I will personally staple your clothes to your body."

A joyless laugh slips out before I can stop it, but it's drowned out by the growl—yes, a growl—he gives me, and I gulp, yes, again, and stutter out, "U-Uh, deal."

Ham glances sideways at me. "For the record, I'm glad you saved her from Brett."

My chest warms. "Yeah?"

"Yeah, but don't you even think about touching her."

"I won't," I quickly reply as I pull out my phone and open my contacts, scrolling right in front of Ham. "Now, help me make a list of the dweebs—*I mean, harmless men*—who we can set Lottie up with."

Hiking a brow north, he gives me an angled stare. "So that's your master plan?"

"I told you, I don't have a plan!" I screech. "Do I look like a man with a plan?" I urgently gesture to my phone, which only has hockey players in my contacts. Even if her mom said it was okay for her to fake-date a hockey player, there isn't a single guy in my phone I'd be okay setting Lottie up with. The thought of watching her go on another date—even a fake one—makes my chest nearly convulse. I don't know how I'll survive this.

"I'll tell you what to do," Ham says thoughtfully as he squares his body with mine. "You need her to go out with someone who is single but still in love with his ex. Then you know the relationship won't progress."

"Great idea," I mutter sarcastically while I scroll. "Let me put an ad out for that. 'Seeking fake date who is in love with someone else, so he won't fall for the perfect woman.'"

"Whoa, bruh." Ham tips his head closer. "This is my sister, dude. She's not perfect."

"She is to me." I barely get the words out. I still can't believe I'm finally honest with someone about my feelings for Lottie. Sure, it's not Lottie. But telling Ham is even harder. Maybe if he has time to get used to the idea, he will eventually help me. At this point, I'll take all the help I can get. I just can't lose her now—not after all of these years. "I don't think the ad's going to work." I lower my phone, giving up on my list of contacts. "I need to be creative and take her somewhere to meet some dweebs in person."

"Oh, yeah?" He hikes an eyebrow at me. "Do you know such a place?"

Scratching the back of my head, I rack my brain. Jocks are clearly not safe. I need to avoid any and all gyms, parks, or places where sports are played. I don't want anyone staring at her, so we will also avoid beaches and pools. No serial flirts either, which means no bars or restaurants. I need to go full-on pocket protector for this operation. Engineers would be a dream, but it's not like I can walk into an engineering firm and start chumming it up with the nerds by the water cooler. They are too hard to get to.

Nah. I need somewhere public, packed full of dorks like a library or museum.

I look to the side as an idea forms.

I've got the perfect place!

Eight

Tyson

"Ahhhh." Tipping her head all the way back, Lottie stares at the looming façade. "What exactly are we doing at the Smithsonian?"

"I told you, looking for *dweebs*—I mean, dudes." I adjust the collar on my shirt as I take in the place. I've never been good at anything besides hockey. This is so far away from my normal hangouts, I already feel out of place. But I'm committed for Lottie's sake. "Apparently, there are lots of intellectual gentleman here. You know, men who are cultured, with refined tastes, and likely Ivy League college degrees. Someone who will be perfect for your mother's image boost. We just need to find the right person."

She stares at me as I continue to adjust my collar. I don't remember ever wearing a shirt with a collar outside of game and media days. It's not my thing at all. It just seems silly to have all this extra fabric up by my neck, like it's trying to choke me. Normally, I wear T-shirts or jerseys and athletic pants. Not these preppy dress slacks I'm wearing to impress her today for our excursion.

"Okay, so let's pretend we find such a person," she says slowly, as if this still doesn't make any sense. "You're forgetting I'm still confused about one thing. Just because we lay eyes on someone doesn't mean he instantly assumes the role of my fake date."

"Right," I'm quick to quip back, my fingers moving in a walking gesture. "Then it's the easy part—you walk up and ask him to help you out."

"Are you aware of how insane this all sounds?" She widens her stance, peering at me with narrowed eyes. "There's no one on the planet who'll offer that much help to someone they don't even know"

"It's not insane at all." I press my lips together and shake my head.

As if countering my headshake, she juts her chin. "Nobody will agree to lie for a complete stranger."

I shake my head again. "You only think that because you don't see yourself. Trust me, you can walk up to any guy here and ask him to help you, and he won't hesitate."

Squinting as if confused, she drops her voice to an almost whisper, "Why do you think that?"

"Because ... because you're you." I motion sharply at her—there are no words to explain it, but every guy who sees her will know it.

Her eyes pierce right through me, unblinking, like she's trying to read my deepest thoughts. "What does that mean?"

"It means, you know, you look like *you.*" Dropping my gaze to my shoes, I don't need to look at her to know how this will go. No guy will ever say no to her. "You've got those surreal green eyes, and some hair and arms ..." I gesture vaguely, struggling not to go off about what an absolute smoke show she is.

Lottie laughs and echoes, "Some hair and some arms. Wow, that's a great compliment."

"Not to mention, if they have any sort of a career—which, of course, is why we came to this refined institution—they'll get some serious free publicity dating a senator's daughter. It's a win for them too. Come on. We're wasting time." Before I say something more embarrassing, I wave her forward. It's hard not to glare at the building itself. Even though it's impressive, the simmering dread in my gut reminds me of what I'm about to do. I pray the perfect dweeb is right where I need him to be.

"If you insist," she mutters under her breath, and we ascend the steps. We aren't even halfway up when we pass a guy coming toward us. He's wearing a fitted short-sleeve shirt, showing off his trim physique and sinewy arms. Lottie slows her steps. Like clockwork, her eyes slide over to him as she whispers, "He's sort of cute."

And my heart convulses!

It's all I can do not to dramatically grab my chest and fall backward. I didn't actually think she'd get into this. I'm not cut out for it. Sweat slathers the back of my neck. All I want to do is grab her hand and run far away, but to make her happy, I do an inspection.

Thick, masculine facial hair, neatly trimmed. The dude is practically a model, with a sharp jawline and high cheekbones. Way over six feet tall. Not to mention his glowing white teeth. On cue, he flashes his smile at Lottie. My gaze snaps to her as her cheeks flush pink, and I throw out my arm in disgust, grumbling, "Nah, he's not good enough for you!" My voice squawks as I rush out an excuse to keep walking. "Come on, let's hit up the Apollo 11 Command Module. There'll be much better guys there."

"I don't see anything wrong with him." She plants her feet on the step, her gaze following him. My blood boils. *I'm about to be cooked here!* There is no way I'm witnessing Lottie checking him out. With their matching bright smiles, they would be too perfect together—Barbie and Ken. Her tone lowers as she continues, "I mean, I have to find someone by the end of the day, and beggars can't be choosers."

"Not him!" I jerk my head for her to follow me in the other direction. "He's got ..." I draw a blank as I struggle to find a flaw. He clearly won the genetic lottery, every facial feature perfectly placed. I frantically search for a wedding band. That would be an automatic dealbreaker. There's not even a tan line on his finger. With no way to compete, I freeze. I had envisioned stomach rolls and a bad comb-over. Possibly even a hint of bad breath, so she won't want to stand too close. And yet, it's just my luck that the first guy we see is a young Brad Pitt lookalike ... and he turns, looking up at her as he reaches the final step. I catch a tiny glimpse of a mole on his chin and blurt, "Look! See that?" while frantically waving my finger in his direction. "Contagious Chin Mole Syndrome!"

"Ah, what?" Her brow wrinkles as her gaze stays glued to him while he slowly meanders down the street. She barely looks at me.

"I knew it!" I excitedly go off. "I saw it from the distance, but it's confirmed. It's a new disease they just announced. It's highly contagious, and it shows up as a mole on that exact spot on your chin. But that's not even the worst part. It, ah, basically, um, you just, ah, grow moles all over, and did I mention it's contagious?"

Her bottom lip pushes out as she continues to stare after him. "I mean, doesn't everyone have a few moles? It's not a reason to bully—"

"Not these moles!" I explode, my heart pounding so fast I feel like I'm in an emergency. There's no way she can ever go on a date with Intellectual Young Brad Pitt. A bead of sweat springs on my brow. *This isn't going the way I had planned!* That guy probably has his own apartment just around the corner. I was hoping for some guy who still lives in his mom's cellar. I don't want to lie to her, but I'm protecting her from all the heartbreak that man will bring. That's why I launch into, "Well, these moles aren't regular moles. First, they're just there, but then they start to grow hair. You might think that's okay, but no—it's a lot of hair. Then they start to get infected and rupture at the slightest bump, spewing buckets of pus. And if you touch it, you're cooked. Did I mention already they are contagious?" I stop as she hikes a raised eyebrow at me.

Buckets of pus might have been too far.

I mean, this still has to be believable.

"I've never heard of this, and my mom's a senator." Her voice wavers, and she's no longer staring off in the direction of Mr. Intellectual Young Brad Pitt. "If this were a real disease, my mom would know about it. It's part of her job to make the country healthy and safe."

"Yeah, it's basically like a government cover-up thing," I grumble and stare at my shoes, because there's no way I can lie to her face.

"Okay, Ty." Out of my peripheral vision, I see her fold her lips together and cross her arms. "How about we try this your way. You tell me who I should approach."

Now we're talking.

I lift my chin and scope out the place. We're still on the steps, but the campus stretches out before us. A group of schoolchildren follow a teacher in a perfect row back to their bus. To my right, a small group of elderly women, wearing dresses and matching fancy hats, waltz up the stairs.

This might be harder than I thought.

Releasing a deep breath, I glance up and down the sidewalk, and then I spot a treasure of a lifetime—*the one*!

Carrying a leather book bag and mumbling to himself, a short man, maybe five foot six at the most, stumbles toward us. He's missing the stomach rolls I had envisioned, but he's crazy thin—like he could walk sideways in the rain and not get wet. Not a muscle on his body, and his skin is so pasty pale he looks like he's been hiding in the stacks for days, maybe months. *Oh, and his glasses are perfect!* They are so huge they cover the top half of his face. He's dressed perfectly in a pair of baggy khaki pants and a button-up shirt. Guy's got no game, he even buttons the top button at the collar. To top it off, he's half bald, and hunched over.

Seriously—a back hump!

Nothing is better than that.

I love him already!

When my gaze slides back to Lottie, her hand is planted firmly on her hip. "I know what you're doing."

My head jerks back. "Ah, helping you find a fake date."

She whisper-screams under her breath, "That man has to be at least a hundred years old."

"Age is just a number," I fire back. "Plus, just think about how mature he will be."

"You're being absurd!" She spins on her heel, moving down a couple of steps before glaring at me over her shoulder. "I don't know why you agreed to help me when you clearly have some messed-up version of who is willing to date me. If I showed up with that elderly man, that would be a scandal."

"Pfft." I wave off her concern. "That's the whole point, right? We want the focus to be on you, so it's off your mother."

"Clearly you don't think I'm good enough to get someone close to my age. Maybe let's forget about it." She takes another step down, and my heart sinks with her.

Not good enough?

How could she ever think I don't think she's good enough? *She's a literal queen.*

No, not a queen, but my queen. She'll never need a crown. Her queenship is a different kind. Not over a country, or a kingdom, but my heart. And the wildest part? After all the years of dropping hints, she apparently still has no idea. The thing that scares me the most is that it's not hard to see how perfect she is. Any man she spends time with will be blown away, and I just can't risk losing her like this.

She's too good for anyone.

My heart shatters as her shoulders slump forward. I'm only trying to protect her, which is awfully hard when she doesn't understand the severity of what she's possibly getting herself into. How do I tell her she's too good, and I will die if she dates someone else? "Don't leave," I call after her with a weakened breath. "I wasn't trying to make this hard—"

"Excuse me," a deep voice cuts over the top of mine and pulls my attention to the sidewalk below.

It's Mr. Young Brad Pitt!

My heart comes to a screeching halt.

He's circled back and peers directly at Lottie, thumb hiking over his shoulder. "Excuse me, miss. I hate to interrupt, but is this guy bothering you?"

"No," she's quick to reply. "He's a friend. We're totally fine."

"Are you sure?" His words are perfectly measured. "I saw you both staring at me when I walked by. Honestly, I got a weird vibe from him. If you need help—"

"Actually, I do need help," Lottie blurts out before I can comprehend what's happening. It's like having front-row seats to the most gruesome car accident. I can see it all unfolding, but I'm helpless to stop it.

I open my mouth and reach forward, but my words are trapped in my throat. All I can do is mouth a scream, *"Noooooooooooo!"*

It's too late, he's already in hero mode, trying to rescue her as he raises an eyebrow and leans in. "You need to get away from this dude?"

"No."

That earns him a small smile, and I'm instantly jealous. I want all her smiles. It's not fair.

"He's not bothering me, but if I'm honest, we're talking about a situation I'm in, and, ah, it's strange." She cuts herself with the cutest little giggle, causing my heart to pulse faster.

It's the cutest little giggle *for him.*

I can't do this!

I can't stand here and watch her ask this dude out.

My brain is literally exploding, melting into my skull as every second of this interaction brands itself into my memory. The last thing I need is this moment burned in my brain forever. I'll die with it replaying. When everyone gets a full-life review … not me. On my deathbed, I'll just relive this over and over. It's so nauseating I gag.

His eyes lock on hers, and there's clearly interest. "Are you seeing anyone?" Her voice is surprisingly brave and steady. On another planet, I might be proud of her for taking a risk so uncharacteristic of herself, but not now.

"Like hallucinating?" She laughs at his joke, while I almost choke. Seriously? Why does he have to be funny. That was a great line. I almost laugh but force my lips shut, so not even a smile leaks out. Lottie asking this guy out is not a laughing matter.

"No, like dating." Her voice gains confidence, and her smile widens as she continues, "I'm in a work situation where I need a plus-one for an event, and I don't know anyone. I don't suppose you'd be interested in helping me out." Her words speed up as she adds, "You can totally say no."

His head tips closer to her, but his gaze slams back to me. "You're not together?"

"Well," I quickly say, trying to conjure something that might make him feel threatened, but Lottie steps in front of me.

"Nah, we're friends." She waves her hands in front of her, negating that idea, and my heart squeezes painfully. It's not built to handle seeing the woman of my dreams ask another man out, while basically pretending like I don't exist. I can't listen. I'm not trying to be rude, but I stuff my hands in my pockets and turn away. I don't miss the twinkle in his eyes, lighting up just for her—the exact way every guy reacts around Lottie. It must be a protective instinct, but my brain goes foggy. Their conversation fades into background noise, and I take that as my cue to sulk away.

She doesn't need me for this.

He's leaning toward her with a smile so wide, you'd think he'd just won the lottery.

Only this is better: he's won Lottie.

This is the worst thing that could have ever happened, and the crazy thing is it was all my idea. My heart slams against my rib cage, ricocheting sharp pain through my extremities.

I'm clearly dying.

It won't be long now, and I'll just tip over dead.

I bet she won't even notice. She will link arms with Mr. Intellectual Young Brad Pitt as they step over my sprawled-out body on the sidewalk and stroll off together to live happily ever after.

I grab my throat as I run off from this nightmare.

Unalive.

Nine

Lottie

His chin mole seems to pulse as I reluctantly lower my hand in front of me. "I'm Lottie, by the way. Nice to meet you."

He reaches forward, taking my hand. I hold my breath, unable to help wondering if the mole disease is a real thing. Ty was teasing, right? Nothing about that makes sense. Not to mention, he's the one who convinced me to come here. Why would he try to talk me out of recruiting a guy he basically preselected?

"I'm Bodan." He takes my hand, holding it for a couple of seconds before releasing it. There's no tingling or burning sensation coming in my palm. I don't think he's contagious. I hope.

Tossing a glance over my shoulder, I want to properly introduce Ty into the conversation. To my surprise, I don't see him. Looking to the left and then to the right, my brows knit together. He's clearly left. Distracted from the conversation, I hike a thumb over my shoulder. "Did you happen to see where my friend went?"

"Yeah, he scowled in my direction and stormed off that way." He emits a soft laugh.

Scratching the back of my head, I stare in that direction, hoping to see where he went. It's like he dissolved. With no sight of him, I turn my gaze back to Bodan. "I guess he had to leave."

"I guess so." He smiles at me in a way that makes me feel comfortable. I hate the position my mom put me in, but it is what it is. I came here to get a fake date. There's no point in delaying the ask, especially if he's going to turn me down. Here goes nothing...

Please don't turn me down.

"So, um, like I said, I'm in need of a sort of date thing to make my mom get off my case, and it should not be a lot of hours. I just need to make sure you don't play hockey."

"Hockey?" he echoes, as a chuckle bursts from his lips. "Heavens, no. Hockey is a cult that is under the control of the shadow government. Trust me, I work in the archives. I've seen proof."

"Ah." My eyes move side to side because I don't know how else to reply to that. It's a bit extreme. "My mom works in government, and she's not a fan of hockey but she's never said anything like that."

"She won't reveal all the secrets." His brows stitch together. "I don't trust any activity that requires that many secret hand signals. They're clearly up to something."

"Secrets?" I'm mentally slapping myself, realizing we're not only having two different conversations, but he's starting to show some red flags.

Instead of replying to my echo, he looks at his phone and then back at me. "Hey, Lottie, I hate to cut this short, but I have to get back inside for my shift. But to circle back to your question, I'd love to date you." He hands his phone to me and taps open the contacts. "Can you enter your contact information, and I'll be in touch?"

"*Fake* date." I go hard on the F, enunciating it with everything I've got. "Not a real date. It's just a public thing."

"Right." He nods, and I swallow. This was a bad idea but, apparently, I like bad ideas, because I go right on typing my number and give his phone back to him.

"So, yeah, you should be able to get ahold of me with that." I step back and find myself glancing over my shoulder for a sign of where Ty went. *It's so odd he left me here.*

"Great. Talk soon, Lottie." Bodan throws his hand up in a silent wave and twirls around to walk away.

I stare after him.

This is good.

I got what I came for on the first try.

I got a handsome man to pose as my boyfriend. He works at this museum, and my mom will have to be pleased about that. My gaze drops to the side as I can't help feeling a sinking in my gut.

Why do I feel an impending sense of doom crashing over me?

Ten

Tyson

No matter what I do, I can't get rid of that image of Lottie with Young Brad Pitt. It's swelling in my brain, making me disoriented. On top of that, the pressure riding on me as the team captain makes me want at least one thing to go right, so I arrive to practice early. I shove the door open, finding the locker room empty. With fake courage, I steel myself, square my shoulders, stride to my stall, and drop my bag in front of it.

I'm going to need a moment here. I check over my shoulder to confirm I'm still alone, and then I let out an emotional breath.

It's always surreal seeing my number on the jersey.

I've played for many teams and in tons of tournaments over the years, but it never gets old. Tingles spiral up my spine and all through my extremities, while little fizzling nerve bubbles inflate in my gut. With so many emotions swirling, I inhale a deep breath, allowing everything to soak in. I've never felt so much pride in both my country and myself. I am deeply honored.

I'm captain of the US Stars team.

That actually sounds like I'm flying some sort of spaceship, which makes me chuckle under my breath like an idiot. Captain of the US Stars team, *Crushing Way Too Hard*, reporting for duty. Because I've already gone off the rails, I let myself give in to the daydream for a second. I picture Lottie on the bridge, because she's always front and center in all my daydreams. Her hair is pinned back in her political bun, and she's issuing orders I would absolutely follow without question. She's wearing some sort of spacesuit, and she's hot.

She's always hot.

I'm at the spaceship helm, and she's beside me, helping me navigate this ship. We both know, even though I'm the captain, she's the queen and calls all the shots. She could simply tilt her head, smile that smile, and I'd be like, *Yes, Queen—tell me where to go or what galaxy needs saving. I trust you with my future and my oxygen supply.* Of course, the ship is named after her, something like the USS *Queen Lottie.*

The door swings open, and footsteps echo behind me before a, "Hey."

I straighten immediately, like I've been caught doing something illegal.

"Hey." I nod at Bryce Chambers, who also plays left defense. We both do that half-second pause where we recognize each other without saying it. I met him at the team bonding breakfast yesterday. He plays for Denver, and he seems calm as he walks to his stall next to mine. We turn back to our stalls and find our pads. It's not long before the room fills with more guys. With every guy who joins us, my pulse kicks up another notch.

It's getting real, *real* fast.

Once my pads are on, I grab my jersey. I don't miss the C on the chest. I'll never get used to seeing that. Nervous, my fingers fumble with the bottom seam. I open it and slide it over my head. My big noggin must have found the shoulder, because my head won't go through. I tug the jersey over, pulling it down tight, but my head doesn't budge.

Seriously, I'm trapped!

Pushing my arms in, my new strategy is to get my arms through the armholes and then push my head through. I easily find the armholes, but my hands are blocked too. My arms flail around inside my shirt. I'm getting claustrophobic.

I need out of here, now!

Snickers break out around me. "Bruh, look at Lane," someone to my left says. "His jersey's been sewn shut."

Ripples of laughter burst through the air. Even though no one can see me, my cheeks flame hot. *So much for impressing the team with my great leadership skills on the first day*! I can't even get my jersey on. Seeing there's no way out of it, I struggle to move my hands to the bottom and lift it over my head. Another wave of laughter runs through the room as I quickly examine the seams. Just like they said, my armholes and head hole are sewn shut.

And very neatly sewn shut.

It is almost as if a professional did it.

Taz's threat about messing with my jersey flashes through my head, and I hold back a chuckle because this has his name written all over it. "Very funny, guys." I turn back to my stall and stare forward. Good thing I keep scissors in my bag for cutting tape, but I seriously need to hurry. Sweat beads on the back of my neck as more chirps spiral around the room. It's not the first time I've had a joke played on me, but I've never been so nervous to make a good impression.

My fingers tremble as I dig through my bag for my supplies and find my scissors and tape. It's only half a feeling of relief as I open the blades, aiming the tip at one of the stitches. Most of these guys are already dressed, and only a few have their skates left to put on. I'm racing to get this jersey on before the coach comes in.

With scissors in hand, I glance around the locker room. A couple of guys won't meet my eyes. I can't tell if any of them look guilty. Dropping my gaze to my jersey, I angle the scissors into the first stitch, but to my dismay, the stitches are seriously tight—of course they are—and I struggle to snip them. It quickly becomes apparent I need to cut every single stitch. My pulse ticks up as the vibe changes from casual to locked in.

This can't be happening!

My first day on a new team, and I can't get my shirt on.

"Let's go, boys." Ice forms in my veins. I didn't even hear Coach Badaszek walk into the room. I'm such a fan of his. The last thing I want to do is come off as a slacker.

I work faster, tugging harder while heat creeps up my neck. I don't need to turn to know he's there. Coach's presence radiates pressure from behind me. "Are you planning on joining us today?" he asks.

I straighten, swallowing. "Yeah, sorry, Coach. It's a minor wardrobe malfunction." I don't want to rat out any of the guys, since they clearly were having fun. I also don't want to disappoint him. I turn slightly so he can see my scissors tearing at the stitches.

His eyes drop, and his brows rise. "Jerseys don't sew themselves shut."

A beat passes. I could put the blame on someone else. It might make it easier for me, but I've learned that narcing doesn't earn respect. I bite my tongue.

Behind us, the last guys file out, and the chatter fades behind the door. Now it's just me and Coach, and his gaze pins me in place as I finally manage to rip the last stitch. My fingers shake enough to annoy me. I keep my head down as I slip on my jersey and quickly pull it over my body. I grab my skates right as he says, "Lane, talent doesn't buy patience."

"Yes, sir." I don't even know what that means exactly. I hope it isn't followed by me being fired. He stares me down with his jaw set forward before he turns on his heel and leaves. The door shuts behind him, and the locker room falls silent.

I jam my feet into my skates as fast as I can. My chest is tight, but not from fear. It's determination not to let this first impression change anything. I deserve to be here as much as any of the other guys. I won't give them a reason to doubt it. In fact, I'll work so hard that they'll see why I'm here, and I'll be given the respect I deserve.

Even if I am the last on the ice.

Eleven

Lottie

A LOUD BLEAT OUTSIDE the front door draws my attention, and I scramble to my feet, rushing to apprehend the escapee before Dad discovers he's out again.

At this point, I don't even look. Toast's bleat is loud enough to bust him. Add in the thud of his headbutt on the door and it's good as confirmed. By the time I whip open the door, Toast is planted squarely in front of me, blinking at me with his irresistible little face.

"Well," I exclaim with a sweet smile for the little baby, "I see the gate held up nicely."

He bleats and turns toward the driveway, as if showing me what he's been up to. A shiny black sedan is parked there, and Ty is standing on the bottom step with his jaw clenched and one hand gripping the banister. Gone are his fancy pants from the museum. Tonight it's basketball shorts and a gray T-shirt. The collar is stretched out, hanging loose around his collarbone and giving me something to stare at, because I officially wasn't prepared for the pointed look he aims at me. I don't know if he's annoyed at Toast or mad about the museum, but he's the one who left early.

Toast takes one look at him and bleats again, louder this time.

Ty glares at him. "Is he judging me?"

"Yes." I dredge up a smirk I hope passes for playful, even though my mind is taking me on a winding detour of thoughts that are anything but playful. The silence tightens between us as he shifts from one leg to the other. I crack under the weight of the tension and ramble. "He does that. He's better than any guard dog. Plus, he might be jealous of you since Crunch likes you, and they have this weird rivalry thing going."

"Just what I need—to be in some weird goat-jealousy triangle." Ty chuckles softly, then flicks his gaze over my face like he's reading my mind. His stare is so intense it feels like little pinpricks pulsing across my skin, and I turn my head to look at the barn. Eventually, he takes a tiny step toward me, as if he's risking his life to move in front of Toast, and his gaze stays locked on me when he asks, "Hey, are you okay?"

"Uh, yeah." I keep one eye on Toast, who is miraculously standing still now. "Why? Is there something wrong with *you*?"

Shrugging, he takes another step forward, and I tuck a loose tendril of hair behind my ear and process how close he is. His presence sets my mind off on a game of mental hopscotch, because he always gives me such direct eye contact. It's so gentle, I can't help but think there's something else woven in there. Yet aside from that one time in the car when he tried to kiss me, he's never made a move. It's all confusing, but boy, is it hot out here. I swipe at my brow at the same time he says, "I'm alive but a little bummed, because we had our first practice. Let's just say I failed to impress."

"I'm sorry." I feel that like a tug behind my ribs. "Do you want to share what happened?"

"Nah, it's not worth wallowing over." He glances down the long driveway. "Ham invited me for dinner. Is he around?"

"He's inside." I jerk my thumb over my shoulder, motioning toward the open door. "You can go in. I should probably get Toast back in his pen."

"I can help you." His gaze meets mine, and the offer softens something inside me. Or maybe softens isn't quite right. It's more like an opening ... to a trap door I know better than to tiptoe around.

"Ah ... I'd like that." Even with the tension, I'm honest. I've always treasured our weird alone time, even if it means he's ditching Ham on whatever plans they had. Ham can wait. It's not like he has anything going on.

Just then, my fake date Bodan's silver SUV rolls down the driveway, coming in too fast for having animals roaming around the yard. Throwing my head back, I slip out a moan as I remember my mom inviting him over for dinner so she could "preapprove him" before we go public. He clearly wasn't warned about the goats, and I cringe as I frantically search for signs of Crunch and Cinnamon. When I don't find them, I'm a tad relieved.

Bodan pulls right up to the front of the driveway and steps out of his perfectly polished SUV, wearing a patriotic navy blazer, as if my mom already prepped him. He waves as he rushes up the walkway. "Hey, Lottie," he says brightly. "Your home is incredible." He does a double take at Toast. "Is that a goat?"

"Yes," I say. "I have three, and they are master escape artists who never like to stay in the pen. Just a FYI, it's always good to watch for them when you are coming up the driveway, and it's best to drive slowly."

Ty stiffens beside me. I feel it without looking. When I glance at him, a harsh smirk takes over his face. Bodan must feel it too, because he sticks out his hand. "I'm Bodan, the new-hire boyfriend. You must be—"

"Ty." Ty takes Bodan's hand, his face shifting into neutral, with no hint of a smile. "Longtime friend. I saw you at the museum, remember?"

"Oh! Great." Bodan bobs his head. "Lottie has told me all about you."

My brows pull together. *That's a total lie.* I haven't said anything. Aside from those few minutes outside the museum when we exchanged numbers, I've barely even talked to him. To hide a flicker of disappointment, Ty's eyes cut to me. It hits me harder than it should. It sounds like Bodan and I have been talking a lot, when clearly Bodan was just sucking up to him—but how do I explain that to Ty?

"Hey, Lottie," my mom's pleasant, speech-giving voice cuts in from behind us. "If our dinner guests are here, please don't make them stand on the porch. Show them inside."

Rolling my eyes, I wave my hand toward the open door. Bodan goes first, glancing in all directions. Ty steps forward, stopping behind me, and grabs the door from me. "Go ahead."

I want to go in because I'm starving, but my attention drifts to Toast, standing on the bottom step now. "Are we going to let Toast roam free?"

"Sure. Why not?" He shrugs. At this point, I'm about to give up on Toast ever staying in his pen, and I turn on my heel, leading the way inside. Ty follows closely, shutting the door behind him.

The house smells like whatever expensive candle my mother is currently obsessed with. The old dining room waits beyond the foyer. It has original décor, with dark wood paneling, and a table long enough to seat an army. A crystal chandelier throws soft light over the linens, and it's honestly so formal that it feels intimidating, even to me. Every time I see this show I fight the urge to roll my eyes. We aren't this fancy.

This event is all about onboarding Bodan.

Clean-shaven, my dad is seated at the head of the table, wearing a dinner jacket, just as my mom insists he be. His focus is out the long window. "How did the goats get out again?" he asks, to no one in particular.

"Opportunity," my mom inserts herself into the conversation, already focused on Bodan. "So, you must be the gentleman Lottie told us about." My mom spares no mercy as she gestures to the chair across from my dad, requesting him to sit. When he does, she plops down next to my dad and gets right to the questions. "Bodan, it's wonderful you're willing to work with us, especially on short notice. Think of this dinner as the orientation to a new job. Now, tell me, are there surprises in your criminal record we should know about?" she asks this so sweetly, I have to blink twice.

"No felonies, if that's what you mean." Bodan pauses to insert an uncomfortable laugh. "Or anything on my record, other than maybe a parking ticket."

"That's excellent news." Mom is practically drooling, but it's not from the salmon the staff just served her. She doesn't even acknowledge her food or say thank you when the waiter bustles around her filling her glass. "And as far as the job goes, we aren't looking for a hard sell," she goes on. "Everything will be done with the upmost professionalism. A couple of photo ops, tops."

"Looking forward to it." Bodan pokes into his salmon, taking a bite without bothering to use a knife.

"I bet he is…" Ty mumbles so softly I think I'm the only one who hears it. I don't miss Ty's mouth twitching as he takes a seat by Ham, sitting as far away from me as possible. I'm assuming that much space between us wasn't intentional, but yet it feels like he's somehow expressing disapproval by not taking one of the closer chairs.

Swallowing, I shift my focus to my mom, who is now glaring at Ty. He's never been a stranger, since he and Ham are usually inseparable when they are in the same city, but my mom also has a way of making it known that he's beneath her. "It's so nice you could join us too Mr. Lane," she says.

It sounds sort of supportive.

But it's far from it.

It's her fake attempt to smooth over that foot she still has stuffed in her mouth.

"Yes, ma'am." Ty nods. "Thanks for having me over again."

The staff finishes floating around us, placing the last of our food on the table. I don't think I'll ever get used to this lifestyle, but Bodan appears to fit right in as he doesn't seem to find it off to have waiters in your own home. Maybe he lives this kind of life too? I guess I never asked about his upbringing. I could ask, but I really don't care. Not to be insensitive, but my mom's the one who wanted him here. She should talk to him.

I'm more concerned about the way Ty stares at me, making all my words dry up. When I grab my water and sip, I don't miss, the moment I lift the cup to my lips, Ty looks away. He always does that, and I always find myself studying him, even when I try not to. I'll never be able to rationalize how much of my brain is devoted to indexing everything about him. It's embarrassing to admit, but he's carved out a whole territory of brain cells just for himself.

"Well, Tyson," my mom's tone is soaked in stuck-up approval. "It appears you're doing well and staying disciplined. You know, discipline is important."

The way her eyes flick to me when she says that makes my chest tighten.

What does that mean?

Aside from the fact, every time I lift a fork or a cup to my lips, Ty looks the other way, dinner passes in a blur of conversation. Bodan fits in effortlessly. He's actually a little over the top, throwing his head back and belly laughing at my dad's lame stories. He even makes a point to compliment my mom's blazer, which, as it turns out, perfectly matches his. My mother beams with pride. Oddly, it feels like they could be friends. I will never admit my mom had a good idea with this fake-dating stunt, but Bodan will be good for ratings. He's charming in all the ways my mom notices. And I don't even notice his chin mole.

I mean, I hardly notice it when I accidentally look at it.

I don't think it's contagious.

After all, my mom would be one of the first to know about a new disease.

Across the table, Ty cleans his plate without saying another word. As soon as the plates are cleared, he slides his high-back chair away from the table and says, "Thank you for everything, Mrs. Halloway, but I should get going."

I stand, not waiting for Ham to offer. "I'll walk you out."

"Oh, nonsense." My mom makes a sweeping gesture to control my movement. "You can sit while we have coffee with Bodan. That is, if he will stay. Ham can see his friend out."

I freeze.

Bodan looks pleased and raises his brows at me. "If that's okay with Lottie, I'd love to stay for coffee."

"It's fine," I hear myself huff, as something in me cracks a little.

We all stand at once, like we're being directed by a conductor, and move to the living room, where the staff has coffee and tea service set up. My eyes lock on the floor as I move all the way to the end of the biggest sofa. I hope Bodan takes the hint not to sit next to me. Out of the corner of my eye, I see Ty leave without looking back.

In the oddest way, my heart stumbles. It feels like I'm losing something I never had. As happy as my mom is, I know without a doubt this fake-dating thing is a terrible idea. I'm lying to myself, and it's sending the wrong message to...people I care about. Shame rushes through my gut, scraping at my intestines like shattered glass.

Bodan lets out a pleased sigh as he sits beside my mom on the other sofa, already laughing at something she says.

Everyone looks happy.

The waiter comes over and hands me a piping coffee cup, which is good in a way because it gives me something to stare at. I can't help wondering why it feels like I've somehow hurt Ty.

That's crazy.

All I did was exactly what he agreed I should do.

Twelve

Tyson

HAM COLLECTED A RANDOM hacky sack from somewhere and tosses the knitted ball from hand to hand. "So, how's this new celebrity team going?" He opens the front door more with his elbow and crosses the porch with me.

"Celebrity," I echo with a forced chuckle. "Whatever, you say."

"So, ah, this might seem out of the blue, but I was watching you watch her tonight." He tosses the hacky sack one-handed and catches it, seeming to avoid looking at me. "Have you ever...told—"

"Nope." I cut him off before he says anything. I can't hear any words about Lottie and my feelings. It's as if hearing them will make them even more real. I'm having a hard enough time ignoring them as is.

His lips part as he tilts his head and squints. He focuses on me in a way that makes my cheeks burn, like he somehow read all my hidden thoughts about Lottie. "Dude, I don't understand it." He swallows hard, almost as if he's suppressing throwing up. "I mean, she's my sister, but maybe you should talk to her."

"I can't." I steel my jaw and take a step toward my car. This conversation is risky, and on the off chance I accidentally say something I shouldn't, I'm ready to bolt. "She's too perfect."

A whip-loud chuckle cracks out of him, and I startle. *Is he mocking me?* In my defense, I go off, "Maybe at one time I could have tried to say something. Things were easier years ago—especially when we were at the lake—but now your mom has this whole issue with hockey players, I need to stay away. This isn't blowing over, and I wouldn't want to put Lottie in a weird position. Plus, my grandpa used to tell me something." I drop my gaze to the ground, knowing it's cheesy, but I trust my late grandpa more than most people. "He said, 'If a woman likes you, she'll let you know. Until then, it's the gentlemanly thing to not push her.'"

He blows out a breath as he tosses the hacky sack again. "I think that advice might be a little outdated, but whatever." I shrug and can't reply before he rushes on, "You have to remember, my mom's had Lottie in a bubble. She doesn't date—ever. She more than likely doesn't know how to tell you she's interested—*if* she even is. But"—he arches his brow at me, tension building from the sharp angle—"it's just, you know, you sort of look like you're going to be ill. I hate seeing you like this."

With my words frozen, I give him a *I'm-clearly-in-pain-but-I'm-dealing-with-it* shrug.

He seems to catch my drift and looks away. "Hey, do you have a few seconds to fix another gate? Toast is on your car."

"What do you mean, Toast is on my car?" My eyes zero in on my car, a goat glares at me from the roof. "That's not even my car! It's a rental," I grumble as I fly forward, waving my hands and yelling, "Shoo!"

"Look at it this way." Ham laughs, moving forward to assist me. "If he punches a hole in it, you'll have free air-conditioning."

"That's the dumbest thing I've ever heard." I grab the goat by the leg. He bleats loudly as I pull him down. Since nothing in my life is ever easy, he fights back, showing me his ninja kicks. Eventually, I get him on the ground, and then it's like a switch is flipped—he trots off down the hill like he has no intention of ever going back in that pen. I glare after him, shaking my head. "Why on earth does Lottie bother with these nuisances? There's no way she likes all this trouble."

"Why do you love Lottie if you know you'll never tell her?" His face is dead serious.

My chest caves, and I shoot back, "Why do you breathe if you know you're going to die?"

"So, you admit it—you do love her." Ham chuckles.

"Well." I can't say *it* out loud. My head starts to bob in a yes motion, but I'll never be able to speak it. I turn back to my rental and place a hand on my hip. "I should leave before that goat comes back—or, you know, I have to look at Bodan with Lottie again ..." My voice trails off as my gut tightens even further.

"See ya." He's almost taunting when he sidesteps, tossing the hacky sack in the air. "It's probably no use, but I'm going to try to fix the gate again." He slides two fingers into his mouth to whistle. Miraculously, the goats round up and follow him down the hill. I get in my rental and slowly back away, making sure not to accidentally hit one of the goats. Even though, at this point, it's a tad tempting.

I would never do that to Lottie.

Of course I wouldn't.

A blur of something catches my eye in the rearview mirror.

Lottie is on the porch, giant tears streaming down her face.

And Bodan is nowhere around.

As much as I'm over this fake-dating orientation, I could never turn my back on Lottie crying.

My foot stomps on the brake.

My heart crawls into my throat.

Thirteen

Lottie

I'm standing on the porch like an idiot, arms wrapped around myself. There's no doubt my mascara is absolutely not holding the line. I swipe at the tears on my cheeks like I have the power to erase the evidence of crying. Up the drive, brake lights flash on Ty's rental, and...I'm busted.

I slipped out here for a safe place to cry. There's no way I can cry in front of Bodan. When Ty stops his car in the middle of the drive and steps out, my stomach flips. His gaze locks on mine instantly, searching. "Lottie, what's wrong?"

I don't say anything.

He jogs toward me, asking a follow-up question with a growl in his throat, "Where's Bodan?"

"He's fine. I know what you're thinking. This isn't about him." I shake my head a little too fast, making me dizzy. I grab hold of the rail and steady the spinning. "He's inside. My dad took him to see his collection of fountain pens that have been touched by presidents. I just needed some air, and seriously, he's fine. I'm fine. Everything is fine."

I'm only halfway lying about the part that I'm fine.

I'm not okay with a lie so big it's starting to choke me. How am I supposed to go onstage and act like I'm in love with someone I can't even look in the eye because I'm that shy? I've never had a boyfriend, never known what it's like to go on a real date—unless you count that bar encounter with Brett, but I've long since burned that from my memory. Or at least that's what I tell myself.

I'm mad as a wet cat at my mom for willingly giving away my dates like they mean nothing and are all for her political gain. Dating someone—even if it's fake—should mean something. I couldn't even sit next to Bodan on the couch because it felt too intimate. I know it shouldn't, but when you have zero experience with that stuff, everything feels heightened.

Ty stalks toward the porch, his eyes stay locked on my face. "So..." he says gently, like he already knows. "Bodan is fine, but you're not, and you can't lie to me. What's wrong?"

"I'm fine." The lie falls apart immediately. My voice cracks, and I look away, staring at the porch railing. "It's just...it's stupid."

He stops a few feet in front of me, but he's close enough that my breath catches. "You're crying, which tells me it's not stupid."

I almost manage to swallow everything down, but he tilts his head, and his warm eyes soften so much it's like they back me into a corner. Something in me snaps. "It's that, you know, I love my mom. I want her to succeed, but this is too far," I blurt. "Lying about a boyfriend. I mean, come on!"

He blinks but doesn't say anything, and I rush on, "I mean, Bodan is being a great sport about this, but he has no idea what he's getting dragged into. I'm so mad at my mom I can barely breathe, and it's just—man—it's so awkward. I don't want to be close to a man I don't even know. You know me. I don't date much. This is a whole new thing, and it's so—" I bubble out an embarrassed laugh as I picture myself sitting on the exact opposite side of the couch in the living room. "I refused to sit by him. Something in my body spasms just thinking about getting closer to him. How am I supposed to get onstage and pretend like we're in love in front of the whole world?"

Ty steps forward—not in a creepy way, but more like he's trying to be a source of support. "It'll work out." His voice is rough, cracking with honesty. "You're always amazing."

I shake my head, surprised by my own level of honesty. "No, for real. Have you forgotten how shy I am? I've never even held a guy's hand before. How do I do this in front of the whole world and not crack?"

"Well, that's not true." He hesitates, like he's choosing his words carefully. "You held my pinky once when you got stuck on that rock ledge, and you needed to be rescued. Remember?"

My face warms without permission. I remember that encounter all too well. "Ah, yeah, remember how I refused to take your hand, so you basically gaslit me into believing that I'd die if I didn't at least take your pinky."

"That wasn't gaslighting. I saved your life, but nice to know you appreciated it." He exhales and shifts his weight until he's leaning closer, and I can smell his warm amber scent. I close my eyes, wishing I didn't even know Bodan.

"You're forgetting I'm comfortable with you, but that's taken years. I don't have years to get used to him." A brittle laugh leaks from my throat. "This would be so much easier if my mom hadn't made that rule about hockey players and you could just help me."

"Okay." He straightens up as if accepting a challenge. "Just because I'm not your fake date doesn't mean I can't help you. So, you're worried about holding hands. That's not too bad. It's just a technical skill, like anything. If there is anything I know, it's how to teach yourself new skills. First, you need to manage your stress. Relax your shoulders. You carry stress right here." He gestures vaguely near my collarbone, sending a ripple of goosebumps through my body. "People read that before they hear anything you say."

I blink. "I—what's wrong with my shoulders?"

"Nothing is wrong with them but try to keep them loose—it'll make breathing easier. And when you're next to him," he continues, like this is the most normal thing in the world, "don't overdo it. You don't need to make some grand gesture to make people believe you love him. Small things work too. Lean in when he talks and make sure you look at him. You know, act like now that you've found your person, you never want to be away from him. You can give that little smile you have—the one that makes you lower your lashes, almost like you have a secret."

My breath catches. I have no idea what smile he's talking about. I stare at him, my heart pounding. "Ah ... you just randomly thought of all that?"

"It's not random at all. I know your expressions." A corner of his mouth lifts. "And you can do a lot with just expressions, so you don't have to touch him if that makes you nervous. But if you want to try hand-holding..."

As if my heart could take any more probing, he reaches for my hand, slowly, like he's giving me a chance to back away. My confusion mingles with curiosity. Suddenly I yearn to feel what it's like to touch him. I mean, I've touched him before, but not like this...whatever this is that makes my skin heat. I don't pull away as his fingers skate over my palm. Our hands connect, fingers locking together in a perfect fit, like some unspoken skill we're both discovering. Electricity sizzles through my throat, my gut, even in my toes. The fizzle-popping explosions are relentless, and I clear my throat, hoping it will help simmer the sparks. No luck.

"Good hand-holding is comfortable," Ty continues quietly. "Don't go overboard with the squeezes or making it super tight. Just act like you belong there."

The fizzle stops as my whole body goes numb.

What in the actual—

I gape at my hand in his and can't miss that we fit perfectly. Suddenly it's that summer again, back in that Land Rover Ham and I used to share. I refuse to sell it even though it's old. Ham has long since gotten a new ride, but me, I'll never be able to let go of that moment when Ty's breath was too close. That single moment where everything tipped, and we almost kissed. All the years of wishing for it came together, but I pulled away because...because...I don't really know why! I've forgotten and remembered that moment more times than I care to count, always stuffing it down before my heart feels it. The memory hits so hard my knees threaten to give out. I swallow, and my fingers tremble in his. I'm painfully aware of how perfectly we fit together—and how wrong it is.

What planet am I even on, when Ty's holding my hand, and it feels like the most natural thing in the world...while he's telling me how to date another man? As if this whole fake-dating thing wasn't already out of hand, now this is completely undoing me.

My fingers twitch in his.

It's not dating advice anymore. It's him and me and everything we never said that summer. And all the summers before that.

It spirals up my chest, filling it so full of pressure it feels as if it's about to break. I pull my hand back decisively, like touching him any longer might crack something open I can't afford. "Yeah," I say, forcing a breathy laugh that sounds wrong even to my own ears. "You make it sound easy."

His hand drops to his side. "I'm just saying," he replies in a low voice, "you don't have to pretend so hard. Just be you. Whoever's standing next to you is lucky."

The words slam into my chest.

Does he know what he does to me? He's the one standing next to me. He has to know.

I meet his eyes—warm, deep.

For half a second, I forget what we're talking about. "You shouldn't be this good at this," I murmur, rolling my hands into fists to stop myself from acting on the impulse to touch him again. "It's confusing."

His brow furrows. "Confusing how?"

"Never mind." I shake my head, already retreating. "It doesn't matter. You're being a friend and helping me out." The word *friend* is deliberate. I need a guardrail, even if it costs me something.

He studies me as I try to hold back my expressions, but at least five different emotions rush over me. There's not a planet I can exist on where I can stand next to Ty, hold his hand, and act like my brain isn't consumed by him. Steeling my face, I clench my stomach and give everything I have to pretend he isn't unraveling me.

Lucky me, the front door flies open behind us. "Lottie!" a cheerful voice calls. "I was looking all over for you."

I stiffen as Bodan joins me on the porch, his eyes flicking between us before settling on me. "Hey. Is everything okay?"

"Yeah." I sigh a little too heavily. "I'm *fine*."

Behind me, Ty shifts, adding more physical space between us, but I hardly notice, because our emotional connection is still throbbing in my brain. I don't look at him because...well, I can't.

Bodan is waiting.

Fourteen

Tyson

I'm last to step off the team bus, trailing behind everyone as we file into the practice facility. The cold air hits my lungs like it always does. It feels amazing, especially since it's over a hundred degrees outside, and I'm here to play the best hockey of my life and earn everyone's respect.

The guys chat as we travel down the hall. My mind reels, and I stay quiet. I'm three steps into the locker room when the chattering turns to chirping—trash-talking and taunting. It doesn't seem aimed at anyone in particular, but after yesterday, goosebumps dot my spine.

Avoiding all distractions, I focus straight ahead. Yesterday was my turn to be humiliated. I took it and forced myself to laugh it off. There's no way they'd go for me twice in a row. Even pranksters have a sense of balance. Right?

My gaze sweeps the room.

Hartman is leaning back on the bench, his shiny new helmet dangling from his fingers. When my eyes meet his, he suddenly finds the ceiling fascinating. I don't know if it's guilt or what, but my intestines tangle.

I shake it off and keep walking.

My stall comes into view, and that's when I see it—my jersey. It's hanging where it should be, but something is wrong. It's clearly inside out with little stickers all over it.

Rocket shaped stickers with a zoomed in photo of Taz's face!

Groaning, I step closer. My fingers brush the fabric, and my heart sinks straight through the concrete floor. The snickering isn't subtle anymore. Bryce is standing next to me, his face split into a full grin as he chuckles. "Bruh." He throws his hands up defensively. "It wasn't me."

"Nope. This sure wasn't your work."

This stunt has Taz Houlihan's face all over it. Literally. Rocket is his nickname, and I hate how clever he was to put these cutesy little stickers all over my jersey. I hate even more that I know I'll be laughing about it in six months. He must have been behind yesterday's trick too—this is his thing, trying to make me crack.

My hands feel clumsy as I pick at the stickers, reliving all the panic from yesterday. Of course they're super sticky—glued on or something—and I have to scratch at the edges as they peel off slowly.

This is taking forever!

Houli is so lucky we're friends, or I'd kill him for this.

The heat of everyone's eyes warms my cheeks. My fingers tremble no matter how many times I curl them into fists and tell them to stop. It's not a big deal—they're just stickers—but I'm so nervous, my fingers don't work fast enough.

The room snaps to attention as the door swings open and Coach Badaszek strides in. All the laughter evaporates, and my chest locks up. I'm nowhere near ready—I'm still picking stickers off like it's my first day of preschool.

Coach's gaze pins me. "I—" My voice doesn't cooperate. I swallow and try again. "Hey, Coach. I'll be ready."

I'm sure he's seen the splattering of stickers over my jersey, but he doesn't acknowledge them. He lowers his voice, but somehow it feels louder when he says over my shoulder, "You're wearing a letter for a reason, Lane. Leadership isn't just what you do on the ice. You're not getting these guys on your side by playing with craft supplies."

My jaw tightens. I nod because arguing won't help. Explaining would sound like I'm making excuses. He turns away and takes a spot near the front of the room. I barely hear what he says, which I know is not very captain-like, but I'm stressing to clean my jersey. Coach says what he needs to say, and one by one, the guys file out.

I'm alone.

Again.

I stare at the jersey in my hands, and I let out a slow breath, swallowing my pride along with it. These stickers won't come off. I'm going to miss practice if I stay stubborn about it. Instead of fighting it, I turn my jersey right-side out, slip my arms in, and pull the jersey over my head.

Houli will skate with me today.

And then I'll kill him later!

When I stand, my hands steady. With my chin held high, I stride out, shoving the door open with both hands, ignoring how stiff my jersey feels.

Fifteen

Lottie

THIS IS A HORRIBLE idea!

I freak out the moment Bodan takes a spot onstage. Not because Bodan isn't attractive. He checks all the fake-date boxes in the all-things good-looking category: inviting smile, fit physique. He obviously came to slay the press in a dark suit that fits his broad shoulders perfectly. Honestly, he is sort of born perfect for this role.

No, he's the reason I'm crashing out.

Who am I kidding?

I'm crashing out because I'm ME!

"Hi, again," I say meekly as I take the final steps to close the gap between us. I never knew I could take such baby steps—my feet barely move. Yet I know they are moving, because he is, in fact, getting closer, and I am, in fact, starting to sweat. "Err, um, I'm glad you made it," I squeak out.

"I'm honored to be here." He grins an easy smile that, frankly, makes me jealous. I've spent years standing on these stages next to my mom. It's never been easy. Add in a fake date, and it's deadly. "You look ravishing," his casual compliment floats out.

"Well, I don't know about *ravishing*." I let out a small chuckle. That's an awfully nice compliment, even if I think he's exaggerating a little to cheer me up. If he's offended I don't return the compliment, he doesn't show it.

He scans the room, which is quickly filling with reporters. He slides his hands behind his back, clasps them, and whispers, "This room is terrifying."

"Yep." I follow his gaze around the hotel ballroom that is practically glittering with donor money. Dozens of linen-draped tables hold tall floral arrangements in patriotic colors—that part I'm okay with. It's the banner with my mother's face blasted across it that makes something twist in my stomach. It's just another one of my mom's political fundraisers. I should be used to them by now, but instead of getting easier, each one cranks the nauseating dial higher than the last. "It can be terrifying," I murmur. "Just smile a lot and act impressed when you hear phrases like *grassroots* and *bipartisan support*."

"And if I panic?" The dreamboat smile he gives me is so far from panic, I raise a skeptical brow. He's clearly enjoying the spotlight.

"Start chugging water," I say dryly. "They usually have that expensive sparkling water. It goes down easy and helps settle the nerves."

He laughs an easy chuckle. He doesn't look like he's struggling with this at all, which makes me wonder if he's just saying that to make small talk. For a moment, I feel sorry for him. He's merely another one of Mom's props—a temporary solution to move the current conversation in another direction. I hope this doesn't backfire on him. If all goes according to my mom's plans, he'll get a giant credibility boost when this is over, and no harm done.

But if I'm honest, it's the "no harm done" part that I can't seem to get past.

Since when does lying not cause harm?

"Okay," I say through a fixed smile as reporters position themselves in the front row. "Remember, if we do this right, we won't have to do it again. It's awkward, but let's try to sell it."

"I've got it all covered. I listen attentively. I laugh at the right moments. I say things like, 'Lottie is the most remarkable woman I've ever met.'"

I shoot him a look as his lips tilt into what feels like a flirty smile. "Don't overdo it," I caution.

"I'm a professional." His smile fills in even more, confirming it's definitely flirty.

I let out a shaky sigh and mumble, "I'll never understand why you agreed to do this. My mom must have some serious blackmail on you."

He laughs, showing all his perfect teeth—even his back molars. Either he had some serious braces or just perfect genes. "No blackmail at all, but she did promise to throw a little extra attention toward the museum. I'm hoping to get a promotion when my boss sees how 'important' I am." He inserts finger quotes as he speaks, and it hits me. Here I thought he was doing a good deed, but seriously, everyone uses everyone.

My attention shifts as my mom strides through the open double doors, and her sharp eyes zero in on me. "Great," I mutter.

"What?" He leans in, acting concerned.

"My mom has arrived."

"We should probably act like we're a little more comfortable with each other then." His words are laced with logic as he holds his hand out like an offering. "Do you want to take my hand?"

I stare at his palm. Nothing weird about it—not even a single mole—and I double-check just to make sure. I'm not worried about his mole disease, but I don't like these weird games. Before I take his hand, I glance back at my mom. Sure enough, she's boring into me, like I'm taking some test. Against my better judgment, I slide my palm into Bodan's. His skin scratches against mine as we shift, trying to figure out how to get comfortable. It doesn't feel natural at all; his arm seems extra-lanky and gangly. I practically have to drop my shoulder to line up our palms.

Is it supposed to be this hard?

My mind snaps back to holding Ty's hand—how our hands were magnets, connecting without effort. After another few awkward shifts, Bodan bends his elbow, and it feels a little better. Enough that I can step forward to play the role of the "good girl who dates perfect boys." It sounds easy, but my pulse echoes with the memory of the way the other hand fit so well. I can't help but feel like the other wasn't finished.

"Lottie!" Mom exclaims, air-kissing my cheek for attention before turning fully to Bodan. "So glad you could make it. You look handsome."

Bodan's hand tightens around mine, a little too snug, so my pinky has to slide under my ring finger to make it fit. Maybe he's nervous too, but everything feels forced, like he's trying to hold me back from running away.

Oh, good idea!

I should run away.

Oh, is it too late to run away?

I look toward the exit, and see people pouring in, filling the room all the way to the back. There's no way I could sneak out now.

"Thank you for having me," Bodan says smoothly to my mom. "It's wonderful to be here supporting your amazing work."

Eating that compliment right up, Mom beams as if she's the one on this fake date. Then she squeezes his forearm, claiming him for her campaign. "Well, Bodan, I think it's time we introduce you to everyone."

My stomach plummets. I get that's what we're here for, but we don't need to make a big spectacle out of it...or us. "Mom, speeches haven't even started—"

"That's even better," she cuts me off sharply. "Let's do a lap around the perimeter of the room together."

Bodan raises his eyebrows fractionally, then smiles at me. "Sounds like a plan."

Mom pulls us into the crowd and leans closer to Bodan. I catch her whisper, "You're doing well, but make sure not to leave Lottie's side."

He tilts his head toward her. "That shouldn't be a problem." My pulse jumps as his eyes find mine, and he smiles down. "I don't want to leave her side."

Great.

This fake date is already getting complicated.

He better not be catching feelings for me, because I didn't sign up for that!

My mom turns abruptly, steering us into a small group of people. "Oh—wonderful," she says loudly. "You're all here already. I want to introduce you to someone new."

My stomach has now taken to somersaulting. I didn't know it was this athletic and had so many routines. Gritting my teeth, I walk forward, noticing mostly familiar faces from past fundraisers or events. Reporters. They swivel in unison toward my mother, ready to hang on her every word.

"This," Mom announces, sweeping her arm in my direction, "is my darling daughter, Lottie, as you know." She pauses, flashing a smile that makes me want to gag, then continues, "And this is Bodan, her boyfriend." She inserts an airy laugh and leans in, "I suppose we might as well get the news out now. It's probably already leaked."

My jaw clenches.

Leaked. As if my mom hadn't meticulously planned this herself. I don't doubt she had Brett draft a full-page press release that's been emailed.

Bodan doesn't miss a beat. He stares at me like I'm the only thing in the room. I fight the urge to grind my teeth. One of the reporters leans in, tilting her gaze toward me. "Lottie, is this true? Do you confirm you're a couple?"

All eyes swing to me.

The moment stretches. I try not to glare at Mom's expectant smile. Maybe he feels the tension, because Bodan drops my hand to slip his arm around my waist, applying soft pressure that pricks my skin. "Yes," I say, because apparently this is my life now. "Bodan and I are *dating*."

There it is.

The official statement.

Everything is public now.

The things I do for my mother.

Does she even appreciate it?

"Well, congratulations, Lottie. We had no idea." The reporter smiles, pulling out her phone and positioning it in front of her. "Would you mind posing for a quick photo?"

My heart lurches as Bodan answers for me, "Sure." He leans in, murmuring into my ear, "Don't worry. I've got you."

My stomach finds a new trick—like it's being sliced down the middle. I don't like lying. Sure, on the surface, no crime is committed. Bodan is more than willing, but it feels immoral. The reporter takes the photo just as Bodan's arm tightens around me in a perfect photo pose. I force a smile. Not a happy one—not a real one—but it's the default I perfected years ago.

Click. Click. Click.

I hold my breath, waiting for everyone to take their turn like I'm some zoo animal on display. All the while, Mom beams from the side. At one point, I hear her correctly spell "Bodan" for a reporter, glowing as if she's already won the next election. "He's a scholar who works for the Smithsonian," she adds. After the final reporter moves on, my mom walks off, leaving me with an unsettling truth that stings far worse than it was supposed to.

This was supposed to be simple.

But I've never felt more guilty.

A weight feels tied to my flattened stomach, swinging there as it drags my gut lower and lower. Bodan must sense my unease, because he lowers his hand from my waist and steps aside, giving me space. "Is everything okay?"

"Ah." I shake my head, my eyes darting from my mom to him. "I don't know. I didn't expect this to feel so heavy, but I guess...whatever. It's done." I swallow quickly, hoping to avoid further emotion. It seems like everyone has already moved on. Speeches are about to start. No one is even looking at me anymore. This is the perfect time for me to leave.

Normally, I'd stay until the end to help my mom. Tonight is different. She pushed too far. "Boy, I'm struggling to breathe in here." I'm not being the least bit untruthful. "If you don't mind, I'm going to step outside, but you're welcome to stay as long as you like."

"I'll walk you to your car." Bodan stays at my side as I search for the exit. Running a hand over my cheek, I flounder for the right words. "I should be fine, but thank you. It was a pleasure working with you." I nod politely, then speed away, cringing. The bad news: he's right on my heels. I guess it's the gentlemanly thing to do—but I hate it.

A boundary I never knew I had was crossed tonight.

My mom and I have never been friends, but there was always a level of respect. Tonight, I was used.

My. Mom. Used. Me.

My heart cracks right down the center, shattering the place reserved to hold all the love and loyalty a girl has for her mother. Even though our relationship never felt normal, I protected it, but I know now, a line has been drawn. Forever.

Sixteen

Tyson

THE VOLUME ON MY phone is low, but the captions scroll as I slouch in my bus seat. When Lottie's face pops up on the bottom of the screen, the air leaves my lungs like I've been punched.

She's standing in a crowd, her hair pinned back in that effortless way. She smiles like she always does when she's trying to keep something from showing on her face. The closed caption reads: "Senator's daughter confirms new romantic relationship with notable scholar."

Bodan is next to her—*his arm around her waist!*

My gaze trails along his arm, and I grit my teeth as the mere sight of him touching her feels like an axe to my gut. The reporter leans in and asks her a question. All my blood rushes to my head, and I can't read what she asked. Lottie nods and smiles, her gorgeous smile stretching even wider.

It's fake.

It's fake.

It's all a big fat lie.

I chant to myself, but it doesn't stop my heart from feeling like it's being bludgeoned. I also know Lottie's smart and not the type to get caught up in some fake-dating scheme. Right now it doesn't matter. A wound tears open right between my ribs. It kills me to witness her next to any guy, fake or not. I hated seeing Bow Tie with her. This is maybe worse.

Around me, the guys are loud, riding the post-practice high. Someone's laughing about how tonight was the first time I actually made it onto the ice on time. Thankfully, I didn't get a prank ambush today. I should feel good about that. Instead, all I can see is Lottie smiling at Bodan.

Maybe I'm a sucker for punishment, but I open my texts and scroll to the one person who knows what's going on, hoping for another point of view.

You off work?

The dots appear almost immediately.

Ham: Just wrapped up the fundraiser. About to head back to the farm. Why?

My stomach's in knots. I'm not hungry, but I can't think of another excuse to get him to meet me.

I reply:

Dinner?

A pause.

Then: **Yeah. I can swing by the hotel and grab you.**

A minute later, the bus slows, and the blinker ticks as we pull into the hotel lot. The guys talk over each other as they grab their stuff and head out. I hang back, waiting until the aisle clears, then step down onto the pavement. The hot, muggy air hits my face and burns in a way that almost feels needed.

I don't wait long before Ham's truck pulls up like he timed it to the second. I shove my phone into the center pocket of my hoodie. Stepping off the sidewalk, I open the door and immediately groan when I see the inside of his truck. "Dude. What is all this?"

He laughs, waving his hand around like he's presenting a prize. "It's the fundraiser aftermath."

There are signs everywhere: poster boards, rolled banners, stacks of leftover programs, and boxes that smell like coffee. I wedge myself into the passenger seat, barely fitting. "Too bad you don't drive that Land Rover any more. I see Lottie still uses it, which I was surprised to see. It has way more room in it than this," I mutter as I shove a box of brochures aside.

"Complaining already?" He pulls away forward. "If I'd known you'd be such a downer, I'd have left you on the curb."

My zip hoodie is puffed up around my neck, trapping heat I don't want right now. I always slip it on after practice because the arena is cold. I clearly don't need it anymore, and I shrug it off. Since there's no room to put it next to me—and I'm afraid it'll get lost in the sea of stuff in the back seat—I shove it behind me. Then I let out a sigh when I'm finally able to breathe in the muggy air. "So," I say, trying to sound casual and not like I'm still recovering from seeing Lottie touching skin with Bodan, "how'd the fundraiser go?"

"Good." He checks his mirrors and pulls forward. "Looks like my mom's approval points are climbing back a little, and Bodan went over well."

I squawk a laugh as my throat constricts, and the sound that slips out is terrifying.

He taps his brakes and jerks his gaze over at me. "You good?"

Turning my attention out the window, I watch the streetlights scroll past the windshield. I don't need to tell him everything, but Ham and I have always been close. "I saw the Bodan announcement on the news."

He takes a left. "Yeah."

"I didn't think it would bother me." I rub my eye, not because it itches. My nerves drive me to fidget. "I know it's fake. I know why she's doing it. I'm happy she's helping your mom." The words tangle on the way out. "I didn't expect it to feel like that."

"Like what?"

"Like losing something I never had." I give him a side-eye, half expecting some cocky smirk that reveals Bodan was some elaborate joke he cooked up after I admitted I like Lottie. But he's not smiling. It's not a joke.

He keeps driving, one hand resting on top of the wheel. Maybe I should keep my mouth shut, because it has to be weird for him. She's his baby sister. But my chest is so tight it doesn't even feel like my chest anymore. It's like I've been body switched. Is that even a thing? I don't know what to do with it.

I hope it's not too late. I hope I didn't push Lottie into something that's going to mess up any chance we might have.

Crashing out, I ramble, "Dude, I know she's your sister, but I think about her all the time. I tell myself it's just a crush and it'll pass in the next month or so, but then I see her like that, and it hits me that it's not just a phase. It's her. It's always been her. For years. I don't even remember a time when it wasn't her—"

"Bruh!" He holds up one hand to his ear like he's plugging it. "Got it. That's enough! I get it. Totally. I don't need any more." He shudders as he takes a left and turns into the shopping center parking lot. He parks between a burger place and a barbecue joint and kills the engine. Neither of us moves. After a moment he adds, "So this might be too simple, but maybe you need to tell her already?"

"No, the timing is off." My throat tightens. "At first, I seriously thought it was fate bringing us together this summer, but everything changed when your mom had to make that big deal about hockey players." I shake my head as it hangs even lower. "Seriously, it's not even a hobby. Hockey is my job, and I'm good at it. And your mom knows me. Why would she ban Lottie from seeing someone in my profession?"

"Maybe my mom feels the tension, and she doesn't want it to affect Lottie's focus," he says, before adding, "not that it would."

"And I get that. Really, I do. I've tried to be rational about this. Trust me, I don't want these feelings. It makes everything so much harder." I drag a hand over my face. "I've got this insane soul tie or something, where I'll be doing the most normal thing and suddenly I'll see a white Land Rover with a woman with long blond hair driving it—and my chest just collapses. I just can't breathe. She's ruined me from white Land Rovers for life."

I shake my head. "Dude, the day I moved away from Mapleton, I was bawling at a gas station because I saw a bag of plain M&M's, and they are her favorite. Everyone knows the peanut ones are way better, but she's so loyal to the OG." I let out a slow breath. "I don't know when it started, but it almost happens daily—these little pulls I can't shut down. She's perfect."

"Brah, she's really just another chick. If you lived with her, you'd know she isn't perfect." Ham chuckles but I can tell it's not a real laugh. It's more what you do when you try to forcefully lighten the mood. "She leaves all this hair in the shower drain. It's disgusting. She's terrible at taking care of those goats. Like, they are ruining our lives—"

I flick my hand out, cutting him off. "See, I don't see those as liabilities. I find them adorable."

"You wouldn't think her hair in the shower drain is adorable if you saw it. It looks like a dead rat." Sighing, he flicks his finger forward, pointing to the burger place. "You still want to eat?"

"Yeah," I say. "I do."

Opening his door slowly, he mumbles, "Well, let's stop emoting about Lottie then."

I open my door and grab my sweatshirt. It's hot outside, but everyone always has their air-conditioning cranked so cold that I like to wear it indoors. As soon as I swipe it from my seat, something slides free and hits the pavement with a soft tap.

It's my phone. The screen lights up, flashing bright.

Lottie's name glows on it.

For a second, the world narrows to that single word, pulsing like a secret I didn't mean to reveal. Then it dawns on me.

It's not just her name

It's a call, and it's connected!

Somehow, I called her, and she's on the other end.

I grab my phone, my fingers trembling, and slowly raise it to my ear. The line is dead silent as I speak quietly.

"Lottie, are you there?"

Seventeen

Lottie

BODAN WALKS ME TO my car with his hands tucked into the pockets of his blazer. We stop beside my door. "Well," he says, smiling in a careful way, "goodnight, *girlfriend.*"

"Goodnight," I echo, cringing as I try to ignore that other word. I'm very aware of the keys clutched in my hand. The moment feels so unbelievably awkward. He reaches out and brushes a loose strand of hair away from my face. I get it—it's a sweet gesture, meant to show me he notices me—but I turn my head at the same moment my phone rings.

He lifts his hand in a small wave, stepping back. "Text me tomorrow, and we'll talk about the parade."

"I will." I climb into my car, shutting the door with more force than necessary, and answer the ringing phone.

"Hello?"

There's silence.

Oh, wait—no. Muffled voices.

"Dude, I know she's your sister, but I think about her all the time," the voice says. *"I tell myself it's just a crush and it'll pass…"* It muffles for a bit and then cuts back in, *"But then I see her like that, and it hits me that it's not just a phase. It's her. It's always been her. For years. I don't even remember a time when it wasn't her—"*

My stomach drops when I recognize another voice. Ham cuts him off, and I grip the phone so hard my knuckles ache.

I know the other voice too!

Oh, my!

That's totally Ty!

Oh, my Ty!

I should not be listening to this!

What even is this?

Is this a prank?

Everything muffles again but I can't stop listening. After a good minute, I hear, "Hello? Lottie, are you there?"

"No," I say quickly, then burst out laughing because clearly, I'm here. "I mean, yeah, I'm waiting for you. You called me, but you didn't say anything."

"I didn't call you," Ty rushes out, but then adds in a cautious voice, "How long have you been waiting?"

"Not that long," I quip, then bite my lip hard.

"Did you hear anything—"

"No," I interrupt, but my voice is forced and strained. "What did you want?"

He clears his throat. "I didn't mean to call you. Must've been a butt dial. I was sitting on my sweatshirt."

"Okay. That's fine. I better go. I'm driving. You know, I should pay attention to the road." It's not like he can see me, but to prove my point, I crank my engine, shift my car into gear, and pull out.

"Yeah. Talk later."

We hang up, and I drop my phone onto the passenger seat like it's a burning lump of coal. I robotically take all the turns I need to get home, but I remember none of them, because my mind keeps replaying what I just heard Tyson say to Ham.

It was muffled, but not so muffled that I couldn't make it out.

He said he thinks about me.

He has for years.

I thought I was alone in my feelings for him, but I guess not...

I'm dead.

An hour later, I pull into my driveway, not remembering a single thing about the drive. I park and step out of the car. Something shuffles behind me, and I don't even need to look to know it's a goat—one that isn't in his pen—coming up to greet me.

"Seriously?"

I slowly turn. Sure enough, Crunch is trotting toward me. I'm in a mood and yell, even though I never yell at my goats.

"Get in your pen!"

My heart won't slow as I chase him across the yard.

All I can think about is what I heard.

All I can feel is my heart slamming against my chest, sending little ripples through my veins. Each one feels like it is changing me.

Changing what I thought I knew.

About myself.

About Ty.

And now, as I run after this goat like my life depends on it, my whole life flashes before my eyes.

It's the oldest story in the world.

One day you're driving home from work, and your brother's best friend is just your shy brother's best friend, the one you've known for years. Sure, you have a crush on him, but that's cliché. And he's off-limits because he's your brother's best friend, and he's a hockey player your mom hates, and okay, he's hot but he's definitely not into you.

Then suddenly everything rearranges.

All my memories.

All my emotions.

I press my hand to my chest.

He likes me back.

I didn't imagine that.

Just like I didn't imagine we almost kissed that one time.

A lump swells in my throat.

Oh my Ty. Apparently, that's my new slogan or something. I sort of love it. I whisper it out loud, loving the way his name sounds when it rolls out of my lips, "Oh my Ty..."

Eighteen

Lottie

THE FLOAT IS SO much smaller than I expected. Mom's been
planning this for months, and she made it sound like we'd have
a huge semi-trailer, but this is basically a small flatbed pulled by
Ham's truck. I settle on a hay bale—because Mother thought
they'd be festive—and wedge between her and Bodan's very solid
arm.

I have one hand wrapped tight around Cinnamon's ribboned
leash. Of course, my mother thought it would be good for her
wholesome branding to bring one of the goats. I was stunned she
even suggested it, because hello—has she seen what kind of trouble
they get into? But I know better than to argue, and I loaded up

Cinnamon, because she's the best behaved of the three. Down deep, part of me thinks this is going to be hilarious.

Before I know it, the red, white, and blue bunting flaps against the trailer, and we inch forward in the parade lineup, the unforgiving July sun beating down. We barely start moving when Cinnamon rears on her hind legs, her front hooves skidding toward the edge as if she's ready to launch into the crowd. I can't imagine how insane my mom would go if that happened. "Oh no, you don't," I hiss, pulling her back just as she tries to leap.

Bodan laughs. "She's feisty. Kinda like you."

I give him a look, but he only grins wider. I'm not really into the random flirt attempts. I'm glad they're rare; he's professional. But ever since we held hands on that stage, he gives me the ick. I turn away.

My mom clears her throat, her glare drilling into the side of my face as she subtly nudges me closer to Bodan. "Remember to stay in character. People are watching," she murmurs through a smile. "Try to act like you're in love."

"What do you want me to do?" I mutter through clenched teeth, my distain for her lying scheme boiling over. "Make out with him in front of everyone?"

Her smile stiffens. "No. But you need to sell it. You could at least hold hands."

That's when Cinnamon headbutts my mom square in the butt.

Exactly what I was thinking about doing.

Man, I love this goat.

Yep. I couldn't have planned it better.

She yelps as her foot slips, her arms flailing backward in slow motion. Gasps ripple through the crowd as she tumbles right off the trailer, landing in a heap of patriotic streamers. The spectators hush, then rush forward to ensure she's okay.

Call me cruel, but I'm laughing.

I can't stop. Laughter bubbles out of me like it's been waiting my whole life for this exact moment. She's clearly not hurt. Her pride will be bruised, but honestly? It's worth it. She needs to be put in her place. I'm giving this goat a hoof massage later because she just made my year.

While I'm laughing, Bodan seizes the opportunity to hero up. He hops down from the float and goes straight to my mom, helping her to her feet. "Hey, Senator Halloway, are you okay?"

Cameras are going wild, people crowding in from every angle, and my mom smiles at them all, milking the attention. "I'm fine, everyone."

Bodan helps her back onto the trailer and then rejoins me at my side. His hand finds my arm and lingers there. I want to roll my eyes. Instead, I let him touch me, but I turn the other way. My mom looks like she might combust, but the photographers are eating it up.

"Seriously, this is fun," Bodan says quietly, leaning in. "I'm having a great time. Thank you for inviting me. You're amazing at what you do."

I open my mouth to respond when Cinnamon comes to my rescue, choosing violence again. This time she clamps her jaws on Bodan's pressed blazer sleeve.

"Sorry," I say, tugging her back. "Apparently, she doesn't like anyone today."

"Yeah, sometimes sorry isn't enough." He tries to laugh, but it's clearly fake. I let his odd reply hang in the air. It strikes me that if he were Ty, he would have told me not to apologize. I don't hear what Bodan says next, because something catches my eye.

Not just something, but someone.

Walking alongside his teammates is Ty. Sunlight hits his summer tan just right, and he looks so unfairly handsome as he smirks at the crowd. He carries a hockey stick, shaking hands with as many people as he can as he moves along. Then he gets distracted and looks my way.

For a second, our eyes meet.

I forget where I am.

I forget the cameras.

I forget Bodan's arm brushing mine.

Unfortunately, Bodan uses that moment to slide his arm around me. Tyson must see it, because his gaze jerks away.

At this point I want to elbow Bodan—even though he's doing his job. Thankfully, I don't have to use any force, because Cinnamon jerks the leash again, pulling me away enough that we're no longer touching. I wobble as my heart races and grip the leash as tight as I can, since Cinnamon is doing everything in her power not to behave. I force a smile for the crowd, but nothing about it feels happy.

Of course, the one guy I have feelings for is watching me fake date someone else while I wrangle a rebellious goat in front of the entire city.

Can this get any more ridiculous?

Nineteen

Tyson

So much for earning the team's respect at the parade—not only did I split my pants in front of everyone, the guys somehow tricked me into eating horse treats. Thankfully Brenna, Kingston Brewer's cousin, carries a sewing kit wherever she goes because she's a wedding planner, and she was able to sew my pants. But seriously, I'm over being embarrassed. The chirps never stop. I'm never going to win their respect. There's so much pressure to be better, I can't take it. Still lugging my last hockey stick to give away, I peel away from the team at the first chance I get. I don't know exactly where I'm going, but I pull up the parade map on my phone, trying to plot the best spot to "casually bump" into Lottie before they leave.

It's easily ninety degrees, if not a hundred, and my practice jersey is soaked in sweat. I peel it off and drape it over my shoulder. I've got another shirt underneath, so I'm still warm, but it's a tad easier to breathe.

I spot Lottie near their trailer, parked at the end of the route. She looks incredible in a bright pink sleeveless shirt that shows off her arms. I didn't know I had a thing for arms, but now I do. Or maybe just when they are on her.

She's standing between Bodan and her mom, who is in full shark mode, practically yanking pedestrians off the curb and forcing them to shake her hand. Instead of business cards, she's passing out garden seed packets, pretending to know something about gardening in a bid to be relatable. Her approval rating must still be in free fall because I've never seen her this desperate.

"I'm telling you, daisies are the heart of my garden!" Senator Halloway's voice carries over the crowd. It makes me chuckle—I'm one of the few people who know her precious garden is all a farce.

Lottie catches my eye, and an exhale slips out before I can stop it. Her face instantly brightens as she smiles at me. "Ty, are you coming to save me?"

"Rough morning?" I grin, stepping closer. I nod a quick hello to her mom, then ignore Bodan standing next to her. He's not a bad guy, but my brain refuses to acknowledge any man standing next to *my* queen.

"Not really rough," she sighs, looking down at the leash in her hand. "Cinnamon has decided today is the day she enters her terrible teen years."

I give the goat a side-eye and Cinnamon returns a very judgmental expression. Lottie isn't exaggerating. "Hey," I say, holding my hand out cautiously. I smell like horse treats, and I half-expect her to bite me. To my pleasure, she lifts her chin and ignores me.

I lean in, holding up my hockey stick. "Hey, I have to hand this out for PR. If you need a break from your mom, you can walk with me until I find someone to give it to."

"Ah, sure." Her gaze flicks to her fake date before she steps forward. "Bodan should be okay with my mom." Without hesitation, she pulls the goat along. Technically, I could give the stick to anyone right here, but it might feel like part of her mom's campaign. I respect what she does and all, but I don't want to be associated with the campaign. Plus, I need this moment to walk next to Lottie. We haven't had much time together, and it's certainly not like our Julys at the lake. I don't think we'll ever get that feeling back.

The heat is thick, and we haven't gone fifty yards when a tiny kid with a beaming smile wanders into our path. "Wow, what kind of dog is that?" The kid's eyes are wide at the goat.

"It's a goat, buddy," Lottie says, tugging the leash and holding her back from jumping on the kid.

Sweat drips from my face, and I don't care to loiter longer than necessary. I raise the stick toward him. "Do you like hockey?"

The kid's face lights up like a Christmas tree. "Yeah!"

"Well, it's your lucky day, because I play for the US Stars team, and I have a stick to give out. Would you like it?" I push it toward him, making sure he can see my signature. He takes it and excitedly runs to tell his mom. I'm so focused on watching him scramble away with his prize that I don't notice the weight shift off my shoulder.

I'm grinning when Lottie giggles. "Ty, did you notice you lost something?"

I whirl around. Cinnamon has my jersey in her jaws. From the looks of it, she's already managed to swallow half a sleeve.

"Hey! That's not a snack!" I lunge for it, but she plants her hooves and pulls back.

I don't want a tug-of-war with a four-legged vacuum, but those jerseys are expensive. Lottie is doubled over, laughing so hard she's clutching her stomach. "Not to be gross, but I think she smells the salt from your sweat. She loves salt."

"That's nasty!" Reaching forward, I grab it with a sharp tug, and the jersey pops out of her mouth with a sickening *rrrrip*.

I stare at a gaping hole, right through the sleeve.

Lottie drops to her knees in front of the goat. She cups her little face in her hands, looking her dead in the eyes. "Cinnamon Halloway," she coos in a high-pitched, sugary baby voice. "You didn't mean to eat Ty's shirt, did you? You just couldn't help how great it smelled, right?" Cinnamon lets out a soft noise and nuzzles her palm.

I stand here, holding a ruined shirt, and I can't even be mad. Watching her talk to a goat like it's a toddler makes my chest flip. She glances up at me, cheeks flushed from the heat.

Man, she's stunning.

"Sorry," she says, still smiling. "She's—"

I cut her off. "Don't apologize. Actually, I won't be able to wear it anymore with the extra ventilation. It's full of holes now." I make a split-second decision to toss the mangled jersey to her. "You can keep it."

She catches it with her left hand, hugging it close to her body. "You're giving me your jersey?" She eyes the hole, then back at me with a playful glint in her eyes. "Boy, that makes me feel pretty special. I didn't think you guys just handed those out."

My heart slams into my ribs.

I hadn't planned it to *mean* anything. It was purely an impulse—her goat ate it, so it felt like a "you-break-it-you-buy-it" gesture. But now, with the way her eyes are glinting at me, I've changed my mind. I've never actually given one of my jerseys to a girl before. Suddenly this moment feels heavier, like one that matters. "Yeah, I guess I am giving it to you," I say, trying to keep my voice steady. "You should wear it to one of my games."

Her expression softens. "My mom would forbid it," she whispers, glancing back toward where her mother is still doling out fake gardening advice next to Lottie's fake boyfriend. "You know, with her whole scandal and all." She looks at the jersey in her hand and back up at me, a defiant little smirk forming. "But, ah, I'll see what I can do, Ty."

I swallow, hanging on to the way my name sounds on her lips.

Like she made it extra soft and gooey.

Ah, she's just being friendly.

Is she?

I don't need to catalog the way her eyes linger on mine. I drag a hand down the back of my neck, trying to ground myself.

Say something normal, I tell myself.

Anything!

Instead, I huff out a breath that's halfway to a laugh, because I'm not convinced anything coherent will come out. She has no idea she just knocked my world off its axis. All I can do is stand here, pretending I'm not unraveling from the inside out as I picture her in my jersey.

What if she comes to one of my games?

I'm already a nervous wreck without her there.

But wait...what if she comes?

My gaze drifts to the side.

She's not interested in hockey.

If she comes, that means she's interested in something *else*, right?

That something...would be *me*!

Twenty

Lottie

SOME DAYS REQUIRE COPIOUS *amounts of Diet Coke!*

I chug from my freshly popped can and gaze around the dining room table as the air keeps getting thicker. I tried my best to go to the game, but my mom had already planned this kiss-up-to-billionaires dinner. Now my phone is face down on my thigh, buzzing softly with game updates, and I'm doing my best to hide it from my mom.

Mom cooked chicken herself instead of letting the usual caterer handle it. That alone tells me how badly she wants tonight to go right. The table is set with the nice plates again. Actually, every time we eat in the formal dining room, those are the only plates we use.

Across from me, Beau Tucker, an oil tycoon billionaire, grins politely. He's next to another billionaire, Trey Michaels, who made his name in tech. I've met them before at fundraisers. Of course, I was trotted out to shake hands. This rubbing-elbows thing isn't new. What's new is the way their attention keeps sliding back to me, like I've got mashed potatoes smeared in my hair.

"So," Trey says while cutting into his chicken, "I heard on the news you're dating someone. Congratulations. It sounds like it must be getting serious."

My stomach sinks straight to the flower flip-flops my mom didn't notice I snuck in with. She hates open-toed shoes. I hate any kind of shoes in July. It's a month meant to be barefoot, in my humble opinion anyway. I lift my fork and take a bite, which I don't taste—or maybe I do taste it, but it's mostly just cardboard flavor. After chewing for a ridiculous amount of time, I mutter, "So I guess I am."

Mom's smile is sharp as she kicks me under the table and then speaks for me. "Very serious."

My phone buzzes again. I sneak a glance while casually lifting my Diet Coke to my mouth. I've got lots of practice angling the screen just enough to catch it. The arena lights explode in blue and white, and the crowd blurs as the camera scans all the fans before zooming in on the guys skating out.

My heart stutters as I squint and zero in on Ty. I've never been one to ogle hockey players, or really any guy, but why have I never noticed before how handsome Tyson looks when he's in his jersey and pads?

"Who's the lucky guy?" Beau asks, interrupting my game sneaking.

I look up from my phone too late. Everyone is watching me. "Oh, my boyfriend, um," I drag in a breath and swallow. "He works at a museum. The Smithsonian."

I catch Mom's jaw tighten as she takes her water glass and sips from it.

"Oh?" Trey adjusts in his seat, sitting more upright as he finally cuts into his chicken. Eating is a good sign. That means he can't ask me more questions. "I've always been a huge fan of the Smithsonian. Is he one of the curators?"

Wrong.

Apparently, he can eat and be nosy.

I take another sip of my Diet Coke to buy some time. My phone vibrates again, and I slide my leg back, pressing it against the chair, doing my best to trap it so no one can see it. I wish so badly I could see why it updated. "Um," I say. "I should know what his position at the museum is ... but, hmm. He might be a curator. That sounds smart, and he's very smart."

Mom exhales loudly. "They met through mutual connections," she adds quickly. "Lottie isn't one to spend too much time at museums. She doesn't understand the organizational structure."

My brows pinch together as I glare at my mom. She's making me sound stupid. Sure, it's my oversight that I didn't get Bodan's exact job title. In my defense, I have only hung out with him two times. Both times she was breathing down my neck.

"What's he like?" Beau leans over the table, still grinning. "Personality-wise."

"Well, he's smart since he works at the museum." I stir my potatoes with my fork. Not because they need it. It's just nice to have something to do with my hands. "He's busy, and he's very handsome."

"I think the handsome part is mostly keeping her preoccupied," Mom says with a chuckle, and everyone laughs. I shouldn't risk it, but I steal another glance at my phone. Tyson's skating fast, his jersey clinging to him, and he looks so good my eyes practically pop out of my head.

Why didn't I start watching hockey earlier?

My cheeks ache from the effort of not smiling.

"Are you going to try long-distance dating?" Trey asks, keeping the conversation going. I'm starting to resent that nobody has anything else to talk about.

"No," I say too fast. Then I slow myself down. "We shouldn't have to do distance. He lives here, so while the Senate is in session, we'll be together, but even when Mom's not in session, our family has been spending more and more time in DC. I'm not sure we'll head back to Mapleton. I guess there's really no reason for me to. It's a little too soon to think that far. We'll figure things out."

Mom's hand lands lightly on my wrist. It's clearly a warning disguised as affection. "Lottie's been balancing her new relationship with work so well. Bodan is a joy to have around."

I smile a toothy grin, even though the only thing I'm managing is not tilting my phone so the whole table sees exactly what I'm watching.

The questions keep coming. Where did we meet? What do I like most about him? And on and on. I answer with borrowed details, trying my hardest not to flat-out lie. My knee bounces when I can faintly see Tyson score a goal. At that point, I have to cough to cover my excitement.

Finally, Dad changes the conversation to talk about crypto investing, and I slink down into my chair and wait for everyone to finish their food. By the time chairs scrape back on the marble floor, it feels like this dinner has taken an eternity. Everyone is polite as Mom escorts them to the door. She's laughing in that polished way she reserves for people she considers important.

The second I'm dismissed, I bolt upstairs.

Relieved to be free, oxygen fills my lungs all the way. Rushing to my room, I flop on my bed and pull out my phone, turning up the volume. The game is almost over. It's third period, and people are booing.

The Stripes pull their goalie, and my eyes glue to the screen. The puck is in play, and the guys spar pretty hard until someone on Ty's team makes a shot that goes right into the empty net, bringing the lead up to 4-1.

"Since when do *you* watch hockey?" Ham's voice cuts through the air.

Startling, I jerk my head back and nearly drop the phone. Ham leans in my doorway with his arms crossed and a smug expression on his face.

"I don't know what you're talking about." I slide my phone behind my back.

"You think I don't recognize what you're doing?" He gives a quiet laugh. "The real question is, why the sudden interest? Is this payback for Mom making you fake date to cover for her hockey blunder?"

"I seriously have no idea what you are talking about. I wasn't watching hockey. I was reviewing notes." I smash my phone screen down on my comforter. "I want to make sure I don't forget anything when I introduce Mom for her big speech next week."

"You're a terrible liar." He slowly shakes his head. "Now, tell me why you all of a sudden care about hockey, and I won't tell Mom you were watching it all through dinner."

I straighten, letting my eyes drift around the room. Ham and I aren't exactly close, but we get along. I could come up with some lame excuse, but the truth is, as Tyson's close friend, Ham's in a position to help me. Maybe I'll regret it, but I take a risk. "So, the other day, you and Ty were talking about me, and I heard everything he said through his butt dial."

His brows bend down as if he's remembering. "Wait. What did you hear?"

"All of it," I add quietly. "About how he thinks about me, and...the truth is, I can't stop thinking about him, and it's been like this for a while. Maybe we are both infected with some thinking disease. I also can't stop looking at him. I mean, have you ever really watched him play hockey before? He's HOT!"

"Seriously, Lottie." He makes a gagging noise as he turns his back to me for a second and pretends to be ill. "He's my best friend. You're my sister. Why is this getting weird?"

"I didn't do anything to make it weird." My hand flies forward in a gesture that mirrors the desperation that's budding in my chest. I never asked for things to be this complicated, and I'm at such a loss of how to fix it.

He studies me for a long second before he sighs. "You know Ty really well. I mean, you probably know him almost as well as I do. I hope you aren't just curious because he's getting a lot of attention now with the tournament and you're bored, because what I saw in his face when he confessed that all to me is he really cares about you."

"I heard it too in his voice."

He peers out into the hall, making sure the coast is clear before looking back at me. "If you're serious about liking him, then stop pretending you don't want it. He's a good guy, but he's not one to play games with. He won't handle you leading him on and then ghosting him."

"I'm not going to lead him on," I hesitate, "but are you forgetting I'm not supposed to date hockey players? And I have a new fake boyfriend the whole world is fascinated with?"

He lifts one shoulder. "Since when has Mom forbidding you from doing something ever stopped you?"

It's my turn to shrug. I'm not rebellious.

"Just—" he adds, softer now. "Look, I'm headed back to my place for the night, and I don't care to get in your business. This whole thing is cringe to me. I can't tell you what to do, but I know he has feelings for you—and they are genuine. You two need to talk before this fake-dating mess gets any worse, and before someone else decides your life for you."

I swallow hard because he has some good points. As he turns on his heel to leave, my heart races. My gaze snags on my phone.

Should I call him tonight?

That sends a rock to the pit of my gut.

I wish I knew what to do.

Twenty-One

Tyson

IT'S GAME TIME, AND the second my skates hit the ice, nerves fire through me. Instead of fighting them, I let them fuel me. When the puck drops, my team quickly takes control of it. Within moments, it comes my way, and I don't even have to think. I'm open, and I shoot a clean wrister with an easy release. It goes exactly where I want it to go.

For a split second, the arena goes silent, or maybe that's in my head. I have tunnel vision as I watch the puck slide across the ice and into the net. When it hits the back of the net, the crowd explodes.

Stone is on me first, slamming his glove into mine. Kingston jumps on me next, and it's knuckies all around as the horn blares. That does nothing to silence the crowd as it continues to lose its mind. I can't hide the fact I'm relieved we got the first goal. I'm even more relieved I finally did something that might make it look like I actually deserve to wear this C. This is how respect is earned, and I'm here for it. The pressure in my gut doesn't release though.

Unstoppable, my goal song, plays as I skate back to the bench with a niggling thought popping into the back of my head. *Is Lottie watching?* Yeah, she said her mom would never allow her to come in person. Maybe she's at home with the game on? My chest tightens, but I don't have time to overthink it, because the game gets chippy fast. Houli gets into it with Leniecker behind our net. I sort of want to laugh, because Houli has it coming with all the pranks he's played this week. Shoves are exchanged. Even though no calls are made against either side, my stomach knots anyway.

Stuff like that has a way of boiling over later.

Then Jeremiah Precio gets called for holding Baptiste Marchand, and suddenly we're a man down. The Stripes team gets a power play and keeps the puck moving around our zone. I count every second until we finally survive the penalty.

I breathe, but only enough to maintain consciousness.

We get lucky when DiFranco snaps a shot past the Stripes' goalie. It's clean and fast, and now the scoreboard glows a beautiful 2–0. The arena erupts again, but I don't celebrate. It's too early, and too much can happen.

Next, Otto Stagmeier trips Jake Twiles, which gives us a power play. We set up, but they kill it off like it's nothing.

With a minute left in the period, the East presses hard. The puck gets jammed in the corner. Every player piles in. They manage to dig it free, and it slides to Ted Powell, who takes off like a maniac in a breakaway.

It's him and Blake Davis that I skate after. Everyone crashes the net, and I have laser focus as I dig for the puck until the whistle finally blows, announcing the end of the period.

As I skate to the bench, my lungs burn. I glance once more toward the stands and then toward the cameras.

I don't know if she saw any of it.

But I felt her the whole time.

"Undefeated!" I announce as I bust through the locker room door. That earns a chorus of cheers. Someone lobs a roll of tape at my head. I'm in such a good mood, I burst out laughing.

Heading straight to my stall, I listen to all the side conversations about blocked shots and busted plays. We won in a blowout, and I couldn't be happier about my goal. Still, I don't kid myself—something is bugging me. I didn't see Lottie in the stands.

Sure, she doesn't really care about hockey, but the smile she gave me when she took my jersey meant something. Now I'm hyperfixated on my phone, and I quickly pull it out to check.

Nothing.

I'm still holding on to hope that she'll be randomly outside when I leave, and I'm craning my neck in every direction, willing myself to see her.

Does it work?

Nope.

It isn't until I'm on the team bus, heading back to the hotel that my phone finally buzzes, and my heart actually skips a beat.

It's not Lottie. It's Ham.

> **Dude, this is going to wreck you, but I talked to Lottie tonight. She heard us the other day, and she knows. I don't want to get in the middle of your business, but you guys need to talk.**

I don't know what I'm doing faster, blinking or typing, but both are happening simultaneously.

> **What do you mean, she knows? She knows! She knows what? She knows I like her.**

> **Yeah, she heard your butt dial, and you need to call her before the fake date gets real.**

I reread his text, trying to decipher what he means. He didn't exactly come out and say she likes me too, but he's also not telling me to stay away from her. I'm about to reply when another text comes in, and my heart stops—it's Lottie.

> **Hey. Sorry I couldn't come. My mom had another donor dinner at the house, and you know how she feels about hockey. I couldn't escape. But I watched as much as I could on my phone under the table. Congrats on your goal. You were incredible.**

I stare at the text. I picture her surrounded by people in suits while she's hiding her phone in her lap. Too funny. It's not the same as her being in the stands, but it probably took twice the effort. My thumbs are moving before I can overthink it.

> **Thank you. The win feels pretty amazing, but it's just the start. We have to win two more times.**

I take a breath and Ham's words about needing to talk to Lottie echo.

It's seriously now or . . . never. Swallowing, I let my fingers do what my words could never have the courage to do.

> **I was wondering if you want to hang out. I can squeeze an hour off after practice tomorrow. Maybe somewhere a goat can't eat my clothes?**

The typing bubbles appear, then vanish for a long beat. My gut drops all the way to the floor. When they finally return, I hang on to them.

> **I want to, but my mom's been watching my schedule like a hawk since I announced my fake relationship. She doesn't want me to do anything that could expose her lies. If someone saw us together, that would really upset her.**

I lean my head back against the seat. I'm not losing to her mom's schedule. I think about her stupid fake date. Well, not that Bodan is stupid. He works at the Smithsonian. He's probably brilliant, especially compared to me. The situation is stupid.

> **What if you tell her you're going to the museum to meet up with Bodan for a lunch break? If the press or any of her friends see us together, you have a built-in excuse. You're hanging out while you wait for him to get a break. Totally innocent.**

I hold my breath while I send it.

> **Using Bodan to our advantage, huh? It could work. I'll text Bodan and see what time works for him, and we can meet there.**

I exhale in relief and grin. Tomorrow just became the most important day of my life. It's the day I finally tell Lottie exactly how I feel.

If everything goes well, we'll finally be together.

Twenty-Two

Lottie

I TELL MY MOM exactly what she wants to hear. I'm going to the workshop Bodan is teaching at the museum.

It's technically not a lie.

I'm going.

I'm just going with Ty—one of the people my mom despises. On top of that, he accidentally confessed his feelings to me, thinking he was only talking to my brother, and now he acts like it never happened. The tension is so thick, I know that as soon as we get the right moment to talk, it will all be ripped wide open.

When I arrive, I find him standing near the stone steps, hands in his pockets. He's got that lazy, one-sided grin that unravels any defense I may have had, and my heart lurches. I didn't know I had a rebellious streak in me, but the fact my mom has forbidden this makes this excursion all the more exciting. My entire life has always been neatly balanced on the edge of perfect public perception.

Frankly, I'm sick of the pressure.

His lazy smirk grows when he sees me. Rebellion seems to be calling my name, and I plow forward. "Hey, you."

He's wearing a dark button-down with the sleeves rolled up to his forearms. When he waves, the fabric pulls just enough across his chest to steal my breath. I wonder if he planned to look this good? The moment our eyes meet, something ignites.

"You came," I say, which is stupid because obviously he did. He wouldn't be standing here otherwise. My gut is doing gymnastics, sinking low with nerves, soaring high with anticipation, pulling taut with hope. I don't doubt if this continues, at some point I will just stand and grunt as I clench my stomach, praying to steady it. Ever since I found out his true feelings for me, my bodily functions haven't been cooperating.

"I said I would." His eyes sweep over my face, and his lips part as if he wants to add something, but then he dramatically looks behind me and declares, "I was half-expecting you to show up with Toast or Crunch."

"Don't worry. I left them all at the farm," I say solemnly. "I still feel terrible about your jersey. I'm so sorry."

"Don't apologize. It's not your fault." He chuckles quietly, like it's just for me, causing something to loosen in my chest. Without another word, he opens the door, and we head inside, falling into step with each other. I stop when I spot a low-hanging banner with Bodan's face. The title of the presentation reads: *250 Years of the American Story*, as presented by Bodan Bowey. There's nothing wrong with the photo, but it hauntingly reminds me of the banners my mom makes for herself. I stare at the sign, and a shiver—definitely not the good kind—spirals up my arm.

"That sign is uneven," Tyson whispers.

I squint and follow the horizontal line it makes, and he's right. It is noticeably higher on one side. "Great," I mumble, with an air of teasing in my voice. "Now I can't unsee it, and it's all I can focus on."

"Welcome to my world." He chuckles. "I always notice things like that."

"Sounds rough."

"It can be." He grins at me, and we slow near a display case. Wanting to talk about something other than the sign, I lower my voice to change the subject, "So, how was practice?"

"Good." His smile twists wryly. "We've got a practical joker in the locker room. At first, I thought it was Taz. My jersey was sewn shut the first day, and then at the parade he was hanging out with someone who had a professional sewing kit. It was just too perfect—I still think he pulled some pranks—but now some things are happening that I don't think he could manage. It's been... interesting. And since the first couple of days, when the jokes were aimed at me, I ended up completely frazzled. Honestly, I probably didn't make the best impression on the coach."

"That's not good."

"Yeah, you know how first impressions linger, but I'm determined to win him over, and the team too. Scoring in the game helped." His shoulders lift in a stiff shrug, though it's not convincing. "It's a tough situation since we only play together for a few weeks, and everyone is pushing to do their best. I really want to earn their respect."

"From what I saw on my phone under the table, it didn't look like you were struggling at all. You were amazing."

"Oh, yeah?" His gaze holds mine, his teeth pressing into his bottom lip, that telltale pause when he's figuring out what to say. "That's your professional analysis?"

"It is." I tilt my head. "Well, at least the free one. If you need a comprehensive one, I charge extra."

He chuckles, crinkles forming by his eyes, then sobers quickly. "It's just frustrating. I have never had tension with a boss before."

The words hit closer to home than he knows. "Trust me," I say quietly. "I know exactly what it feels like to not get along with your boss."

The lobby fades into the background as his eyes soften. "You handle your mom so much better than I would," he says at last. "If I didn't know your family personally, I'd never guess there's any conflict, especially with the press. You are truly brilliant at what you do."

Caught off guard, I blink. It's far from the first time he's said something nice to me, but knowing what I know about his feelings, everything feels different now. "Brilliant is a bit generous," I say. "Most days I just bite my tongue and I perfectly time my eyeroll for the exact moment she looks away."

He laughs like that's the funniest thing he's heard all month, and he flashes his perfect lazy smile at me. "If there were medals for handling the worst boss, you'd podium."

It's my turn to laugh, heat rising up my cheeks. Again, he's always been sweet to me, but it feels like he's layering his compliments thicker and *flirtier*. "Wow. That's a nice thing to say."

"I'm serious." His voice softens again. "You're so good to her, even when it costs you something, like having to go along with this whole Bodan thing. You didn't want that, but it helped her. You also didn't ask for anything in return. That's pretty selfless."

My throat clenches. I open my mouth to deflect, but he beats me to it. "Also," he says, eyes glinting, "I respect your ability to still hang out with me, even when your mom has expressed her disapproval. It's a risk, but don't think it's lost on me. I appreciate it." He fixes me with a look that says just how much he *appreciates* me.

For a second, I forget where we are.

I forget who I'm supposed to be dating.

I forget the lie waiting beyond the auditorium doors.

Heat rises up my neck, and I feel like I might melt to the floor.

I swallow and lift my eyes to the auditorium looming ahead like an eerily haunted house. I don't want to go in—it'll only deepen the lies. What I want is right here, yet I feel completely stuck. He notices me staring at the doors, and his smile fades. "We can go in when you're ready."

"Never," I whisper, savoring having Ty all to myself. Then I remember something Bodan said the first day I met him and giggle. I whisper, "So I forgot to tell you, but Bodan has these crazy conspiracy theories about hockey. He fits right in with my mom, but if you get any weird vibes from him, that's probably why."

He's laughing when he says, "Now you tell me."

I'm not laughing. Everything instantly feels heavy as I spot Bodan. He's wearing a full tailored jacket, and he is surrounded by coworkers who, if I had to guess, have definitely read the headlines about him dating me. As soon as he spots me, he declares very loudly, "There you are. I'm so glad you made it, *honey*."

The random nickname burns in my gut, which makes me wonder if I ever had so many stomach problems before this week. I don't recall. It's like my digestive system is trying to slowly kill me. I flatten my palm on my stomach, hoping to calm it.

Before I can respond, Bodan's coworkers bumble forward. With huge, eager smiles, they shove their handshake greetings at me. Their gazes flick between Bodan and me, and my stomach drops again, making my brows draw together in worry. At what point does my stomach just land on the floor? It can't go any lower. The thing about having a fake public boyfriend is that it's actually *public*. I shouldn't be surprised, but I never expected his coworkers to react like this.

Tyson goes still beside me, and it brings me back to the present. "This is—" I start, then pause to carefully choose my word, "—this is my friend, Tyson. He's in town for the week and wanted to check out the museum." Every word tastes like chalk. It's completely true—even if I've left out a lot about how he loves me and I love him too, but neither of us has the courage to say it aloud.

Tyson offers a polite smile and shakes hands with a couple of people who step forward to welcome him. His jaw tightens enough that I notice. Then we're ushered to the front row, where Tyson and I sit next to each other. It's another moment before Bodan takes the stage and launches into his lecture. He really is confident and engaging. Looking around the room, I notice it's almost full, and everyone is hanging on his every word.

Turning my focus back to Bodan, I last about three minutes before a yawn bubbles out of nowhere. My eyes drift sideways, where I see Ty's elbow propped on the armrest with his chin resting in his palm. More alarming—his gaze is pinned on me. When he catches me looking, his eyebrows hike, and he makes an exaggerated face like he's fighting sleep. I bite my lip to keep from laughing.

I turn back to Bodan, who is apparently a lot smarter than I'd realized. Most of his intellectual jargon sails right over my head. Thankfully, he's not talking hockey conspiracies. Truthfully, he's handsome up there with his neatly gelled hair, but I am struggling to care. My gaze slips back to Ty, who catches my eye again and mouths the word, "Help."

I shake my head, struggling not to laugh. We are definitely on the same page. As the lecture drones on, I don't hear a word of it. Somewhere in the middle, Tyson starts bouncing his knee like he's got ants in his pants. That wouldn't normally bother me, but every few bounces, his leg brushes mine. Accidental or not, lightning rockets through my thigh.

Every.

Single.

Time.

Too distracted to care about what Bodan is saying, I wish Ty and I were somewhere else. Somewhere private, where we could talk. I could tell him how much I hate pretending I'm dating Bodan, how much it feels like something's been growing between us, and how sick it makes me to think I'm wasting all this time that we could be spending being honest with each other.

Maybe at some point, I need to stop blaming my mom? I mean, I'm not a little girl anymore. I can make my own decisions. My breath catches as I think about the fallout. There's no way I could turn my back on her and still work with her every day. I'd have to get another job, which I know exists, but it's hard when this is all I know. I majored in political science at George Washington University and was so determined to do this career I graduated in three years, even while working full time for my mom. When I say I put all my eggs in one basket, they are stacked heavy.

The thing I didn't foresee? Even well-stacked eggs can crack.

Applause fills the room. I missed the ending of the lecture. Bodan grins at me as he steps away from the podium and walks downstage until he's right in front of me. "Thank you again for coming."

"Of course," I say automatically.

Cameras flash around us. A few people line up to talk to Bo-dan. In a way, it feels like the room is closing in. The weight of expectations—to be perfect and pretend to be in love with this guy—squeezes around my ribs.

Ty leans in, whispering, "You look like you need some air."

"I think I do." I exhale, relief flooding through me. Waving at Bodan, I smile and say, "I'm grabbing some air while you wrap up questions." I don't wait for a reply. Ty and I slip away together, heading outside, where the air feels instantly lighter, even in July. The sun isn't as hot as it could be, cloaked behind a promising gray cloud. We haven't had much rain this summer; cooler weather would be nice, though I'm not getting my hopes up.

We walk a few steps while my brain buzzes, and I struggle to find the right words to explain what's going on inside me, finally blurting, "That was interesting. What did you think?"

"I don't know if I found it interesting, but it was okay for a change of pace." His eyes never leave mine, wicked flickering happening. "But if I'm being honest, I think the goats are more fun."

I laugh, even though my chest aches to spill out what I really feel. That I hate pretending to love Bodan while denying that I love *him*. "Next time," I say with an irritable nod, my intestines twisting in protest. I'm starting to wonder if they will stay like this forever.

"Oh, next time." His smile is instantly playful. "Does that mean you're asking me to hang out again?"

"It sounds like you are upset about missing the goats. I'm not going to deny you the goats, if that's what you want. We can go to the farm, where it's just us—" I cut myself off, realizing how that sounds. I meant where there are no fake dates or crowds of people, but it's too late to walk that back. Heat flushes my face as I fumble for a rebuttal, but Tyson makes it easy.

"Just us." Without missing a beat, his smile tips higher on one side. "Is that a promise?"

Dropping my gaze to the sidewalk, I finger the hem of my shirt. It's not unusual for him to ask to hang out, especially since we only have a short time. It's getting harder to pretend all of this attention is easy for me. "Yeah, just text me when you have time off." I try to sound as casual as possible and toss out a joke, "I'll make sure Bodan has to work, so we don't have to hear about—" I stop, because I have no idea what he said. After wracking my brain for a solid ten seconds, I give up. "You know ... whatever he just talked about for the last hour."

I wait for him to chuckle, but his eyes continue to glint at me in a way that makes my knees weak, and his voice deepens into something caramelly. "I'll text as soon as I look at my schedule."

"It's a plan." I start to back away before I say something I'm not ready to say. "Anyway, I better get back to the office. I only marked myself out for an hour lunch break."

"Same. I need to get back to work too."

I wave over my shoulder as I turn. As we part, I can't stop thinking about all the mounting lies.

I'm lying to the world about Bodan.

So is my mom.

Technically, Ty has been lying to me, because he hasn't been truthful about his feelings. I don't blame him for that though.

I'm technically lying back to him.

It's getting hard to keep track of. Shaking my head, I let out a sigh. I don't know if I'll ever be brave enough to tell the truth. I hope I am. It's the right thing to do. Even if it's the impossible thing.

Twenty-Three

Tyson

It's been over twenty-four hours since I saw Lottie, and I'm still hung up on not being able to say what I needed to. I wanted to so badly. As much as the museum seemed like the perfect place to meet up, it was, in fact, not. It was too public, and the vibe was off.

Not to mention the fake date lurking around.

That's not to say I didn't enjoy my day with her, but I failed. I had one task; tell her how I feel. As my frustration mounts, I zip my bag, and it's all I can do not to hurl the whole thing at my stall. Not wanting to draw that kind of attention to myself, I carefully stow it.

I'm only here for a few weeks. Every day that passes is another day she's spending with Bodan. Sure, she says it's all business ... but I don't trust him. I've seen the way he looks at her, and he loves every minute of her attention. I would put money on the fact he's waiting to make his move.

To top that off, it's game day, and I've developed a lump in my throat. I'm chalking it up to the pressure riding on me to perform. I've done enough deep-breathing exercises to know this lump is going nowhere. There's a low murmur from the guys as they pull on gear. I don't engage much with the chirping, but as team captain, I make sure to give everyone a nod. I mostly hover near my stall.

Taking another deep breath, I focus so hard on filling my lungs, I barely hear the vibration. When it buzzes again, I realize it's my phone. I've got a few seconds before I need to get on the ice, but I grab it, and my stomach drops like I've taken a punch.

> **Lottie: Hey, just letting you know I made it to the game, and I'm wearing the holy jersey.**

Chuckling, I catch what she did with the wordplay—from holey to holy—and I smile. Sure, it's not the wag jacket I often pictured her in, but my jersey feels special too.

But then the room tilts as it sinks in.

She's HERE!

My pulse is suddenly everywhere—in my throat, in my ears, in the tips of my fingers—as I struggle not to drop my phone. Seriously, did she tie her mom up and lock her in a closet?

Okay, that's a little extreme.

Excitement surges through my veins, racing all through my extremities until even my toes tingle. I text back fast, tossing a look over my shoulder to make sure no one has left the locker room yet.

> **How are you here!?**

With wide eyes, I wait for a reply, because she's not supposed to be here—because her mom hates me and hates hockey even more—and because if she's recognized, this could turn her fake-dating situation into a scandal.

No response!

Around me, the guys snap helmets on. Bryce slaps my shoulder on his way out the door. My feet won't move. One by one, the stalls empty. The knot in my throat swells as my time runs out, and I reluctantly curl my fingers around my phone. I'm about to stuff it back into my bag when it buzzes!

> **I know, it's shocking. I asked Bodan if he wanted to go on a fake date to see the game. My mom was excited about the potential photo of the two of us together. Every time they go viral, her ratings go up a point. So, we're here together. Perfect decoy, right?**

My chest hollows out in an instant. Of course she's here with Bodan.

Her public boyfriend.

The one who can sit beside her without anyone questioning it.

I picture it without meaning to. Great, now I'm going to throw up. I can't stop the image from replaying in my head—her leaning toward him to pose for a photo. She's playing her role. I get it, but I don't trust he won't try to swoop in.

The sting rises in the center of my chest—hot as blue fire.

But then something else pushes through, stronger than the sting.

She came to my game.

Even though her mom hates hockey, Lottie risked being here. She wanted to be here so badly, she brought Bodan just to make it possible. That feels like it means more than it does on the surface.

I'll find you.

My heart pulses in my throat as I can't stop thinking about her sitting next to Bodan, knowing he's working hard to win her over. Any guy would. I force a grin despite myself, tuck my phone away, and hurry out of the locker room.

The arena's roar crashes over me as I take a warm-up lap. Scanning the crowd, it's effortless to spot her. Our gazes are so in tune, we connect instantly.

She's a few rows up, and like she warned me, she's tucked beside Bodan. He has no clue how lucky he is to be on a date with Lottie, even if it is fake. When she sees me, her mouth curves into a smile I swear she's been saving just for me.

I lift my glove and wave.

She waves back.

Bodan waves too. In my opinion, he's a little too enthusiastic and obvious, like he's greeting a best friend across a parking lot. I chuckle under my breath. *Buddy, you have no idea.* I shake my head as I get ready for the puck drop.

Everything narrows, like it always does, to just the ice and the puck.

The first period is a little out of sync. It feels like everyone's trying to establish dominance. Despite that, we get control of the puck, and Jake Twiles takes off on a rush that makes my stomach clench. It's looking good until their goalie shuts him down with a glove save that brings the crowd to its feet.

Emotion rises in my throat as I steal a few seconds to look at Lottie. Sitting on the edge of her seat, her gaze fixes on me with so much focus. Not at all like she sat at the museum lecture, which makes me chuckle. Poor Bodan. He has no idea … What is that, like the third time I said that about him? That's like his slogan. No-idea Bodan. I like it.

Back in the game, Twiles gets loose again.

He snaps one on a breakaway. I skate past our bench, my jaw twitching as I force myself not to look at the crowd. *Stay focused, Ty.* For the most part, I do. It's easy to be consumed by the game. It's a first language to me.

Late in the period, Taz catches a cross-ice pass and snaps the puck toward the net. It goes in clean. The horn blares, announcing the tie, and the sound punches straight through me.

The Stripes take a second to celebrate with a few fist pumps, but my eyes lift up to the stands. Lottie's on her feet, and the expression on her face makes my chest feel too full for my ribs.

The game grinds on. In the second period, Stripes' player Chas Sullivan buries a one-timer from the left circle, and the arena explodes. My chest constricts, my airway narrowing even more.

In the third period, Jeremiah Precio gets a shot in for our team, and thankfully everything is tight again. That's not the only thing that's tight though. The tension coils tighter with every shift.

Midway through the final period, Baptiste Marchand slaps one home. Suddenly, the Stripes are up again. The cheers vibrate through my chest protector. In a risk I'm not sure I'd take, Coach Badaszek pulls our goalie, and my palms start to sweat. We gain a skater.

My teeth clench as my attention snaps back to our unguarded goal. If there was ever a time to show the team what a defenseman can do, it's now. I dig in, pulling every last ounce of adrenaline to drive my skates faster. I block a shot that rattles my shin, but I don't stop. I chase down the puck as if my life depends on it. The crowd erupts, and it looks like we got this.

With seconds left, East player Reeves fires it from the red line, and when it slides into our empty net, the Stripes win is sealed.

The horn sounds.

I barely register it.

My heart is in my throat. This isn't how I wanted tonight to go. As I skate off the ice, I toss one final glance toward Lottie, who's politely clapping when her eyes lock on to mine. A jolt of electricity shoots through me. I may have lost the game tonight, which sickens me, but in a tiny silver lining I didn't see coming, something else is slowly, and *finally*, coming together.

Twenty-Four

Lottie

From the porch, I study Maddie's camper parked next to the barn. It arrived a couple of days ago, but I haven't had a chance to visit with her yet. According to Ham, she needs a ride to the hockey games. I was going to drop by and say hello and confirm the time, but she doesn't seem to be around. I turn on my heel to head back inside just as Tyson's rental car putts up the driveway, kicking up dust in the late afternoon light. My heart rate increases as he climbs out with that hesitant confidence, and I find myself scanning everything else because I can't bear to meet his eyes.

This is so different for us.

Although we are both naturally shy, we've never been quiet around each other. Here I am, checking the camper again, then the barn, even the fence line, searching for anything that isn't Tyson Lane.

He seems to notice me scanning everything, and he does the same, taking in the place from every angle. A slow grin tugs at his mouth. "Is Ham around?"

"Well," I say after a beat, "he stayed late with my mom for some meeting. They should be back shortly. It's just me right now." I sink my teeth into my bottom lip. Saying we're alone out loud feels like stepping into a giant spotlight. I rush to change the subject, "So, uh, your game yesterday was amazing."

"No, it wasn't." One eyebrow cuts up. "We lost."

"You guys all played well though." I hesitate, then continue, "Isn't it more about how you play?"

"No, it's about winning." He shoots a clipped nod at me before lowering his voice into a grumble, "Taz and I have played with and against each other for years. It's almost a bad thing—he knows me so well he's always one step ahead."

"I wish we didn't live so far from each other, because I could get used to coming to your games." I hold his gaze and wait to see if he picks up on the subtle hint. I know it's subtle—maybe too subtle—but I'm not good at this.

Deep down, my overreactive digestive system kicks in again, loud and insistent. "Even though I'm not good at this, I'm tired of this. Stop dancing around the issue." Yes, it actually said all those words. I know, because I speak colon.

Shifting his weight from one foot to the other, he clears his throat. "So, uh, how was Bodan?"

"Well, he's Bodan." I tug on the hem of my shirt as I study the perfect straight seam like it's the most fascinating thing I've seen all day. "I think he had fun. He's one of those people who does well wherever he is, and he's not shy. He likes the attention."

"That sounds promising." Tyson's voice is dry, as if he can barely force the words out.

"He's not a bad guy," I say honestly, even though neither of us wants to talk about him. He's basically my coworker at this point. With only a few minutes—or maybe an hour tops—before Ham and my mom come back, I'm struggling to steer the conversation to where I need it to go. Shoot, my dad might even pop in sooner. I so desperately want to talk about all the things Ty and I need to talk about. *But how?* After a pause, I swallow, mustering up all my courage, close my eyes, and drop a hint bomb. "Yeah, Bodan is fine to hang out with, but I don't think he's the one for me."

Just like that, the air thickens.

Like, *so* thick.

How did that happen in a single second?

Someone cranked the oven dial to a hundred and ninety. I open my eyes right as Ty tosses a look over his shoulder, scanning the property as if he expects my mom to materialize. When he turns back, he scratches the back of his head, like he's solving the hardest math problem ever. "So, just to be clear. No one's here? We're not having a family dinner. You just invited me to hang out?"

"Like I said, if you're already bored, Ham is on his way, but honestly, I was hoping we could talk." I take a tiny step closer, careful not to touch him. I'm not brave enough for that yet. Sure, I've accidentally touched him plenty of times over the years, even shared friendly hugs, but the tension is now suffocating—I can't move another inch.

"Talk?" His voice pitches up and squeaks, causing me to stifle a giggle. He evens it out and adds, "Sure. We can talk."

I hate having to initiate this. I've never done this kind of thing before, but I get why he's not saying anything—because one, I have a fake boyfriend, and two, my mom made it clear we can't date. The air is muggy as it should be in July, but it layers sweat on my lower back that's distracting. Needing my head to clear, I nod toward the front door. "Why don't we go inside, where the air-conditioning's on?"

"Sure." I wait for him to say more than a single word, but after he tacks on a cheesy grin, I realize this is weird for him too.

Why is this so weird?

It's Ty!

I don't doubt that once we get over this weird initial step, every-thing will be perfect—but neither one of us has ever been much of a talker. I lead him inside, where my plan to sit down and relax completely backfires. Somehow, it's worse here. It might have to do with the formality of our living room, with its high-back chairs and giant portrait of my mom above the fireplace. We sit on opposite ends of the couch like we're waiting for a mediator.

"So," he says, his eyes glued on the portrait of my mom, "your mom wasn't upset about you going to the game?"

"No, her approval rating went up another point." I deflate a little. This is way too awkward. He won't open up like this. I stand abruptly and say the first thing that comes to mind, "Do you want to walk the goats?"

A teasing grin spreads across his features. "Should I be scared?"

"Nah, they always behave perfectly." I'm already grinning wider, eager to get somewhere that feels more natural.

Clearly, he likes the idea, at least better than this, because he's on his feet. I think we're both grateful to have something to focus on, and we quickly scramble outside, grab leashes, and wrangle three very opinionated goats. Even with the struggle to get them all leashed, we're interacting more naturally. Crunch butts Ty's leg and tries to nip at his sleeve. Ty's quick to jerk his arm away, and we laugh. Our chemistry clicks into place again as our eyes meet, and we hold a long, unbroken gaze.

This is how we work.

Not sitting and staring at each other.

We steer the goats out of the pen, letting them roam the pasture. The silence is no longer awkward. My stomach relaxes, and I find a way to ease into conversation, "I'm sorry about Bodan being at the game."

Even though he's not looking directly at me, I can tell he rolls his eyes. "Why are you apologizing?"

Wincing, I struggle not to apologize for apologizing and settle on a one shoulder shrug. "I guess that's what I do."

His bottom lip rolls under his top, as if he's fighting not to say something. When his lips finally purse, he says, "You know you say sorry too much."

I smile faintly. "You've told me that before."

"Still true." We pause near the barn, letting the goats snoop around, and he nudges a rock with his shoe, like he's not ready to stop moving. "You care too much about making everyone else happy. Hence, you got sucked into this whole fake-boyfriend thing."

"I won't argue with you there. I do that a lot." Biting the inside of my cheek, I give my shirt a nice tug again. My poor shirt will have loose threads when I'm done with it. "I guess I was hoping, if I did this for her, she'd finally see me a little differently. Like, not just an extension of her, but me for me. You know, I just always feel like she sees me as a tool or a resource but the rest of me is invisible."

"You're not invisible." His gaze snaps over, and his voice lowers when he asks, "What about your happiness?"

"Oh, I'm fine." I wave him off. "Bodan is a gentleman. A perfect fake date. My mom is happy." I swallow, the words I refuse to say stick somewhere behind my growing lump.

"I didn't ask about your mom's happiness." His jaw twitches. "And why don't I believe you when you say you're fine?"

My gut reacts, plummeting lower. "Well," I start, then stop. *Why is this so hard?* I know he likes me—I heard him say it—but I can't tell him that. It's too direct, and we don't have that kind of boldness going on. "I don't know ... maybe, I'm confused."

"Confused about what?"

Exhaling, I check on the goats, who have found a patch of wild grass to devour. I'm glad they aren't after my mom's flowers. It means I can focus on Ty. My stomach is looping, but it's seriously now or never. His question is the perfect prompt, and it won't get easier. I look him dead in the eyes, but my tongue ties.

As if to take the pressure off me, Ty dips his head toward me and softens his voice. "Lottie, be honest. I talked to Ham. Did you hear what I said to Ham when I butt-dialed you?" The sun catches the side of his face, lighting up his eyes, and the familiar—but now somehow terrifying—pull to him comes roaring back. He's giving me the bait to shift this conversation exactly where it needs to go.

I pray that admitting I heard him is the right thing to do. Once the words are out, I can't take anything back. I'm terrified of making a mistake. My face heats under the pressure of the cracking silence. "I heard it. Ham and I chatted about it the other day, and he confirmed what I heard was true."

A slow grin spreads across his face. "Well, I guess Ham's officially banned from secrets now." His voice softens even more. "But since we're being honest, I'm relieved you heard it."

My palm presses to my chest in a reflex I couldn't have planned. My heart pounds so hard, I feel compelled to hold it. I've never felt so brave before, yet I've also never felt so at ease. When Ty looks at me with the softest glint in his eyes, I breathe out softly, "So ... are you confirming that's true?"

He steps a little closer—not enough to crowd me—just enough to make the air feel warmer, which is wild since it's already about a hundred and ninety out here. "Lottie, you've been on my mind for a while." It sounds so casual now compared to the way he confessed everything to Ham. I get he might be playing it cool. His voice lowers when he adds, "How does that make you feel?"

Phew!

I look down for half a second, then back up as courage pools in my chest. As I focus on his warm, chocolate eyes, my breath evens. It's just us and our honesty. I don't know what I was afraid of. When we connect like this, my reply floats out, "Right now, I feel like I'm where I'm supposed to be, but ..." I exhale and rush to add, "I might also feel like I'm in trouble."

"Trouble?" he echoes, his voice fills with concern.

"Not in a bad way," I say quickly, hoping to distill any anxiety. Crunch tugs on his leash, pulling my attention to him for a second. He's seriously worse than triplet toddlers. I could drop the leash and just let him graze ... all the goats are doing right now is eating. In a normal situation, I'd never let them go, but I'm right here. I risk it—only for Ty—and drop the leashes, giving them freedom. Then I turn back to Ty, whose eyes are so wide I feel bad for leaving him hanging, and I take the biggest risk yet. "I think about you too."

"You do?" A slow smile dawns on his lips. "Good," he says gently. "Because I was hoping I wasn't the only one feeling that."

A quiet chuckle slips out. "Wow," I say, shaking my head.

"Wow is right. I didn't expect today to turn into this." His smile blooms wider. "But ... I'm really glad it did." I wait for him to say something else, perhaps ask me out on an official date. I don't know the proper procedure. He clearly already has my number—we've been talking for years. Nothing about our situation makes sense. I look back at him, trusting he knows what to do next.

Some moments feel slow because they are boring or painful.

In this moment, time *stops* as it suddenly becomes *scared*.

I stare into the depths of his eyes as this moment, more than just a moment, quickly becomes my favorite memory. Ty's eyes visually caress my face, as he slides a foot forward, closing the gap between us. I wait for him to say something, but to my surprise, he risks everything, his hand sliding to my hip and drawing me to him. My body responds instantly, as if hypnotized, and I move with him into an embrace. He leans close, and my heart races, expecting a kiss—but instead, he lowers his face to my cheek and presses a soft, chaste kiss in front of my ear. The touch is so gentle and feathery light, that tingles flood the side of my face. It lasts only a second before he pulls back. "Is this okay?" he asks, his voice barely more than a whisper.

I don't trust my words, so I let my fingers curl into his shirt and I nod. He brushes his thumb along my cheek. A swallow pulses my throat as I melt into his embrace. He lowers his face again, exactly as before, as if to drop another sweet kiss on my cheek, but I turn my head and part my lips, hoping he takes the invitation.

We share a beat of deep eye contact that travels to my toes. His lashes lower, I tilt my chin, and our lips brush together in the slowest setting—like the whole world has been put in slow motion. His breath is warm, pulling me in, and as I relax into his lips, his hand wraps fully around my back, tucking me into his chest. All my nerves unwind, and I drop the guardrail I've held between us for years. Kissing him is everything and nothing like I thought it would be. He's so careful, yet attentive to every tug of my lips, it's like we practiced for years.

When he pulls back again, he lets out a satisfied exhale. I can't help but chuckle, even though I'm breathless. There's nothing funny about this moment—the tenderness is still palpable. "Sorry if that was out of the blue," he says, a little winded. "I'm terrible with words, as you can probably tell. I'm much better with action. I just needed you to know … you know, exactly what this moment was doing to me."

I bat my lashes at him. "Don't say sorry."

He grins at me like he's about to lean in again, and my lips tingle in anticipation, but this time our lips fail to touch because Crunch suddenly leaps between us, bleating for attention like a tiny horned chaperone.

Ty lets out a laugh, and I take a step back, brushing my hands down my jeans. "Okay," I say, steadier now. "I know what I need to do."

He watches me closely as I find Crunch's leash dragging in the dirt and I pull on it to keep him from butting Ty. It's not working, and Ty laughs when he looks back at me. "Lock them back in their pen?"

"That too, but I need to talk to my mom," I say. "And Bodan. It's the only way we can have a real shot at this."

"A real shot." He goes still, and his eyes widen. "Is that what you want?"

Maybe it should feel presumptuous to assume that's where we're headed—especially after just one half-conversation and a kiss—but everything in my soul tells me: This. Is. It.

After all the years of putting everyone else first, I'm ready to focus on me. Ty is worth it. "Yeah, it is."

His hands curl at his sides as his gaze drills into mine, like he's searching for something. "Lottie, I don't want to be something you feel you have to convince yourself into, or something that will mess up things with your mom. But if you're sure you want this, then just know we'll face the fallout together."

Relief washes through me, forcing a long exhale. He seems to already know my anxieties before I even identify them. Knowing he understands everything I'm facing makes me even more certain I can do this.

He sidesteps, collecting the other goat leashes, and I swallow hard, planting my feet like I might actually need the ground beneath me. He doesn't know what my mom is capable of. Sure, he knows her a little, but he's still naïve. He hasn't seen how fast she can turn on someone.

My fingers tighten around the leash, bracing for the risk I'm taking. But when I meet his eyes, I melt into warm, velvety goodness, and the fear loosens its grip. The look of pure admiration fuels me, and somehow, that's enough.

I hope.

Twenty-Five

Tyson

IN ALL THE YEARS we've been friends, I've never once visited Ham at work, which is probably why I have no clue what he does. Sure, he's the security manager for his mom. It sounds impressive until you realize he's not a frontline guy. He's never the guy standing next to his mom. That spot is reserved for a guy with muscles. Once I learned that, I just assumed he schedules the guys who do the real work.

I take the bus to the closest stop and walk until I'm on the edge of the office complex, craning my neck at the building. Then I glance at my phone, check the address to confirm I'm at the Hart Senate office, and look back up. So, this is where they all work—Ham, Lottie, and their mom. An American flag snaps stiffly in the wind, welcoming me forward. In my head, I mutter, *This office is way scarier than I thought.*

My stomach twists as I step inside the door. Before I can take another step, a uniformed officer shifts subtly in my direction, like he clocked me the second I crossed an invisible line. "Can I help you?" he asks.

I lift my palms, suddenly very conscious of how out of place I probably look. "Yeah, I'm here to see a friend, Hamilton Halloway. I called ahead. He said I should be on a list for a visitor pass or something."

The officer's expression flickers. "What did you say your name was?"

I step forward. "Tyson Lane."

The officer speaks on his phone. After a moment, he turns back to me. "You are cleared to go through the metal detector."

Taking a cautious step forward, my eyes flick from the uniformed officers stationed at every corner to the throng of visitors moving purposefully through the doors. I get in line with them and follow them through the checkpoint. The second I step past security, I'm in a hallway where Ham's waiting. "Ty," he says slowly, scanning all around me. "I'm so touched you are visiting, but also a little suspicious. Care to tell me what's up?"

I try to smile, but the guy works security for his mom. Which means two things:

>   1. This is the worst possible place for me to show up to see
>   him.

2. He already knows something is wrong.

"I just need to talk," I say, rolling my shoulders. I look around at all the rooms and nod toward a dark one. "Can we go someplace private?"

His eyes narrow, his feet planted firmly, making no move toward a quiet room. "You *never* 'just need to talk.' Last time you showed up to talk unannounced, it was in Mapleton when you got traded, thus breaking up our friendship—"

Cutting him off before he gets ridiculous, I spout back, "It wasn't a breakup."

"It felt like it to me, because we both cried." He jerks his chin up, like he's trying to rush me, or maybe he's on to me. "Anyway, you're in a federal building, so I know you did something wrong, or you wouldn't be bothering me at work. What did you do?"

I rub a hand over my face, as this is insanely impossible. There's no way I can tell him what's transpired in the last twenty-four hours, especially here in the open. Doing my best to create a private place, I slide my feet back until I'm against the wall. Ham narrows his eyes until the crease between his brows melts into one giant unibrow. I've seen a lot of intimidating faces before on the hockey rink, but this one is giving "I'll kill you if you BS me" vibes.

He follows me until my back hits the wall. I swallow hard, as if I'm forming a launch pad for all the things I need to confess. I can't hold back, and the truth explodes out of me like a bomb. "I kissed Lottie!" My arms fling out as if they too can't hold back, and I slam my lips together, gluing them shut before anything else can escape. I wait for him to scream.

He simply tilts his head toward me. "What do you mean, you kissed her?"

I rush on, unable to stop reliving the kiss in this very moment, relishing every detail. "It was a real kiss, with my arms wrapped around her, and it was everything I ever imagined. She kissed me back with passion, and my entire soul reorganized itself around her existence. My life officially has a before-and-after moment now, and—"

"STOP," he barks, physically gagging. He scans down the hallway as if regretting not letting me into a private office. Then his voice drops. "Oh, Mylanta! Dude. No more talking. That is my sister!"

I wince, realizing I was reliving it all out loud. "I didn't mean to—"

"You kissed Lottie." His nostrils flare, eyes pinning me in a threatening glare. "With your mouth. Don't say you didn't mean to. You can't accidentally smash your mouth onto someone. You did it on purpose. Don't lie to me."

"I mean, yes, I meant to kiss Lottie, but I didn't mean to upset you. You cut me off with that murderous look before I could finish." I need to giggle—saying it out loud fills me with little happy bubbles that flutter up my throat. "It was life-changing."

"Stop!" He points at me. "I swear if you say one more thing—"

I can't help but smirk, slipping back to that magical moment. "She smelled like—" I start, but he doesn't let me continue. He jerks back so fast, letting out a choking noise somewhere between a cough and a shriek.

"I *hate* you!" he yells, flailing one arm as if I've thrown a live grenade at him. "I don't need these mental images." Though his words are mean, I know him well enough to know he's not serious about the hate. He's a tad dramatic.

I lean back, pretending to shield myself from the imaginary attack. "That's fair."

He staggers a few steps back, waving both hands like he's fending off a swarm of angry wasps. "No! Seriously! It's too much. Don't talk about it in any detail, or I will barf."

Holding back a laugh like my life depends on it, my lips twitch. "Was it the part where she kissed me back with passion?"

He throws his head back dramatically. "It's all of it!"

We stare at each other before he shakes his head, muttering, "I knew this would happen. I *knew* it."

"You did not."

"I absolutely did. You look at her like she's—" he cuts himself off and gags. "Dude, this is so weird."

"The gagging is a little dramatic." I gesture forward but don't dare move. My back is still smashed flush with the wall. I bet he's regretting not going into the private office now.

He sighs, scrubbing a hand over his face. "Okay. Okay. I get it. It was bound to happen, but please don't ever tell me about when you touch her again. Or anything."

As much as I'm glad to have this off my chest, my stomach drops. There's more I need to confess. Now I'm the one checking up and down the hallway to make sure no one is listening and I continue in a lowered voice, "Lottie is going to tell your mom about us. We don't want to hide it. We want a real shot at something."

"She is?" He groans as his eyes roll back in his head.

"Yes." I take a fast breath before adding, "I was hoping you'd help."

He gives me a look like his brain just hit the "panic" button. "I'm not helping you get killed."

"Please. Your mom isn't a murderer. I mean, I don't doubt she's not above a nice revenge plot, but do you really think she's capable of murder?"

"Honestly? With her track record? I wouldn't even bet on you living past lunch."

That throws off my swallow, and a laugh bubbles out. "Ha, ha. You're kidding."

He shoots me a sharp side-eye, and nerves spiral up my arm as I start rambling, "Seriously, bro, it'll all work out, but Lottie needs a buffer—and you are perfect for that. You know me best. You can vouch for how loyal I've been to this family; how spotless my criminal record is. You know what she cares about. But if all that fails, I also know her perfect Pinterest garden is a total farce she uses to make voters think she's more domestic. I could totally blackmail her—"

"Stop." He throws his hands up. "You aren't going to blackmail her, but you're right, even if it's cringe." He paces to the other side of the hall and stares out a window before he says calmly, "I hate this idea, but if Lottie has to be with someone ..."

I don't breathe.

He shifts his weight and looks across the hall at me and sighs. "…
I guess it could be worse than my best friend."

My eyes pop wider as I can't believe what I'm hearing. Is he
accepting this? I cross the hall in three big steps and pat him on the
shoulders. "Just think, if I play my cards right, we could be brothers
for real."

"Don't give me a visual!" He throws his hands up in warning.

"A visual of what? Our wedding?"

Just then Senator Halloway barrels down the hallway like the
building is on fire. "Emergency," she announces toward Ham. "We
have a situation."

Both of us straighten.

"Bodan," she says dramatically.

My blood boils. I can't wait until he's out of the picture, and I
speak up before Ham can. "What about him?"

"His grandfather just died," she says grimly, "and this is terrible
for us."

Ham and I exchange a look before he takes the bait. "How
terrible?"

"It's all over the media," she says. "Breaking news. It turns
out Bodan's grandfather is Pulitzer Prize–winning author Hank
Bowey."

My stomach sinks.

I'm not a reader, but I know the name. He's practically a treasure
who wrote a novel about America before the republic, and it's been
added to every required reading list in every school on the planet.

"And," Senator Halloway continues speaking as she plows toward her office, "the media is already speculating whether 'girlfriend, Lottie Halloway,' will attend the funeral…" Her voice trails off as she doesn't pause to talk and disappears into her office. Silence crashes down in her wake.

Ham slowly turns to me. "This is getting out of hand."

Dread curls deep in my chest. *Lottie can't publicly break up with Bodan now.* It will destroy her mother if she dumps Hank's grandson on the eve of grandfather's death or really anytime soon. She'll have to wait for our country to mourn the loss of this great man, and we'll have to wait to be together.

I've waited my whole life for her. I will wait the rest of it if I have to, but my heart plummets, heavy like an anchor dragging it down. It takes everything in me to murmur, "Yeah, it's already gone too far."

Ham looks in the direction of his mom's office, shaking his head in disgust. "Lottie's going to have to go to that funeral, or else it'll backfire."

Somehow, as bad as this feels, something tells me it's only the beginning.

Twenty-Six

Lottie

I STAND IN THE middle of my mother's closet, which is the size of an average person's apartment, and I wring my hands together as I work up the courage to say three words. Okay, maybe not a full-sized apartment, but definitely closer to the size of an average bedroom. But that's neither here nor there. The real issue at hand is *I kissed Ty!*

Between the kiss and the conversation we had, I seriously need to tell her I'm done with Bodan and that whole charade.

But how do I say such a thing?

Mom, don't freak out, but Tyson and I are … well, what are we? I mean, we aren't really dating since we haven't gone anywhere together yet. We kissed. Well, just one amazing, knee-shaking kiss, but that still counts. I'm sure there will be more. Or at least I hope there will be more. We are mostly talking at this point, but we're being honest.

Oh, how do I say Ty and I are being honest? What even is that?

It doesn't matter how many words I attempt, everything clumps in my throat as my mom glides past me in a long black dress that probably cost more than my car. She pauses in front of the mirrored wall and flashes duck lips at herself. "What do you think, Lottie? Is this too elegant for a day funeral?" she asks, already knowing the answer.

"Yes," I say automatically. Then, before I lose my nerve, I add, "Mom, I need to tell you something."

She lifts a pair of silver hoop earrings from a velvet tray and holds them up to her ears. "Maybe if I avoid diamonds, I will look more casual. You know, you should start thinking about what you're wearing to the funeral. It's two days away, and the press will be watching every move. It's events like these that can really shape the public's opinion of you."

"Mom, do you seriously think you are going to that poor man's funeral? It seems pretty shallow to attend for PR."

She glances over her shoulder. "We'd be foolish not to be strategic."

My stomach twists. "You never even knew him."

"I knew him in spirit," she says, turning back to the mirror.

My brows draw together as I process what is possibly the dumbest thing I've ever heard. "That's not a thing." A sound escapes me somewhere between a laugh and a scream. "You don't attend someone's funeral for a photo op."

She plucks a pearl necklace from a hook on the wall, extending it toward me without looking at me. I don't take it. Instead, I give her the crazy eyes she deserves. Undeterred, she presses the necklace closer. "Try this on. It might help make your neck look longer."

Great, now I'm wondering what's wrong with my neck. I grab my throat and mutter, "No."

Her reflection stiffens as her gaze locks on mine. "Excuse me?"

"I'm not doing this." I push the necklace back toward her. "I'm not dressing up to pretend I care about someone I've never met so you can look compassionate to a bunch of strangers. Maybe you can take Ham or Dad. I'm not going."

"This isn't about me." She turns fully toward me now. "This is about Bodan. He's your boyfriend. Everyone expects you to be there for him."

I inhale sharply. *She's delusional!* She knows he's not my real boyfriend. It's all a farce. It's completely disrespectful to Bodan in his time of grief to even think I'd be invited. He needs that time with his family. I will not turn his tragedy into a mockery. "Actually, Bodan needs time to grieve, and it's best we just call off this whole thing—"

"Why would you do that?" Her brows shoot to the ceiling. "It's just getting good!"

A rush of nerves hits me. If I'm going to say anything, I need to rush all my words before she interrupts me again. "Mom, I need to end the arrangement with Bodan, because there's someone else—an actual, real man—who I, uh, want to date—"

"Oh, honey, you can't cheat on Bodan," she interrupts briskly.

"It's not cheating!" I blurt out, my face growing warm. "This is the perfect time to respectfully stop working with Bodan. Then I can move forward with a real relationship."

Her expression stays neutral. Without even acknowledging my news, she hands me a padded hanger with a black dress on it. "This dress always photographs well. You're a little hippier than I am, but if you add a belt, you should look nice in it."

"I said *no*." I push the hanger away without looking at the dress.

Her lips press into a thin line and her head tilts into a disapproving angle. "Boy, Lottie. This is so unlike you. Why are you being so difficult?"

"I'm not being difficult. I'm being honest," I snap. Real anger I've never allowed myself to feel toward her starts to simmer in my gut. Why can't she see me for me? It's like I'm a phantom she can look right through. Before I lose my cool and start screaming, I try one last time to speak calmly. "I'm seeing someone, and I need to respectfully end the Bodan arrangement now, which actually works out perfectly, because he needs to grieve instead of playing these stupid games."

Without waiting for a reply, she turns back to the mirror, holding the dress up to herself and admiring every angle. "Or maybe I should wear this dress?" she mumbles, lost in her reflection.

My mom is completely ignoring me. Not surprising though. She's never seen me. Clenching my fists, I inhale deeply. "Mom,

I'm sorry, but I'm not going to that funeral." I try to end the conversation with a civil statement, but Ty's voice echoes in my head.

You say sorry too much.

I straighten and glance over my shoulder, half expecting to see Ty standing there. When I don't see him, I turn back to my mom and swallow.

He's right.

He's been pointing it out for years, and I'm only now seeing it for myself. There is no reason to apologize to my mom for doing what I want with my life. "Actually, I take that back. I'm not sorry."

She freezes, giving me a bewildered look in the mirror.

"I'm not sorry," I continue as my heart pounds. "It's time to break up with Bodan. He'll understand, and he can move on with his life and properly grieve his grandpa. You can put your dresses and jewelry away, because we aren't going to that funeral."

Her eyes flash. "Oh, come on, Lottie. Snap out of it. You can't break up with him now."

"I will. And I'm done pretending." Spinning on my heel, I do something I know she'll consider rude, but I don't care. I storm off before she's done speaking.

Behind me, she scoffs, "You're making a mistake!"

For a brief second, doubt creeps in. A public breakup is never easy. I'll likely be painted in a bad light, but it needs to happen. I can't lie anymore—not to the public and not to myself. "Maybe I am making a mistake," I whisper, careful she won't hear my reply.

She'd just come back with some rebuttal I don't need. "But at least it'll be mine."

With that, I leave her standing in front of her mirror, continuing to admire a version of herself and a life that I'm finally done trying to fit into.

It's time for me to be honest with what I want.

It's time for me to make my own decisions.

And I've never felt better.

Twenty-Seven

Tyson

Riding the team bus to the arena, I can't stop replaying this morning with Ham. I left without getting a chance to tell Senator Halloway about Lottie and me. She'd dramatically insisted she and Lottie needed to take off the rest of the day to "prepare for the funeral."

I didn't even get to talk to Lottie, because her mom was panicking so much. I have no idea if Lottie's even coming to the game tonight. Honestly, I doubt it. The only way it wouldn't be a huge fight is if she drags Bodan, and he's clearly not going to a game the day his grandpa died.

Following the guys, I step down from the bus and suck in a huge breath as a throng of reporters crowd the sidewalk, cameras ready. It's always nerve-racking, but I remind myself it's an honor to be representing our country in this tournament. I have a duty to appear friendly, and I wave as we file past the crowd. Once inside, I exhale. It's quiet here; the doors are still locked to the public. Only arena staff and team members move through the hallways.

Imagine my surprise when I round the corner and nearly slam into Lottie. I do a double take and stop so abruptly that I almost trip over my own feet. "Lottie? How'd you get in here?"

She looks wrecked. Her hair is half pulled back, like she tried for a neat little bun but gave up halfway. Stray strands frame her face. Of course, I think she's stunning, but this is far from her usual perfect hairdo.

She's not crying, but her eyes are red, evidence of earlier tears. That scares me more than if she were crying now. My heart ticks up a notch as I step forward. "Hey, what's wrong?"

"Ham's friends with the security here, and I begged him to help me get in here to see you. I don't have long," she says so fast, I barely catch it. "I know you have a game."

I reach for her without thinking. My hand brushes her wrist, then I pull back—remembering we aren't public yet. My fingers twitch to touch her again. "Slow down."

"I tried to tell my mom about us," she says, throwing her hands in the air, "but she won't listen. She kept looking at herself in the mirror, like she was imagining herself sitting next to celebrities at the funeral. She's insisting she's going to this funeral for PR, but there is no way I can go."

Her mom is so infuriating that my jaw tightens, but I manage to keep my voice even. "Okay."

Lottie's words tumble out in a rapid procession, "She says I have to keep fake dating Bodan through the funeral, and even longer, or it will make me look heartless." Her eyes lift to mine. "I can't do this anymore."

"Slow down. I'm confused." I step closer, as my heart slams into my chest with worry. I hope she means she can't listen to her mom, but if she thinks she can't tell her mom about me ... I don't think I'm ready to hear that. "What aren't you doing anymore?"

"Lots of things, but for starters, I'm being honest, and I'm done apologizing." She exhales hard through her nose. "For wanting my own life. For wanting *you*."

That affects me more than any body check I've ever taken. And her hands—literally shaking like she's standing on the edge of a cliff—make it worse. I swallow hard, aching to grab her and pull her close. Her perfect sea-green eyes glint back at me, and I squeeze a fist in frustration. Man, I wish I had time to do this right. To hold her properly, to tell her everything I feel. But I can't be late for the game. I glance down the hall as the last of the guys disappear into the locker room. I have two, maybe three minutes, to talk.

I've waited years for a moment like this. I'm not wasting my chance now. She's wrecked, and she needs to hear that I'm all in. "I want you too," I say with force. Since we're alone in the hall, for now, I lift my hand and blot my thumb on her cheek, brushing beneath her eye. No tears remain, just the faint stain of one, and it breaks me that she cried alone over this. "Listen, Lottie, I can't talk right now," I say, hating it. "But you need to know I'm not going anywhere. Whatever happens with your mom, we'll figure it out together. But you are right. You need to do what's best for you."

"I know." Her expression smooths over, as if every worry is being carefully tucked away. "Thank you for ... you know for—"

"Lane!" Coach hollers down the hall, cutting us off. My stomach plummets. I'm really trying to give this team everything I've got, but somehow the coach has perfect timing to catch me at the exact moment that makes me look like I'm slacking.

Gritting my teeth, I tear myself away from her. Clearly, she understands, as she turns and runs off, throwing her hand up in a wave. "Good luck!"

"Wait for me after the game!" I call over my shoulder, then sprint to the locker room. I've played a lot of hockey in my life. Most of the time, I play for goals and trophies. Tonight feels different. Tonight, I play for Lottie. Like I'm meant to prove not only to Lottie that she isn't making a mistake by choosing me, but also to her mom.

Tonight, I know exactly what I'm playing for.

Coach's voice carries through the tunnel. I nod like I'm listening, but my head's still with Lottie, replaying how she chose me, risking everything in her life. Her job, her relationship with her mom, and, if I really think about it, even the roof over her head. Pressure surges to perform, not just for the team but for her.

I'm first on the ice tonight. Houli leans over the red line during warm-ups, grinning like he always does. "Well, are you ready to cry tonight?"

I shake my head. Normally a little jab from Houli would fire me up, but my chest is too tight.

It's no surprise—he wins the opening face-off against Leinecker. He's untouchable. Everything he does shows his A game. My team fights hard, firing shot after shot, but nothing goes in. Jeremiah Precio cuts behind the net, and the puck comes to me along the boards. I don't even look at the net—Stone is already crashing the slot, pulling coverage. That leaves the back side open. I snap the puck down low, and right at Precio.

A sharp *thup*—his backhand lifts—and the red light flares.

The crowd erupts, and I'm already pointing at him. Normally I stay humble early in the game, but we take a moment to celebrate our first goal. Adrenaline roars through my body. The next thought I have is of Lottie. It's crazy how suddenly I'm playing for us. I scan the crowd and spot her sitting alone above our net. She's cheering, and when our eyes meet, she waves. It gives me a boost of something I didn't know I was missing.

Things get even better when Stone scores a second goal. Instantly my chest relaxes, and I breathe easier. We're able to go into intermission with our spirits high.

When the second period starts, the East's Jayce Brady scores just thirty-six seconds in, and the energy does a dramatic one-eighty. I have no idea what they did in that locker room, but whatever it was, it's working. They look like a completely different team now. It only gets worse when they quickly snag a second goal, tying everything up.

Tension is at an all-time high by the third period, and I'm sweating like a sieve. When Chase Sullivan gets the puck, my stomach drops straight to the ice. I can feel it in my gut—this isn't good. He gets it into the net with no assist. Just like that, we are down by one.

I instinctively glance at Lottie. My mind drifts to the promise I made all those summers ago; to be a better man, one who deserves Lottie. As much as I hate to admit it, I yearn to be a man her mom will respect. My throat burns as I sink onto the bench, but I need to sit. My mind is reeling.

Thankfully, Dashiell DiFranco is on fire for our team, tearing up the ice to tie us back up. It's a goal that will surely go viral, and with the tie, the entire arena seems to collectively hold its breath.

His snipe from a perfect cross-crease pass from Ted Powell is a beauty. My heart drops as the momentum slips through our fingers like sand. To add insult to injury, Jayce Brady scores another one for Stripes. I clamp my lips shut and resist the urge to shake my head.

The clock ticks down. Coach pulls our goalie. My heart slams against my rib cage. We scramble at the crease, getting the puck loose for a fleeting moment, all the while the clock's bleeding. The crowd rises, chanting each number as it counts down. Sullivan grabs the puck, steers toward our net, and buries it into the empty cage.

That's it.

The buzzer sounds, and everything inside me explodes. All the thoughts I've been carrying—about earning my team's respect, being the captain they can count on, proving to Lottie and her mom that I'm worthy—crash together. They pile up until the noise falls away, and my body goes numb.

Heading to the tunnel, I don't look back. I can't. Every stride feels heavier than the last, as if the entire arena is full of disappointed faces—all aimed at me.

Some captain I am.

I've been waiting my whole life for this chance to impress Lottie. She's here in the stands, and I couldn't get it together.

What a loser.

I failed my team.

I failed Lottie.

And I failed myself.

Twenty-Eight

Lottie

WATCHING REFLECTIONS RIPPLE ACROSS my windshield, I drum my fingers on the steering wheel in time with the music on the radio. The Stars' team bus idles near the hotel entrance. When the doors open, the players spill out with slumped shoulders and crestfallen expressions. Tyson steps off last. His Stars hoodie rides up in the back, like he forgot to pull it down or he didn't have the energy to care. With how serious he takes hockey, I'm guessing it's the latter.

He texted me after the game to meet him here, to avoid being seen together at the arena. After all the guys disappear inside, I step out of the car and stay in the shadows. The sky is dark, and a bellboy paces near the entrance, scrolling on his phone. As soon as Ty sees me, the invisible knot pulling his face tight unravels. His lips part slightly as he strides toward me. "Hey," I say in a quiet voice, careful not to draw attention.

"Hey." His voice carries a tone of forlornity I expected. His eyes drop to my shoes, then lift back to my face. Since he doesn't mention the game, neither do I. We start walking and close the distance between us until our arms brush. His hands stay shoved in his pockets. Without speaking, we head toward the waterfront park. Maybe it's because we spent so much time together on the water that it's natural for us to gravitate in that direction. As soon as the Potomac River comes into view, my shoulders release some of the day's tension.

Tyson must feel the release too, because he finally speaks, "I hate that when we lose, I can't stop replaying all the ways I failed." His eyes sweep to mine. They are vulnerable in a way that makes my breath catch.

"I didn't see you failing at all." I take a risk by lightly touching his forearm before quickly pulling back. "I saw you playing your best."

His mouth twitches. I can tell he wants to argue, but instead he says, "I want to be someone you can be proud of."

"You are." Without hesitation, I lift my hand toward him again, giving him time to pull away if he wants to, but he doesn't. When I take his hand in mine, my heartbeat stumbles at the memory of how perfect this feels. His eyes drift closed for a second, like he too is savoring the contact and perhaps storing some of the sensation away for when we have to conceal our affections for each other. "I've always been proud of you and how hard you work. I seriously can't wait to tell everyone we're together."

Turning toward me, his hand lifts and settles at my waist. A spiral of goosebumps ripples up my spine as his thumb presses lightly into the fabric of my shirt. I can't help but smile. Even though the team had a devastating loss tonight, being able to finally come together feels amazing. "Yeah, the whole Bodan thing is something I never expected. Three is a bit of a crowd, and I'll be honest, I can't wait until he's out of the picture."

"Well." I slide my lips into a teasing slant. "If you remember, he was your idea."

"No." He shakes his head playfully as he lowers his face to mine. "He was your mom's orchestration. I was only helping to make sure you didn't have to hold hands with Brett."

The mere mention of Brett sends a cold shiver through me. "Yeah, thank you for that. I can't imagine how that would have fueled his ego."

We both chuckle and grow more comfortable until we find ourselves leaning into each other, and his hand tightens at my waist. Without any other cues, we both instinctually sense what's coming. I press my palm against his solid chest, and the warmth that spirals up my arm draws me even closer.

When his lips brush mine, a soft ache spreads through my gut. His kiss is unhurried, almost as if his lazy grin has a matching setting. There's no hint of the game loss, as that all seems to melt away. My hand slides up his chest until my fingers find his collar, and I curl them there, enjoying the unexpected awareness that I can feel the rise and fall of his breathing under my palm.

This isn't our first kiss, but our first one was so unexpected that everything about that moment was fueled by adrenaline. This kiss gives us the chance to explore a little, and his thumb brushes my waist as I find a rhythm defined by the way his mouth moves against mine. When we pull back, his eyes stay closed a beat longer, like he's still not ready to let the moment go, his beautiful dark lashes fanning against his skin.

A burst of laughter spills from somewhere near the water. Reality slams back into place. I have no idea who is out there. Even though it's dark, I slide my foot back one step, almost like we rehearsed it. Without speaking, we nonchalantly turn to the river, like we're out for the view. I watch the faint reflections of the lights in the dark water and pray we aren't recognized. The group of laughing people moves the other way, and we stroll quietly in the opposite direction until we find ourselves alone again.

I've known Ty most of my life. It's an odd—but easy—feeling to transition from friends to something more. We don't need to have a chatty first date about our likes and dislikes. We could probably each write a book about the other without even trying. We know all the details about our families, hometown, and careers. The one thing we seem to need is more physical touch to soak up what this feels like. At least for me, nothing has ever felt more right.

We remain quiet, sharing deep eye contact as the kiss still hangs between us. It's left a warm stain on my lips I don't want to let go of, and I'm craving more of it. So, when we happen to stroll by a large tree and he gets a gleam in his eye, we don't hesitate to slip into the shadows and immediately pull into an embrace.

"I've wanted this for a long time," he says, his voice low. When our eyes find each other's, I smile wider, and he tacks on, "Longer than you probably even realize."

"Oh, yeah," I say with a teasing breath as it's hard to believe. I've been waiting since I was sixteen and except for that one time he never showed interest in being anything more than friends. "Humor me. How long?"

"I knew since the first day I met you that you were meant to be mine, but I didn't really know what that meant, but I asked Santa for you every year."

"You enlisted Santa." I give him a side-eye as that can't be right.

"Every year." He takes a breath before his words rush out like a heavy load he's carried too long and is finally ready to drop. "Do you remember that summer right after you graduated from high school? You were finally eighteen, and we met for July Fourth at your Mapleton house like always."

I remember that summer perfectly.

I remember all our summers together.

I'm not sure why, but my cheeks heat at being put on the spot. Even though this is Ty, who I know as well as my own brother, I'm still shy when it comes to talking about this out loud.

"I had told myself that once you were eighteen, everything would magically click into place. Then, out of nowhere, you announced you were moving to DC to help your mom. I was happy for you, but it was miserable not saying anything."

"I remember that summer, and I also remember *waiting* for you to say something. Why didn't you?"

"I wanted to, and I had planned on it, but I was watching you laugh with Ham on the dock about the first time you drove in DC traffic, and you turned toward me. The way the sunset reflected the water in your eyes, it lit up your whole face. You never looked happier, and I just froze. I wanted to tell you how badly I was crushing on you right there, but I was scared it would ruin your excitement for DC. I had these visions of you moving there and becoming important like your mom. I couldn't fathom you wanting to hold on to anything from your old life. It was best to accept we'd be friends, and I was glad for that at least. I didn't say it, but yeah, I wanted to." His voice catches a little before he adds, "I sealed everything away, hoping one day I'd get the chance to at least say something." His eyes glimmer when he adds, "I need you to know this isn't casual for me. Even though it feels fast and maybe like I skipped a step to express my feelings so soon, I can't risk you not knowing you're everything I've ever waited for."

Understanding exactly how he feels, I smile, surprised by how easy it is to get used to being this close to him. "It's funny how we were both living that experience. Like, on some level I knew we'd end up together. There was never an *if* for me, but there was a huge *when* question I could never solve. Just when I thought, *this will be the summer*, Murphy's Law would come into play, and one of us would be pulled in another direction for work."

A weight has been lifted off my chest and breathing is suddenly easier. It's like all the years I've kept this in—every smile I held back and every accidental touch that haunted me—are finally cut loose. When he dips his head again, I'm relaxed and brush my lips against his. We've certainly gotten used to kissing each other faster than I'd have expected. There's nothing awkward, and at the same time, nothing casual about it. Every tug of my lips sparks something electric under my skin. When we break the kiss, he tosses a quick look over his shoulder and whispers, "We're going to get caught out here."

I laugh, but it's strained. "Maybe we need to get caught, so we can move on with our lives."

"Nah." He eases back, putting just enough space between us to make it look innocent to anyone passing by. "I don't want you to have that stress. We can wait so things are easier for you."

Just then a shadow moves in a way that makes it look like it's heading straight for us, and my stomach drops. "Should we hide?" I half joke as I frantically search for somewhere to go. He's one step ahead of me and grabs my hand, yanking me behind a cement wall. We crouch as low as we can without lying down. Honestly, now that we are here, this is worse than getting caught standing next to each other. The wall is only a half wall, and our bodies press together in totally incriminating positions. At this point we're committed, because if we step out from behind the wall, that's going to look suspicious. I crouch lower as the figure passes at the slowest pace known to humankind. In my painstaking effort to stay perfectly still, I wobble—because, well, I never said I had good balance—and I save myself from toppling over by sliding out my foot to steady myself.

"Ouch!" Ty hisses, grimacing and clutching my ankle.

I look down to find my foot is on his hand, and I mouth, "Sorry," while trying not to notice how unfairly handsome he is this close. I mean, he has stupidly long lashes that give him this sensitive vibe that makes my pulse skid. If we weren't hiding from imminent exposure, I would not hold back from kissing him again. Instead, I focus on not breathing too loudly as the person meanders along. We stay frozen, pressed too close behind the smallest wall ever.

Just when I'm about to peek over the wall to see if the coast is clear, a familiar voice cuts through the tension. "Ah! My eyes!" Ham steps behind the wall while slamming a hand over his eyes. "Lottie, this is what you're doing!"

One side of my brain dials up into panic mode, while the other side crashes with relief knowing it's just Ham. If there's one person who has to find us, I'm glad it's him, especially since he already knows about us.

"This is not only disgusting, but it's completely irresponsible!" he snaps, while seeming to do his best to keep his voice down as he zeros in on me first from behind parted fingers. "Lottie, I almost went blind. You have to be more careful. You *cannot* be doing this. What if you get caught? Can you imagine how that would look with a photo of you two smashed together all over social media, while Bodan is literally getting ready for a funeral?"

I stand slowly and step toward Ham. "I know. You're right. This looks bad, but for the record, this wasn't what we were doing. We were standing here when we saw your shadow. We panicked, fleeing behind the wall without realizing how small it was. We had to smoosh together."

Ty gets up and brushes his pants off. I have a hunch he doesn't care if they are dirty, but it's an awkward moment where he avoids making eye contact with Ham. "How did you even find me?" I look around for a clue I may have left, but it's dark in this corner of the park.

"Mom has your location on your phone turned on, and she was worried about you being out so late. She was coming to look, but I had a hunch you two were out. I told her I was heading into town anyway." He wags a finger at me. "You're lucky I covered for you, but I'm not making this a habit. This was too close of a call."

"I know." I start walking back slowly, and Ty and Ham fall into step with me. It's a little too awkward to say anything in front of Ham, so when we reach the hotel parking lot, I just wave at Ty. "Thanks for tonight. I'll text you."

I think he's going to stay quiet, but instead he leans in close to my ear and whispers, "Always."

A shiver runs from my ear straight down my spine, as his single word echoes in my head. His mouth curves, just barely, like he's trying not to smile. He knows exactly what that word means to me, and to us. It's a lifetime of memories already filed away together.

As I hold his gaze, the teasing drains out of his eyes, replaced with intent that sends a fluttering ache through my stomach. Everything is moving so fast, but after all these years of waiting, I wouldn't want it any other way. He does what he needs to protect me by disappearing into the hotel entrance, leaving me standing there with a hollow ache in my belly and—Ham, who I avoid looking at like he could turn me to stone. I haven't done anything wrong, but he's a reminder of how complicated my life is. It's the strangest dichotomy; my heart feels both full and heavy all at once.

The night is ending, but my feelings for Ty are far from ending. They are only growing stronger with each stolen kiss.

Twenty-Nine

Tyson

I'm a stealth ninja warrior slipping through the hotel's door, finding the lobby hushed and dim. Midnight is coming fast, but I'm not the least bit sleepy. My mouth still tingles from Lottie's soft kisses. I've imagined kissing her a million times. Never did I think it would feel like that. Years of wanting packed into one kiss. We just get each other. No awkward fumbling, no searching for a rhythm.

It's kissing perfection.

Halfway to the elevators, I slam straight into a solid wall of muscle. Or—nope. Not a wall. Just Bryce Chambers, my teammate.

"Brah," I say, looking him up and down. "What are you doing out so late?"

He lifts a crinkly wrapper as evidence. "Snack run." He pulls a few more packages from the center pocket of his hoodie and grins as he fans them out for me to see. "Emergency beef jerky. Emotional support chocolate. You know, all the necessities." He looks at my hands hanging at my side. "What about you? What are you doing out?"

"Oh," I say too fast, and then pat my belly. "Yeah, same. I needed a food run."

He looks me over and grunts. "Where are your snacks?"

"I ate them already," I say with exaggerated confidence, which only earns me a suspicious side-eye. We enter into a bit of a stare down.

"Wait a second..." His head tilts as he ponders out loud, "Do you really think I'm that—I think you were out setting up a prank."

"Me?" I scoff. "No way. I wasn't doing that, but I bet *you* were. You've got that guilty face."

"My face is naturally guilty," he shoots back. "Unlike yours, which looks like you just—"

"Are the fastest guy on ice, ever," I interrupt.

He squints. "That wasn't what I was going for. You aren't that fast."

Chuckling, I gesture to his food-stuffed pockets and give it right back. "Well, maybe if you wouldn't eat so much, you'd skate faster."

That earns a laugh from both of us, and he mutters, "Whatever. I'm headed back to my room. You keep sneaking around to set up your pranks—"

I throw my hands up. "Do you think I'd sew my own jersey shut? I'm not the one setting up the pranks," I try to explain, but he's already strutting away. I wait until he's gone before leaning my hand against the wall, exhaling a deep sigh. I hadn't realized how high my adrenaline spiked until the dip of release hit. Tonight was the most amazing night of my life, but sneaking around with Lottie isn't sustainable—not with so much riding on her professional life. I'd feel terrible if we got caught. Hopefully, she ends this whole Bodan deal soon. I push off the wall, straighten, and peer down the hall.

My attention wanders back toward the snack machines. I could use a little emotional support chocolate too. But not just any chocolate.

I need the plain M&M's.

Thirty

Lottie

MIRACULOUSLY, I MAKE IT up to my room without running into my mom and close the door behind me as quietly as I can, leaning against it. I toy with the end of my hair, breathing hard. Set to sixty-eight, the air conditioner doesn't touch the heat coiled in my chest. My fingers tingle, prolonging the sensation of pressing my palms against Ty's chest. It doesn't quite feel real yet that I get to be with Ty. Even if it stays secret for now, it's the best thing that's ever happened to me. Elation swirls in my heart, spiraling through my body like soft, pillowy cotton spreading warmth.

With a secret smile, I cross the room and pull pajamas from my closet. I tug on the top, careful not to make a lot of noise. Sure, my mom is asleep, but I never shake the feeling of walking on eggshells in this house. Just as quietly, I rise onto my toes, swap my shorts for pajama bottoms, and flop onto my bed with a bit of dramatic flair. I'm irritated at my mom for putting me in the situation.

Yes, I have free will.

Deep down, I follow her plan anyway, because part of me still hopes, if I do *another* one of her requests, something might shift in our relationship. Maybe she will actually be proud of me, or at the very least *see* me as an actual person who has a personality besides being her servant. I understood Ty's frustration tonight when he said he wanted to make me proud, because I struggle with the same doubts. It's weird to crave that from my mom, especially since I'm not entirely sure she's capable of appreciating anyone but herself.

A girl can hope.

Biting the inside of my cheek, I lower my face to my unlit phone screen.

I've been stuck for a long time. Maybe it's the adult thing to do to accept she's never changing. Wasting my life trying to be seen by her is just that—wasting my life. Without overthinking it, I tap the screen and pull up the local jobs board. My expression stays neutral as I scroll.

All I've ever done is what my mom tells me to do. She trained me from the time I was little to be her mini-me. Without varied work experience, I don't even know how I'd translate what I do onto a résumé. *People-Pleasing Doormat.* It's not funny, but I still snicker. And knowing my luck, if I ever do apply for other jobs, she'll find out. She has her ways.

With every swipe, my gut twists with something undeniable; if I quit working for my mom, I'll likely need to move out because of the inevitable friction.

But where would I go?

After years of towing her line, I've never given myself options before. The thought of moving to any city to do anything is overwhelming.

What do I even want?

A thought settles in gently. I know exactly what I want. It's not about the job—some things are more important than that. It's what I've been waiting for. And tonight, I heard Ty say he feels the same way I do.

I can't go back.

I stare at the screen, seeing no jobs that pop out at me. After all the years of networking for my mom, you'd think I'd have met someone who could help me transition into a different job, but my brain is mush.

I'm terrified.

I'm exhilarated.

But most of all, I'm ready.

I'm finally ready for the fallout, and for whatever comes next. There's no question in my mind. I drop my phone on the comforter and lie back on the bed. When I close my eyes, the face I see is Ty's, forever wearing that lazy smile. My heart ticks up a notch as I let the warmth he brings flood in, drowning out any lingering uncertainty and fueling what I need to do in the coming days.

It's going to be worth it.

Since the next morning is Saturday, I don't go into the office. Somewhere in my restless night, I decided I'm not pressing any issues this weekend. Mom will think I'm compliant, but I'm only buying time until I figure everything out. Hiding in my room, scrolling for the last hour has gotten me nowhere. I don't want drama today, I tell myself. I hate I'm still in this arrangement, but I need to check in with Bodan.

Almost immediately, a reply pops up.

My stomach flips. *Meet me?* I wasn't planning on going near his family, especially with the media watching. That was never part of the deal. The fake relationship was only for my mom's events. Confused, I shoot off a text:

His reply comes almost instantly:

> **They watch the news, and they think we're dating. I can't tell them we aren't now.**

Instantly, my blood pressure spikes, and my face grows red hot. I slide off my bed and pace my bedroom as my brain imagines a room full of his family and cameras everywhere.

I can't go to that funeral!

I fire back:

> I've been thinking about our arrangement. This is a good time to call everything off. You have enough on your plate, and you need time to heal. I'm fine being done with this charade. Maybe in a few weeks, we can announce that we went our separate ways but still care about each other, yada, yada—you know—all the normal media spin. We don't have to make a big deal about it, but I don't think your grandfather's funeral needs to be overshadowed by our farce.

I hit send and hold my breath.

The shame I've felt every single day since we launched this fake-dating scheme has been exhausting. As much as I want to call this whole thing quits, we have a duty to see it through in a practical way. We can't live in an imaginary world forever. Continuing to loop our lives further together is not in either of our best interests.

But the phone buzzes again.

We can't call it off today, and definitely not before the funeral. My 95-year-old grandma will croak. I'm her favorite grandchild. She's been following the news, and she is so proud of me for dating a senator's daughter. She told all of her friends, and they will all be at the funeral. Well, what's left of them anyway. Most are dead, but that's beside the point. She's thrilled to meet you. It's honestly the only thing that's bringing her any light in this dark time since her husband died. She even requested our firstborn be named after my grandpa.

My pulse skyrockets. This was not supposed to hit me like this. How did I get sucked into this? I mean, I know how—my mother—but this is absurd.

My legs suddenly go weak, and I lower back onto my bed to keep the panic from spilling into another text to him. My heart thunders. Then what's left of the people pleaser in me pushes forward, conjuring the image of his grandmother. At ninety something, she's wrinkled but spry, and the funeral will likely be the hardest day of her life. She's burying her husband. I'm not so hardened by my mom's selfishness that I can't feel empathy for someone. Somewhere deep down, a stubborn voice whispers, *Grandma needs to have some hope.*

Maybe it's okay if I show up?

Hating what I'm about to do, because the lies are spiraling out of control, I type:

> Okay. You have convinced me to go with you, but it's only because it matters to your grandma. After this event, the score will be even. We've both helped each other. We need to set a timeline for ending this. It's not healthy for us to delay our lives because we're carrying on this charade.

I hit send but immediately regret agreeing to more lies.

This isn't me.

But it's too late, and I'm committed. It's crazy—I never realized before this started how deep this would go. It's only been a week, and it's gotten so much bigger than just my mom's PR stunt. Now it's Bodan's coworkers, his family and his grief. I got sucked right into the middle of it.

I'm right where I never wanted to be.

Ty will be so disappointed to hear I've added more time to this fake relationship.

But there's no turning back now.

Thirty-One

Lottie

THE ONLY THING WORSE than a Monday morning is a Monday morning with a funeral. My lungs feel like they are in a vise that no amount of deep breathing can crack loose. Mom's in my passenger seat, playing the role of a true passenger princess as she's retying her Ralph Lauren scarf for the third time. "This is a funeral, so our game face needs to stay somber," she says in a cheery voice. "You'd be surprised who you can casually bump into at these things. We still want people to like us, so it's best to have a polite smile ready to tack on for those moments."

I grit my teeth.

What I wouldn't do for a flat tire.

I'm not to the point of slashing them myself, but if I see a nail on this road, I'm swerving. Even better if it's a roofing nail. I don't need to mess around with a slow leak. Just give me the blowout. This car ride is endless. Every street sign pulls my anxiety taut across my chest, and a loop of doom scrolls endlessly through my mind.

I can't walk into a church and lie.

There must be a special place for people who lie in a church.

I'm not a liar.

I can't do this.

I say I'm not a liar. Yet here I am, dressed in something respectful, with my hair pinned back, and my crazy mom next to me as we head off to pay our respects to someone we never met. The weight of all the lies crashes over me, so heavy that I slump forward in my seat.

I need this to be over!

"Oh, dear, don't slouch like that, Lottie. It puffs out a stomach roll." Mom reaches across the middle console, invading my personal space to tug at my jacket lapel. "Did you even sleep last night? You look exhausted."

I want to scream!

Or at the very least slam my head into my steering wheel.

Oh, man, what I wouldn't give for a construction site right now. I'd beg for a bucket of nails, and I'd sprinkle them on the road myself. Unfortunately, my tires stay inflated, and we arrive at the church early. Bracing for the whispers, I ease out of the car and do my best to blend into the sea of mourners. It doesn't take long to spot Bodan standing in the back of the church, along with the family as they gather. He's wearing an impressive suit and a somewhat guarded expression.

And just like that, my guilt doubles.

He sees me, and his eyes soften, sending a double dose of shame flooding through me. I weave through the crowd toward him with my mom on my heels whispering commentary, "If you don't know what to do with your hands, just fold them in front of you like you're praying."

"Mom," I hiss, resisting the urge to throw her out the nearest window. Okay, that's a little extreme, but the amount of stress this woman puts me under is borderline inhuman. I plod forward, all the while mentally chanting, *This is the last fake-dating event I will do. Get through this, and it's done!*

Bodan meets me halfway through the swelling crowd. He wobbles a little before settling on leaning in for a one-handed hug. Since we are in a church, it feels appropriate enough. When he releases me, he goes a step further and hugs my mom. That's a good move for theatrics. Bodan is better at this than I am.

He's good, but the Oscar should definitely go to my mom.

She's so good at this lying-through-her-teeth stuff, she squeezes him back, giving him a few pats as she fake-sobs. "I'm so sorry about your loss, sweetie. We are so honored to be included in this celebration of this amazing soul."

"Thank you, Senator Halloway. It's an honor to have you here." Bodan's perfect reply makes me do a double take. He's eating up this display as much as my mom, and he dramatically ushers us to our seats. The problem is, they are in the middle of the family section. It's hard for me to resist shaking my head. I loathe everything about this farce, but Mom's lips tip up like she's holding back from handing out seed packets to all the important people she's been plopped among.

With a packed church, we squish together. Bodan comes around the other side, sliding next to me so closely I can feel the warmth radiating from his suit. I suppose to anyone else we look like a couple. I'm sure there are people who have lied about worse things in life, but my guilt twists tighter with every heartbeat.

Halfway through the eulogy, I steal a glance at him and catch him nodding at his grandma, who is on the other side of him. Almost everyone in the room has at least a sniffle or a tear. Bodan is holding himself together so far. Mom nudges me with her elbow and whispers from the side of her lips, "Keep your shoulders back. It makes you look slimmer."

I close my eyes, silently begging for this to be over. It's funny how it only took a little over a week for one seemingly innocent lie to completely take over my life. The guilt consumes me. I know one thing, once I'm free from all this deception, I'm never lying again.

Not even about my weight on my driver's license.

Ooh, that's a tough one.

Is rounding down lying? I mean, they taught us how to do it in school, so that much should be acceptable.

Finally, the service ends. A shuffle of mourners moves toward the reception hall, granting me brief reprieve from the pressure of having to sit in the front row of a congregation. "I'm glad you came," Bodan says quietly as he turns to me. "I know it's a lot to take in."

I swallow hard, and whisper, "It is. You handled my mom's fundraiser and the parade, and I owed you a favor." My hands clutch the fabric of my jacket as I look around at everyone breaking into little social circles as they meander to the reception room.

"If it's not too much to ask, I'd like to introduce you to my grandma," he murmurs, slipping his hand into mine like he thinks it belongs there. My body doesn't agree, and I immediately miss the way it feels when Ty holds my hand.

I can barely think straight. Everything about this charade feels like a betrayal—not just to Ty, but to myself. Before I can come up with a reason to immediately leave, his grandma makes her way right up to me.

"Oh, there you are," she says warmly. "I told Bodan there is no way you can leave before I have a chancc to be properly introduced to you." Her dull blue eyes sweep over me. "You are Lottie?"

"Yes, ma'am," I manage, dipping my head slightly and praying the lights don't pick up the blush growing on my cheeks.

Her gaze softens, bringing the sense that's she's one of those sweet people who doesn't have a mean bone in her body. "Well, I tell Bodan all the time he's my favorite grandson. Any woman who ends up with him has to be equally as special. When I heard he was dating you, it felt like all my years of prayers came true."

Bodan glances at me as a flicker of guilt crosses his face. When I turn back to his grandma her eyes are bright, spiraling with wishful specks. Maybe he feels the need to be more convincing, because he steps closer and then gestures to my mom, who is still on my side, to bring her into the conversation. "Grandma, this is Lottie's mom, Senator Halloway."

Immediately extending her hand, my mom beams at his grandma. "Oh, please, you don't need to call me Senator. Call me Trudy."

I bite my lip. In the years my mom has held that title, she's never once preferred it not be used. She must be desperate to get these people to think she's approachable.

"Nice to meet you, Trudy," his grandma says, nodding her approval. "It's lovely that you were able to come today."

I force a smile as my phone buzzes in my pocket. Casually slipping it out with my free hand, I glance down.

Ty: Hey, how's it going?

My chest tightens as my thumb hovers over the screen. Indecision slices through me. Bodan's grandmother's eyes are still on us. With a sharp pang, I realize how trapped I am. Even if I could take a moment to reply to Ty, it does nothing to solve the fact I just invited one more person—Bodan's sweet and trusting grandma—into my web of lies. This funeral was supposed to be the end of this arrangement, but with the way his grandma's eyes are sparkling at me, my doom spiral deepens.

I tuck my phone into my pocket. As much as it pains me to put Ty off, he needs to wait. "Who's texting you?" Mom's voice is deceptively casual. I don't miss how sharp her eyes are when she tilts her head in, trying to get a glimpse of my screen before it goes into my pocket.

I freeze. This is where it would be handy to have a life outside of work. Before this last week when Ty came into town, I never went anywhere or did anything. If I did get a random text in the middle of the day, it was always about work—usually my mom's business—which is probably why she feels entitled to know. "Just a friend," I mutter, telling myself that's not a lie. Ty has always been my friend.

She studies me for a long beat, then lets out a sigh before turning back to Bodan and his grandma and saying, "Well, this has been a lovely service, and it was wonderful to meet you both. Unfortunately, I must take off." She turns to me and lifts a brow, like that alone should tell me exactly what to do next.

"Mom—" I start but stop when her brow spikes even higher. I hadn't expected her to leave so soon, since this was her idea to come. Part of me wonders if she's up to something else. I side-eye her, waiting to see what she's really up to.

She bows her head to his grandma again, saying, "My deepest condolences to you both."

"Thanks for coming." Bodan nods, then tilts his head at me, like he's not sure what's going on either. Mom gives a small wave and disappears into the crowd, leaving us alone.

I let out a shaky breath. "Okay. I'm her ride, so I guess I should go too, but I'll text you."

"Sure." He waits a beat before leaning in and hugging me, dropping a quick kiss on my cheek that I'm sure was just for his grandma. I pull away as fast as I can and nod toward his grandma as I'm already spinning on my heel. "It was a pleasure to meet you." She smiles and waves, and I speed out the door, all the while keeping my face down to avoid being recognized. Bodan's grandma's bright eyes burn into my brain, causing my heart to plummet. Nobody was supposed to be hurt in this arrangement.

This was a terrible idea.

It needs to end.

Now.

Well, okay, not now, because Bodan is literally still at a funeral, but very soon.

Thirty-Two

Tyson

It's game four, and I'm taped up and my jersey is on straight with no stickers. I tap my stick against the floor as I wait for the Zamboni to finish its lap, and my legs jitter with restless energy that only shows up when I'm on the edge of something.

Pucks are going to be flying.

I can feel a win tonight.

Call me superstitious, but I know better than to say it out loud. I already know for sure Lottie isn't here. She texted she's a no-go with her mom. She should be in the stands. Instead, she's hiding out and stealing peeks of the game on her phone whenever her mom isn't looking. That's no way to live. The whole situation has added anger to the mix of adrenaline I'm already feeling.

Maybe I have a bad attitude about it.

Okay, not maybe.

I do.

It's been a fantasy of mine for years that I would skate to her section and tap the Plexiglass to wave at my girlfriend. We're finally together, but she can't be here. Well, I'll make someone pay for that. And since I can't get mad at her mom without hurting Lottie, I'm funneling all my emotion into this game.

The Stripes will be eating my star dust tonight.

Three minutes in, and I'm already being handed puck-shaped gifts on a platter. My chest rattles as everything starts breaking in my favor. One of the defenders sends it along the ice like he's leading a retirement community parade, and I'm on him in a second, swiping the puck.

Then I'm gone, charging their goal. It's a clean shot. I fire, and it's a beauty, sailing into the net before the goalie can even react. I throw my head back and roar. Levi crashes into me first, yelling something incoherent. I steal a quick second to close my eyes and picture Lottie smiling. I just need her here with me—even if it's only in my head.

She has to know I'm doing all this for us.

Her mom doesn't like hockey, but it brings in an income and offers a solid career. If I lead my team to victory, I'll be more than an NHL star—I'll be a national hero. Surely, Senator Halloway can respect that.

Unfortunately, the Stripes don't stay down. Mid-period, they respond, tying the game. The plays blur together, and at one point a guy snaps his stick clean in half and gets sent off. Reeves slashes, and we head to the power play. A sting spreads through my gut. I narrow my eyes and focus forward.

All I need to do is look at the puck, and I can sense that it's mine.

I wind up at the point, uncork a slap shot with everything I've got, and I know by the sound it makes that it's pure gold.

And just like that, I score my second goal of the night. When I skate past the Stripes' bench, Houli's smirk is loaded for me. "Careful, Ty," he chirps. "You're going to peak too early."

A niggling in the back of my head warns me to stay humble, but it's Houli. I can't resist a sharp, "You mind your own business." He laughs it off, and the horn blares, bringing the first period to an end.

And what a start that was.

The second period turns into a tug-of-war.

They score.

We score.

They annoyingly score again, like they didn't get the memo that this is supposed to be my best game ever. I've got a woman to impress. Even worse than that, I have a brown-nosing senator to impress. They aren't supposed to have that much stamina. Still, it only pushes me to dig deeper—there is nothing on this planet preventing me from leading this team to victory tonight. Not with Lottie watching at home and her snooty mom turning her nose up at me.

Stripes are going down.

And just like that, we get another power play. I hate to get cocky, but I'm grinning wide. My fingers jitter, waiting for the perfect moment. When the puck comes to me, I don't even skate. I snap it toward their goal.

And BOOM!

Hat trick.

It's official—my first career hat trick! I toss my gloves, and the arena erupts. My teammates pile on me. All of that is nothing compared to the fact I know, miles away, Lottie is cheering. I let out a sigh, sending my thoughts her way.

This is for you, my queen.

All of everything I have is for us.

I hope it's enough.

I'm ready for the game to be over right then and there, but we've got a whole other period to play. I end up nose-to-nose with Taz again, and we're hauled apart. Stripe's player, Dante loses his mind, takes a major penalty, and the Stripes' rhythm visually starts to unravel.

Which is good news for us, because I'm focused. Like I predicted, this game keeps giving us more gifts. Stripes are shooting, but we bury them with our speed, and they can't keep up. When the final horn sounds, the scoreboard lights up with our hard-earned victory. Usually, I'm quick to leave the ice. Tonight I skate to a stop in front of our goal, catching my breath and letting sweat drip from my brow into my eyes.

I'm not expecting to see her, but I look into the stands and imagine Lottie there. She should be here. Yeah, I know she saw it on her phone.

It's not the same.

It's not right.

Something needs to change.

Then I smile anyway. Because tonight, I played the best game of my life, and Lottie saw everything I'm doing is for us.

Even if that means tonight, I go home alone.

It's crazy how in tune my body is when Lottie's around. I don't see her, but I get this notion to adjust my shirt. Right then, I glance over my shoulder, and she's walking my way, wearing a pink sundress that hugs her waist like it doesn't know it has the power to make my heart race. Her hair is loose and down her back, exactly how she normally wears it when she's not working. She's absolutely the most stunning woman I've ever laid eyes on, and I can't believe she's here to see me.

We haven't even spoken yet, but I quickly scan the courtyard. We're behind the National Gallery. I spent an hour researching where we could go today. I didn't want to hide in her car, but we still have to tidy up her arrangement with Bodan before getting careless. I think if we are careful this place is perfect for our first official date. It's right after practice and still early enough in the day that it's not packed with people. The fountain trickles softly, setting the mood. With everything pressing down on us, we need a calm environment.

"Hey, you." She flashes her palm at me, and we sit on the fountain's edge, leaving a foot between us, taking caution before we trust we're safe.

"Hey." I take in every beautiful feature of her face and marvel at my life. All the years of watching her from afar, wishing she'd notice me, tumble into my chest. Though we haven't done anything to warrant a strong reaction, emotion clogs my throat.

Great. I'm already malfunctioning. Swallowing, I push it down. "I haven't gotten a chance to ask you about the funeral yet. How was it?"

"It was a lot harder than I thought it would be, and I didn't go in thinking it would be easy."

"I don't like the sound of that." My jaw tightens before I can stop it. I hate thinking about her with Bodan, even if I trust her. "What happened?"

"Well, my mom was my mom." Her forced laugh is brittle. "That's expected. But Bodan's sweet grandma...looked at me with so much hope. Like I would save her family from all the grief. Maybe I'm projecting, but I could hardly speak to her. I was so grateful when my mom announced she was too important to stay any longer." Shaking her head she adds, "For the first time in my life, my mom's overinflated ego actually saved me."

"Your mom said that?"

"No, not in those words. But you know my mom. It was all in her tone."

"So, how was Bodan?" I try to keep my face neutral, but the thought of her even being next to him makes me fume.

"Fine. He knows the job we're doing. He's professional about it. Though...I started to feel like maybe he's enjoying the attention too."

The hairs on the back of my neck stand in alarm, and I lean in. "How so?"

"I don't know. It was odd. Like, if it were me, I'd protect my grandma from the lie, and I wouldn't want to drag her into it. But he seemed to relish the idea our dating pleased her. It rubbed me the wrong way. I feel guilty. I wonder if he feels the same, now that his whole family is being lied to." She gestures toward me and tacks on, "Trust me, I can't wait to fake break up with him."

"Why wait?" I say, dead serious. "Point me in his direction. I'll do it for you."

"You can't break up with people you aren't dating."

"Watch me." I lift my chin. "I can do it by text or in person. Shoot, I can even write a poem if that's what you need to give me permission. I'm with you on this. Three is a crowd. We need him out of our relationship."

She blinks hard, like she misheard me. "Our relationship?"

The word hangs between us, fragile as glass, until I add a soft, "Yeah."

"Oh." She looks down at her hands, twisting the bracelet on her wrist. For a second, she looks overwhelmed, and my stomach squeezes. I'd anticipated pleasure in her reply, but now I'm worried. "I didn't know we were calling it that," she says after a quiet moment.

"Oops." I try to lighten the mood with a playful tone, though nothing about this feels playful. It's delicate, and I slide a little closer until our arms almost bump and soften my voice. "I've been calling it that in my head ever since we kissed. I'm sorry if that makes you uncomfortable. Maybe I should have asked first…"

"I…" Her gaze lifts, meeting mine, and a zap explodes in my chest. "I don't want to mess this up by rushing."

My chest tightens. This is news to me. I assumed since we kissed, and we've both said how much we care, that we were *together*. That's what I want. I'm not looking at anyone but her. Ever. "I don't want to mess anything up either…" I swallow. "I don't think we're rushing. We've spent years learning about each other as friends. We're allowed to skip a few steps."

A pause clamps my heart in a chokehold. I put my hand over my chest, waiting for her to confirm we are on the same page. When she stays quiet, I blurt, "I want to be with you. This isn't just a hey-we're -in-the-same-city-for-a-week fling for me. Isn't that what you want?"

Her breath stutters, but she quickly says, "It's not a fling for me either."

"Good." I let the moment and my hammering heart settle. I don't want to be confused. "So, we have Bodan, and that's a technical issue we need to sort out, but just to be clear...we're together, right? You want to be my girlfriend?"

Her eyes shine like she's trying not to cry and failing in the best way. "That's all I've ever wanted."

Relief hits so hard I have to chuckle. Without thinking, I slide my arm around her back and pull her close. She tucks her face into my neck, and the skin-on-skin contact ignites a whirlwind of shivers through me.

"So," she murmurs, "you still want to break up with Bodan for me?"

I grin into her hair. "Absolutely."

"No, I was joking. I'll handle it." The softest chuckle leaks from her. "I can't believe we are boyfriend and girlfriend." She goes quiet, like she's letting herself believe it. "This feels unreal."

"Good unreal or bad unreal?"

"Good, of course, but Ham's going to kill me."

"Oh, don't worry. I won't let him." I hadn't planned on kissing her, though it's all I've thought about since the last one. Well, when I wasn't thinking about hockey. I'd forbidden myself to even touch her in public. But when I look into her eyes, normally sea-glass green, they spiral with so many colors it's like I'm seeing an entire forest of happiness. And what happens next? I'll just call it another oops.

One second we're talking. The next, I'm cupping her face in my hand. She doesn't hold back either, leaning in, her fingers curling into my shirt.

That is the part that gets me!

I feel it everywhere!

In my chest.

In my ribs.

In my intestines, which let out a happy gurgle like I just fed them cake.

I hope she didn't hear it.

Did she hear it?

Our lips meet, painstakingly slow, irresistibly slow. I give her time to resist, letting her guide me to where she's comfortable, which turns out to be a pretty good plan, because she melts into the kiss, stealing every last ounce of breath I have.

Crrrruuuunch!

The sound of someone stepping on rocks cuts through the air. I yank back and freeze. A figure lingers off to the side, phone raised as if filming. The fountain? Us? I hate to be arrogant and assume either is important enough to be filmed, but my heart jumps into my throat.

Lottie stiffens, her gaze locking on the person.

"Sorry," the person says, moving into the light. It's a woman, touristy-looking in cargo shorts and a Washington DC T-shirt. Likely photographing the fountain. I hope she was just capturing the fountain. "I didn't mean to interrupt you two," she adds.

"Oh, you're not," I throw out as casually as I can. Thankfully, she lowers her phone and disappears down the path.

"Phew." Lottie laughs shakily. "I thought we were toast."

"So did I," I admit.

"That wouldn't be good." She chuckles, the sound thin. "But I think we're okay."

I toss another look over my shoulder. My heightened senses say not so fast. I want to believe her, but we are in a public place. This might have been a stupid idea. I hadn't planned on kissing her, but declaring we're a couple? That's a huge moment. Standing, I take a step aside. "Well, maybe we should walk. That might appear more casual."

Following my lead, she stands and walks forward. "Yeah, that was close but … worth it," she says like a confession.

"I have to agree." My fingers twitch, hating I can't grab her hand right now. It's a cruel game that after all the years of waiting to tell her how I feel, after I finally do, and we are officially together, I still can't touch her in public. Speaking of public appearances, I bring up something else. "So, tomorrow is the last game. Are you able to come?"

"I don't know." Her face falls a little. "I want to, but I will probably need to ask Bodan to be the decoy, and I don't want to drag this out. The more times we are seen in public, the harder it'll be to break it off."

"Maybe you can come by yourself." I step closer, lowering my voice. "Nobody has to know you are there to watch me. It's not like you are going to wear a wag jacket."

"No jacket but I want to wear your jersey like a true fan." Her eyes flick up, bright again. "My mom would love that."

A chuckle tumbles from my lips. "She'd probably faint."

"She would, but then she'd muster up the energy to kill me. She's superhuman like that." Lottie laughs, and I turn to marvel at how her whole face lights up.

I love looking at her.

"Maybe Ham could be the decoy. He already knows about us, and I'm his best friend. It makes sense he'd come to my game. If anyone asks, Ham dragged you along."

"Ah." She tilts her head, a smile spreading across her perfect lips. "That could work."

"It will work." My chest swells as I imagine her in the crowd. Just knowing she'll be there fuels me even more.

"Okay." She nods with conviction. "I'll blackmail Ham into doing it." She glances back down the path, then back at me. "And I hate to cut this short, but, you know, we almost got busted once already. I hate to push our luck. I should go."

"I understand." I say it, but my body doesn't believe me. I plant my feet, knowing if I move even an inch closer, I won't stop. I hold her gaze instead, because it's the one thing I *can* do without crossing the line. "I hate I can't kiss you right now." The words scrape out of my chest.

Her cheeks bloom pink, and the sight nearly breaks me. She swallows, fingers curling at her sides like she's holding herself back too. "Me too."

I want to tuck her hair behind her ear, but I know even that is too much. Once I feel her hair in my fingers, I won't stop there. As much as I want to kiss her, more than anything I want to respect the place she's in and give her time to clean up the Bodan issue. It would break my heart if anything I did caused a scandal.

"I'm not saying goodnight." I give her a small smile, though it barely tames the ache in my chest. "Because I'm going to text you later."

"I'll text first when I get home." She smiles at me, and even though it's not the goodnight kiss I crave, it's enough to let her walk away. I let her go first, so we don't get caught "leaving together." Every step she takes solidifies in my chest that she is everything I've ever wanted. Wanting her is easy.

It's this waiting that is going to slay me.

Thirty-Three

Tyson

VRRRRRR.

I might as well be half dead, deep in slumber, when my phone vibrates on the nightstand. I'm surprised I even hear it—except it doesn't stop.

Vrrrrrr.

With lazy energy, I swipe my phone off the nightstand and manage to open one eye.

Missed calls.

A lot of missed calls.

I must have been sleeping hard because I didn't hear a single one. Half of these numbers are unknown. I scroll until I see Lottie's name, and my heart skips. It's not unusual to see her name, but when it's in the middle of a dozen unknown numbers, it feels urgent. My heart speeds up as I press Call. Lucky for me, she answers right away.

"Hey," I say, keeping my voice low. "Is everything all right?"

"Weellll." She stretches it out like she's weighing the bad news, and my stomach knots into a ball of nerves. "Nobody died again, if that's what you are thinking, but someone leaked a photo of us from our date yesterday."

Those knots tighten, one by one, until I wince. "Ah, how bad is the damage?"

"Not as bad as it could be. They didn't catch us kissing, but it's obvious. The way your hand is touching my lower back makes it look more than friendly." Her voice wobbles despite her best effort. "It's actually a really sweet photo for our first as a couple. We're both smiling at each other, and you have this soft expression in your eyes, but ... yeah, it's not the best for, you know."

I close my eyes as I hate to ask the next part, "Where did you see it?"

"Oh, everywhere," she says. "The photo credits are *Sport Era Magazine*, someone tagged me this morning. I didn't panic right away, because my mom doesn't read sports articles. But then someone tagged my mom."

My chest tightens so fast, I wheeze. "Aw, that's not good. So they not only recognized me, but you. I'm so sorry, Lottie."

"You don't have to apologize." She chuckles, unamused. "I thought we were careful."

"We were. We just weren't invisible. To be honest, I sort of expected it, because of that lady we saw with her cell phone. It was really odd."

"I was thinking the same thing. People can be so nosy. Like, it's not really that newsworthy, and it's sad they make a living invading others' privacy." She pauses, then says, "I saved the photo as my phone wallpaper."

Chortling, I shake my head because that doesn't surprise me. "Are you trying to give your mom a stroke?"

"This has nothing to do with her. I'm making decisions for me now." She hesitates, then continues, "Like I said, it's a sweet photo of us. You're looking down at me like we have our own little secret world. I love it."

Pain twists under my ribs. "It's not a secret world anymore."

Her voice softens to a whisper, "I didn't think the world would find out like this, but in a way, I'm relieved. I don't want to lie anymore. The photo isn't as bad as it could be. I just have to figure out an official timeline for breaking up with Bodan, which is going to be tricky...since I was just at his grandpa's funeral. Ugh. I hate this." Her voice trails off into a moan.

Sliding to the edge of the bed, I drop my feet to the floor and stretch one arm over my head, anchoring the phone to my ear with my other hand. "You know this doesn't change anything for me. I meant it when I said I want to be with you. Maybe this won't be a big deal, and maybe it will, but nothing changes."

There's a longer pause this time, and my brows furrow, because it's an odd moment not to reply. After a few seconds, I wonder if she's even there. "Lottie, did you hear what I said?"

"Ugh, Brett just texted me," she says. "Apparently my mom is too mad to text me herself, but she wants to see me in her office in an hour, which is dumb, because there will likely be paparazzi there. Why couldn't we talk at home? What a drama queen."

"I can go with you. There's no reason you should have to do this alone," I continue, my voice firm and unyielding. "I don't care if I'm on the front page."

She exhales slowly, like she's still deciding. "You have a game."

"One thing will always be true; I'll always have a game. That's my job, but that doesn't mean I can't be there for you too." I check the digital clock on the hotel nightstand, and it's glowing a few minutes after seven. I stand and grab a pair of shorts from my bag, hurriedly changing. "Besides, I can hurry and be over there to meet your mom at her office."

"I appreciate that, but I don't think it's a good idea to fuel the rumors more—at least not until I figure out a timeline, which I'm sure is what my mom wants to do. You know she's all about damage control. Nothing interferes with her image, not even her daughter's happiness." Her breath stutters. "You know, I'm not apologizing to her or anyone." Her voice grows stronger. "I don't regret it."

"Good." I pace the room. "Because I don't either, and you shouldn't apologize. I'm so sick of hearing you apologize to your mom for things you didn't do. You owe her nothing."

"Okay." Her voice steadies, like she's back in the logical part of her brain. In the background, I hear water running, like she's getting ready. "I need to do something with my hair if I'm going to make it to town in an hour. I'll call you as soon as I'm done talking to her. Is that okay?"

"Always." I don't intend for my voice to sound shallow. The dual meaning of the word makes my voice stumble, and it comes out breathy.

She catches it and echoes, "Always."

We hang up, and I can't help but Google the photo. If I'm going down for something, I at least want to know what it is. The image pulls up, clear as day without an ounce of blur, zoomed in tight on us. You can't even see the fountain in the background, which tells me without a doubt this wasn't an accident.

There I am, touching her back.

Seeing it sends a ripple up my spine, pulling me right back to that moment in the park. Lottie is right. It's a pretty great photo of us for our first "couple" photo.

The caption reads: **Looks like USA Stars team captain, Tyson Lane, has found a way to keep warm while he's in DC. Yes, that's Senator Halloway's daughter, Lottie, who is in a relationship with scholar, Bodan Bowey.**

The photo wouldn't even be bad, but the caption is overkill. Running my hand through my hair, I fight the urge to message the reporter and tell them to kill the caption. It's this kind of thing I can't stand about fame. Who cares who I am standing next to? This has nothing to do with how I play hockey.

I know one thing—whatever comes next, I'm not backing away from Lottie. If anyone asks me about Lottie, I won't lie. I'm not afraid of her mom. Well, maybe I'm a little afraid, but that's because she makes laws.

But seriously, she could send me to prison for all I care.

Wait...can she send me to prison?

I don't think she has that much power.

But she knows people who have that power.

Ugh, I'm getting way ahead of myself here.

Nothing bad will happen.

The truth will come out.

It needs to come out.

Then Lottie and I can finally be publicly together, and people won't care about posting photos like this online. I glance back at the photo still loaded on my phone, and I get an idea. I click on the photo, save it to my phone, and take a minute to set it as my wallpaper too.

Lottie and I are in this together, even if she's talking to her mom alone, I won't leave her alone on this.

Anxiety floods through my veins, and I break out in a nervous sweat. It will take about an hour for her to arrive to the office, and this room seems to grow smaller with each passing minute. My stomach grumbles. Or is that indigestion? Regardless, I need to get breakfast now, or I'll be late for morning skate. So many thoughts race through my mind, it's hard to be focused.

With a Stars hoodie pulled over my head and my stomach knotted in a tight wad; I head downstairs. Thank goodness only a few people are still in the banquet hall, and most seem to be finishing up.

Keeping my head down, I shuffle to the open buffet. The breakfast choices look and smell amazing. I beeline to the buffet and get an everything omelet. Then I take my plate to the farthest table from the entrance and sit with my back to it. I'm not avoiding the fact I'm in the headlines today. It's what happens when any professional hockey player is in the national spotlight. I'm also not the only one making headlines. I've seen Bryce and Taz making their own news, but I don't want to talk about any of it right now. My mind drifts to Lottie and how badly I feel that she has to face this alone with her mom. But she insisted, and I know she can do it.

With my head swirling, I bite into my omelet, and to my dismay, my stomach churns, a bitter taste inching up my throat. There's nothing wrong with the food. Maybe eating wasn't such a good idea. Nausea builds, and I end up discarding my entire plate and returning to my hotel room, anxiously awaiting some news from Lottie.

I sprawl out on the floor and do my stretches, but each passing minute feels like an eternity—an eternity of checking my phone, doing another stretch, checking my phone, doing some push-ups, checking my phone, over and over. Wash, rinse, repeat. A million times.

My stomach knots tighten with each excruciatingly slow-passing minute, until I'm sure a basket has been woven in my gut. With a deep sigh, I open my phone screen and stare at the photo of us.

The phone vibrates and I startle, fumbling the device and nearly dropping it. I'm almost too scared to look.

Lottie: I just parked, and I'm walking to the office. Wish me luck.

Hating I'm not by her side right now, I respond:

I'm leaving for morning skate, but I'm here for you. If you need me there, just say the words.

She doesn't need me. She's tough. I always knew she had that fighting spirit in her. It's hard to explain, but her mom has a way of trying to squash it. As much as this photo wasn't part of our plan, and the timing is terrible, I know she can handle it. I'm proud of her.

I race downstairs, and I'm the last one on the shuttle, before they close the door, and drive off. I close my eyes and try to relax my brain, but after about two minutes my fingers get fidgety, and I pick up my phone.

Nothing.

I tap on my screen, fighting the urge to text to check in, but then I laugh out loud. Seriously, she can handle it.

I stare out the window, all the while my stomach churns with anxiety. Lottie and her mom must be arguing. I should have insisted on going with her. I can picture her mom, snooty chin elevated, staring down at Lottie. It's about time someone put Senator Halloway in her place.

We arrive at our destination, and I jump to my feet. My mind still racing. I don't want drama for either of them, but if it's finally time for her mom to learn a lesson, I won't mind if the whole truth comes out. How Bodan was just a prop. She certainly better not try to convince Lottie to take all this damage and claim she was cheating. That thought enrages me so much my fingers curl into fists, and I fight the urge to punch something.

When my phone finally buzzes, my stomach is in such shambles that I'm half-hunched over. Standing just outside the door, I rush out, "Hey," my voice mostly breath. "I'm here."

She exhales like she's been holding it for her entire meeting. "Well, she didn't yell too much."

I blink. My voice won't work. Even though she can't see me blinking, I hope she knows it's a solid attempt to commiserate.

"She said," she continues in her rehearsed professional voice she uses at work, "that I put her in an impossible position."

I tighten my grip on the phone, fighting the urge to grind my teeth. I am a professional hockey player here. I don't need extra dental bills. "Of course she said that. Like Bodan was all your idea."

"She said I crossed a line I should've known better than to approach."

Shaking my head, I can totally see her mom saying that. I know the exact facial expression she used when she said that—the one where her brows furrow and her eyes practically go cross-eyed. It's one of the scariest faces that woman makes. While I'm ruminating on it, I'm glad Lottie favors her dad's facial expressions more. Lottie never makes that face. "You didn't do anything wrong," I blurt out. "Don't let her convince you to take the blame for this. She forced you to be a distraction from her foot-in-mouth disease."

"She said I embarrassed her," she adds quietly. "And my whole family legacy."

I close my eyes. I also know the face Lottie is making—the one where she pinches her lips together so tightly they pucker in the middle, like she's forming a dam to hold back all the tears she refuses to cry. "You know, Lottie," I say as gently as I can, "it's okay to feel hurt from her reaction. You don't have to hold it all in."

"Honestly, I don't think I could cry right now because I'm furious."

"What are you angry about?" If her mom did something to her, I won't hold back. I can feel my blood pressure spiking.

"I guess, I thought we'd have a conversation, and she'd yell, but we'd figure out a timeline. I started thinking I could say Bodan and I broke up before the funeral, and I only went for emotional support. That we were already done but didn't want to say anything because of the emotional weight of the day. It would've given us an extra day to work with. I was spinning all these lies in my head—for her. I was getting dizzy, but I was going to do it to protect her...and then she kept asking me about you."

"What about me?"

"She doesn't believe we just got together this summer. Basically, she thinks I'm the one lying, and when I realized she won't believe me, I told her the truth—because I don't care anymore. I told her I'm glad the photo is out there, because it's the only honest thing right now. I'm done with the Bodan arrangement. I'm not going anywhere with him anymore. I refuse to make a statement about it, because it's not my mess. It's hers. I told her from now on, I only want to be seen next to you, because we're together."

My pride swells at the courage in that sentence. "And?"

"And she said your career is a liability."

"Of course she did."

"She told me"—her voice tightens as I hear her car start—"these were her exact words: 'Effective immediately, you're no longer needed on my staff.'"

That hits like a clean check to the boards. "She fired you?"

"I guess, but honestly, it's probably better this way. I've needed to quit for a long time but couldn't find the courage. She had this hold on me I couldn't shake, no matter how hard I tried. I guess it's better she cut me out."

My heart hammers against my chest as I shake my head. "That's not better. You know she did you dirty. She used you to clean up her PR mess. When it backfired, she handed you all the damage."

"I know." Her voice cracks. "The worst part is, when the conversation was over, she slid an HR folder across her desk. It already had my name on it, which means she put it all together before I even got there. So, essentially, nothing I said—or could have said—mattered. She had already decided I would take the fall before I even walked in. I'm invisible to her."

"Oh, Lottie." I drag my hand down my face. "You're not invisible. Not to me. You're seriously the only woman I've even seen. I'm so sorry she said that to you."

"So, with nothing else to do, I cleaned out my desk." After a deep sigh, she goes on, "My mom took my keys and get this—she insisted security walk me out. She literally called Ham."

Heat surges through me. "That's—"

"It's okay," she cuts off my fury. "I didn't even cry. Now you know why I can't cry. It's almost like a curtain was ripped all the way open, and I needed to see everything behind it to understand that this is the best thing to happen to me. She's never going to change. I finally saw that if I want to be the best version of myself—and actually live my life—I need to step away from her. She did me a favor."

My arms ache to hold her, to pull her in the biggest, most protective hug. I hate I didn't at least meet her outside the office. I didn't know she'd be fired though. I press my hand to my forehead and steady myself. "You didn't deserve that."

"I know. And that's the problem. I'm finally seeing what I do and don't deserve, and I can't unsee it. As much as I'm irate about how she treated me, I'm mostly relieved. It's weird," she continues, "I'm relieved and angry—and I didn't think I could feel all of this at once—but I'm also disappointed. I've been waiting for a reason to leave. I just didn't think it would hurt this much."

"You're allowed to hurt," I say. "You offered your mom so much love and support, but it wasn't reciprocated."

She goes stone quiet. I cringe, picturing her fighting tears. "Lottie," I say after a long beat of silence. "Can I meet you somewhere?"

"No." Her reply is quick, and then, almost shyly, she says, "Not right now. I don't have time. I need to get to the house to grab some of my things out of my room. I'm going to stay in one of the guest cabins until I figure something out. I can't risk seeing her right now."

"If I help you move your stuff, it will go faster."

"That's okay. To be honest, I need an hour or two alone right now, and I know you have work stuff you are more than likely late to."

"Well, if you insist." I glance at the clock on my phone, knowing the hours will slip by whether I want them to or not. "I'm ready to start practice," I say, then pause, choosing my next words carefully. I don't want her to have any doubts about how I feel. "I want you there tonight."

"Tonight? After this..." She hesitates, then adds, "I don't want to take attention away from the game. If I show up now, who knows what my mom will do. She can't handle things when they aren't all about her. I don't know if it's a good idea..."

"I do," I say gently. "It's the perfect idea. It shows your mom, and the world, that you didn't lose."

"You really want my drama during the most important night of your career?"

I smile, even though she can't see it. "I always want your drama, and if Crunch hasn't completely eaten it by now, can you wear my jersey?"

"I already am," she replies. "I wore it to the office to make my point clear."

That lands somewhere deep in me. I've never had any doubts about Lottie. I love how we're already coming together as our own little team. It's more than I ever imagined. I hate to bring her mom back into it, but I have to ask, "What did your mom do when she saw that?"

"Nothing really. She scanned my outfit, muttered something about decorum in a federal building, and then launched into a speech about how the photo was embarrassing."

"I'm so sorry you had to endure that."

"I'm not, and you shouldn't be either."

My smile spreads wide. I love this new fire in her voice. I always knew it was there. Now that she's finally stepping out of her mother's shadow, I don't doubt she'll take over the world if that's what she wants. "Hey, I'm getting into some heavy traffic. If it's okay, I'll let you go."

"Sounds good."

We hang up, and I scan up and down the street and then look back at the facility. It is exactly how it was one minute ago, but something about it feels different. Like the world is a little bit more still. If anything, the roadblock has been removed. The path forward isn't exactly clear, but Lottie and I are on it together.

Her mom tried to destroy Lottie's life today.

Too bad for her—I'm going to fight with everything I've got to give her a better one.

Thirty-Four

Lottie

MOM WANTS ME TO take the blame for everything and make a statement. I refuse. With Ty working, I need something to do to keep my mind busy, so I spend the day with Maddie, finally having time to catch up with her. We make pizzas for lunch, and my favorite recipe of cereal bars. It's the one where I substitute crispy rice cereal for Cinnamon Toast Crunch, and I call them goat bars. I can't even look at them without smiling, and it turns out being exactly what I need. Before I know it, it's almost time for the game, and I'm giving her a ride, which works out well because I no longer want to go with Ham. After he helped walk me out of my job, I haven't spoken to him. I'm not mad at him, but there's a disappointment I have to deal with.

True to fashion, as soon as we try to leave, Toast has it out for Maddie, trotting in a circle like he's about to lose his mind when Maddie shuts the door, closing him out. I run around like a crazy person to corral him and the other goats, rounding them up and getting them safely into their pen before we head out. The gate isn't busted this time, but somehow they just got it open. Someday scientists will study their escape skills. I'm completely out of breath when I return to my Land Rover.

"Sorry about that," I say, fastening my seat belt and starting the engine. "They don't attack *everyone*. Just people they like. And Uber drivers."

Maddie laughs, a little nasally, like it's stuck in her sinuses. "In that case, I feel so honored."

I back out of my spot, turning around in the wild grass in front of my house, then steer down the dirt road. "Also, sorry if this is rude, but are you sick? I noticed earlier you sounded plugged up."

"Nope. Allergies." She waves a dismissive hand. "Your yard is basically trying to kill me."

"Oh, no. I apologize on behalf of all the flowers. I totally agree they are excessive." I steer around the bend in the drive and pull onto the main road.

Maddie turns to me with a small smile. "So, have you thought any more about what to do for a job?"

I stare through the windshield. "I don't have one."

"That surprises me a little."

I shake my head. "Truthfully, all I ever wanted was for my mom to be proud of me. I had a mission in life; do what she said. It's crazy, but this is the first time I'm thinking for myself about my career, and my brain is blank."

Maddie tilts her head, studying me. "It can't be totally blank. There must be something you're thinking?"

I exhale, not holding back "Well, this week all I can think about is Ty."

"Ohhhh," Maddie draws out the word like it helps explain everything. "Now you confess."

"And it's freaking me out," I add. "I've never been like this before. Maybe it's worse because he's here for a short time, and I know he's headed back to Minnesota. I can't help but think maybe getting fired is my ticket—to not only do something for me, but to figure out a way to live close to Ty. Of course, I have not told him yet ... it's way too soon."

Maddie smirks at me. "For what it's worth, you two are stupid cute."

My heart flutters as I think about the photo I've saved as my phone wallpaper, and I grin. I have a lot of decisions to make in a short amount of time, but going to the game tonight puts things into perspective. This is what I want to do tonight and every night. Show up for my boyfriend.

When I walk up to the arena wearing Tyson's jersey, it takes all of three seconds to know this is better than any confession or public statement I could come up with. Sure, it's not exactly a WAG jacket, but with only one game left, it's too late to buy one. I tug the hem down over my hips. It's so large, it hangs almost to my knees. Wearing it proudly, I get in line with Maddie by my side.

Just as I expected, the stares start instantly. People whisper, a few point discreetly, but I catch them anyway. With the number of glares I'm receiving, you'd think I'd shown up in my birthday suit.

"Just keep walking forward." Maddie nudges my elbow and smiles.

The whispers grow louder, but my heart ticks out a steady beat. This is right. I'm choosing to live my true self. After we pass through the ticket gate, Maddie leaves to find her seat with the Stripes' fans. Going in the opposite direction, I nearly run straight into someone. Instinctively, I cover my face, expecting a verbal attack. When nothing happens, I lower my hand and blink in surprise. And not the good kind. My entire body tenses. "Are you kidding me?" I whisper, glaring at the traitor.

Ham grins, planting his feet in front of me, blocking my path. "You really thought I'd let you do this alone?"

I shake my head, wishing I could kick him in the shin like when we were kids. "You escorted me out of my job this morning!" Emotion surges so fast it tightens my throat. "You really thought I'd let you sit by me?"

"I was doing what I had to do to get you safely away from Mom. You know it was time. If you'd stayed any longer, she would have yelled and made a scene." His gaze drops to the jersey then lifts to my eyes. "I'm here now to support you," he says simply. "And Ty. Work is work and that's business. You guys are family. If you and Ty want this, I'm here for both of you."

"Well, technically, work is family too, because it's Mom," I grumble.

"Come on, Lottie. I'm not letting you do this alone." He looks toward the door and the screaming crowd. Then he turns back to me, opening his arms for a hug. "Truce?" He's not an affectionate guy. We aren't like that. We are more siblings who are rivals. I'm so touched that he's stepping into this drama for Ty and me that I hug him hard, right there in front of everyone.

Until someone elbows me hard in the back.

"Ouch." I startle and look around. People are piling in, and it's getting close to puck drop. I flick a finger toward the rink. "We better find our seats."

We don't speak as we walk together, finding our places as the players spill out onto the ice for warm-up. Ty skates out last, the C on his chest catching the light. My chest flips as it always does when I see him looking so hot. Only now, I don't fight it. I smile and absorb it.

In all the years of hanging out with Ty, I didn't pay much attention when he'd ramble on about hockey. I regret that now because I don't know what's going on.

The puck drops.

I know that much.

Someone from the Stripes team grabs it, and the crowd roars. I lean forward, trying to follow the blur of motion. The Stripes score first. It's clear this arena doesn't have any favorites tonight—half of it cheers while the other half boos. I'm not normally vocal, but I sort of love the booing, and I join in.

Then something happens fast. One of the Stripes players appears to mess up, and a Star player rockets the puck into the net. I jump to my feet with everyone else, cheering. I understand when a goal is made.

I focus in on Ty, who slams his stick against the ice. I'm so glad to witness this in person. It totally beats stealing glimpses on my phone.

The first period ends with a lot of shoving that looks like it should be illegal but apparently isn't. No one goes to the penalty box. I assume it's fine. I hold on to my phone during intermission, thinking maybe Ty will text me, but he doesn't. Clearly, he has a game to focus on.

Ham leans over and casually asks, "Do you think Mom is watching the game at home?"

"Ah, no," I scoff. "Why would you even think that?"

"I told her I was coming with you. She didn't say anything, but you know how she is. If she can't win, she'll find a way to get even."

"She'll never watch a hockey game." I actually giggle, as that's the funniest thing I've considered in a long time.

When the second period begins, so does my emotional turmoil.

The Stripes score again. And again. And *again*. I'm pretty sure that's the technical way of describing it. It's basically a commercial for how great their team is.

The arena is screaming, but I sit back down with the score at 4–1 and my optimism wobbling. I want Tyson's team to win. Regardless, I'm so proud of him and the way he carries himself.

I watch the puck move from one team to the other, and then one of the guys gets tripped with a stick. Even though I'm pretty sure it was an accident, a fight breaks out.

Helmets fly off. Everyone around me jumps to their feet, screaming like fighting is the main event. I scan the crowd for half a second. When I look back, three guys are tangled together. Eventually, the refs pull them apart. There's more booing and cheering, and I'm not sure who won the fight—or if I'm supposed to boo or cheer—so I bite my tongue.

After that the momentum shifts, which leads me to believe the Stars maybe won that fight, because they start scoring. Pretty soon the board says it's 4–4. I'm on my feet again, yelling Tyson's name like he can somehow pick my voice out of twenty thousand people. My heart motors so hard. I just know this is their comeback. Everything falls into place.

Oh—nope. I thought too soon. The Stripes sneak in one more, and they go into intermission with a 5–4 lead.

I exhale shakily.

"It's just a game," Ham says. I'd almost forgotten he was sitting next to me, and I give him a side-eye.

"Maybe for you, but I want Ty to have this victory after everything I put him through this week."

It's his turn to side-eye me. "You really think that?"

"What do you mean? Why wouldn't I want him to have this win?"

He rolls his eyes dramatically and leans in like he's giving me sage advice. "I've known Ty for as long as I can remember. He wants to win, but even if he doesn't, he already got what he truly wanted this week. Believe me, he already feels like a winner."

I don't know what to say. Again, Ham and I aren't usually the kind of siblings who are this supportive. We usually trade insults. Maybe with all the changes I'm making, it's time for me to change our relationship too. "Wow, that's a nice thing to say."

"It's the truth."

I swallow that statement and it settles deep and feels good. I value the truth so much, and I vow to always tell it. No more lies.

Time to turn my focus back on the game. The third period starts with a huge disappointment—the Stripes score again. My heart drops to the floor. I want this win for Ty.

But then something amazing happens. The Stars answer back, and somehow we score two more times after that and tie it up.

It's so exciting, I stay on my feet. I don't know why I never watched hockey before. This kind of action is incredible. Right as time is expiring, something even more incredible happens—our goalie launches himself across the ice like a human miracle and stops what everyone around me swears would've been an empty-net goal.

The buzzer sounds and we're tied heading to overtime!

I don't leave my seat while the guys regroup. I don't even think I blink. I wait as they reset the clock and play resumes. Someone on our team goes to the penalty box almost immediately. Ham mutters something under his breath that sounds suspiciously like a prayer. Apparently, whatever is happening is bad.

But then—

It's an explosion, and my eyes can't keep up. A shot is blocked. There's a pass I almost miss because I'm gripping Ham's arm so tight he yells at me. One of our guys tucks the puck in the net so cleanly it takes half a second for my brain to catch up.

The fans are in a frenzy.

I'm at a loss.

Until I check the scoreboard: 7–6. "Is it over?" I squeeze Ham's arm again. "Did we win?"

"Yeah, the Stars won." A wide smile stretches across Ham's face.

I scream and wave my arms, trying to get Ty's attention as the Stars players pour off the bench and onto the ice. My eyes lock on Ty as he removes his helmet and skates straight toward the pileup; victory written all over his face.

Unable to handle the excitement, I press my hands to my face. The applause doesn't stop. When Ty finally comes out of the pile at center ice, he lifts his glove toward me—and then his eyes find mine.

I sink into the softness of his gaze, and everything else disappears.

I'm no longer hiding anything.

The smile he gives me makes everything worth it.

Thirty-Five

Tyson

THE ARENA EMPTIES SLOWER than usual. It seems like every fan is staying to cheer. This is exactly what I dreamed of my whole life. Most of the guys beam from the never-ending applause. Even with all the celebrating going on, I can feel the question hanging in the air like static. No one said anything about my online drama today. It's almost like they're waiting for permission, which is odd. Especially Houli, who lives for a good chirp at my expense.

When we make it to the hall, Lottie's standing there, right next to Ham. I'm not going to lie, seeing Ham with her makes me a bit emotional. I hadn't expected him to risk his job, or his privacy, for me, and I'm touched.

"It's going to be a while yet," I murmur, trying to keep my voice low. "After we get dressed, we're going out to dinner to celebrate. I'd love it if you could come…"

"I wouldn't miss it for the world." Lottie's expression calms me as she approaches and holds out a marker to me. "But first, I need you to sign my jersey."

A chuckle slips out as I can't believe she's doing this in front of people. I don't know if I'll ever get used to the way my heart flutters from the way she looks at me, but I'm here for it. I take the marker from her and bring it to her sleeve. "Hold still."

It's like every person in the hall takes a collective breath, rising onto their toes to see what I write. I've thought about Lottie so much over the years. It's odd I never imagined this moment. Still, I don't have to think twice about what to write. Leaning in and in my best penmanship—because I want everyone to be able to read it—I write:

To My Queen, Your Ollways, Ty.

I slide my hand out of the way and smile, egging on anyone who wants to gossip. I want everyone to see it. I want everyone to know.

She reads it, her lips tipping into the sweetest smile. "You spelled it wrong."

"Nah." I shake my head, enjoying the deep eye contact. It feels like I can see our future in those sea-glass green spirals, and it's bright. "I spelled it right."

I wink at Lottie, and she gives me a small wave as she moves back toward the door. "I'll watch for you outside."

"I'll find you."

As she weaves through the hall, a sigh of relief falls from my lips that she has Ham with her. He's always watched over her, personally and professionally. He'll make sure she's safe from the reporters until I finish my duties for the team. I turn back and head to the locker room as I step into a new headspace—one where everything feels easy.

We won the game, making us tournament champions.

Lottie and I are together and no longer lying.

Everything has turned out exactly how I dreamed.

Thirty-Six

Lottie

HAM LEFT AFTER HE dropped me off beside my car and made sure I was safely inside with the doors locked. It's less than an hour later, Ty comes running—yes, running—at top speed toward my car. He has an open-mouthed smile that makes me chuckle, and I make a split-second decision to open my door and run toward him. Because I no longer have to hide this, I want to fully experience a hug. He must have the same idea, because he doesn't slow until he's right in front of me. Instead of stopping, he sweeps me off my feet, squeezing me into a tight hug, twirling me around. We both break out laughing.

"You were amazing!" I exclaim when I finally catch my breath.

He stops spinning and lowers me to my feet, but he doesn't let go. His hands stay wrapped around me as he lowers his face to mine. "So were you."

He holds me so close I can feel his heart hammering through his shirt. For a second, I stand here, focused on the steady rhythm of his heart. It's one of the most intimate things I've ever felt. After the silence stretches for a beat, he presses his thumb on my chin, tilting my face toward his. I don't need instructions. I let my eyes drift closed as his warm breath brushes my lips. His hand slides to cup my jaw, and I melt into his kiss. Butterflies break free, fluttering through my stomach like they are about to throw a party. I can't help but smile. It's kissing excellence.

"Why are you smiling?" Ty breaks the kiss long enough to ask before sealing his lips back to mine.

I don't answer right away. I let my smile grow until I feel him smile back. It's fun to tease him. His grip tightens at my waist, and I love everything about this moment.

"Because," I murmur, brushing my mouth against his, "it's been fun to watch you win life this week."

His breath hitches as he pulls back, a soft chuckle sneaking out. "What do you mean, win life?"

I gaze up at him, loving how his eyes never leave mine. "What is there to question? You literally won everything—the game, the tournament, Ham's support, all the fans love you." My thumb traces the edge of his jaw, and I smile at how natural it feels to tease him. "And me."

I expect him to laugh in agreement. Instead, his smile fades into a serious expression. "You know none of that matters if I don't have you." A swallow pulses through his throat. When I don't respond right away, he lowers his voice. "You know that, right?"

Taken aback by how fast the moment shifted from playful to serious, I blink before speaking. "I do now."

"Good." He exhales softly, his expression softening. Then, more casually, he asks, "So...are you ready to go to dinner? I can't wait to introduce you to the team and all the other WAGs."

That word WAGs pings my heart.

Wife and girlfriends.

I can't believe this is my life. It's all I ever wanted. I glance back at my car, then at him. His face is still flushed from the whirl of events. My heart races, knowing we don't have to hide anymore. For a second, I just study him—not because I don't love the sound of it, but because the ease of it catches me off guard. This is us, creating our life together, and no one is dictating it anymore. "Sounds perfect."

The next morning, I wake in one of the guest cabins, Ty's kisses still fresh in my head. It's the first time in forever, I don't go into work on a weekday. I haven't talked to my mom. I'm still mad at her. It will take time before I can see her again, but there is one thing I feel obliged to do. I stare at my phone for a full minute before scrolling to his name and pressing Call.

Bodan answers on the first ring. "Hey, Lottie. Wow, perfect timing. I was just—"

"I owe you an apology"—I hurry to get the words out before my courage fails—"for dragging you into something that got so messy. I should have never listened to my mom in the first place."

I pause, squeezing my eyes shut, as I brace for him to get mad about the hockey game and the photo—but he just laughs. "Oh, don't apologize. This has been the best experience of my life"

My eyes snap open. "What?"

"Seriously, I'm loving this. My Instagram is blowing up," he says cheerfully. "I've got so many women reaching out to me, asking to chat. I've been asked out more times today than I could ever have imagined."

Of course this is happening!

A relieved smile spreads across my face. "Well, I'm glad you're not mad, I'm glad you aren't sorry you got sucked into this mess, and I'm really glad you're happy," I say, meaning it. "And I'm glad I met you."

"I am happy," he says. "And I'm glad you're happy too. Tyson seems like the real deal."

"I think he is," I say softly.

"So, I guess that leaves us as...what? Friends."

"Friends," I easily agree. I start to apologize again, then remember he's happy, and there is no need. "Well, if we're both happy, then I'll let you go reply to all your Instagram admirers."

"Thank you, and good luck, Lottie."

"You too." When the call ends, I stare at his name blinking on my screen. The conversation lasted only two minutes and was much easier than I could have imagined. I got lucky with Bodan. He was the perfect fake date, chin mole disease and all...

The sun is already up, past the time Mom leaves for the office, so it's safe for me to get up. These guest cabins are nice, but I have no groceries. I need to sneak over to the main house for a cup of coffee before I can function. I slide my feet off the bed and stumble down the hall to the door, slipping into my worn flip-flops. I smile and wiggle my toes. It's been a long time since I wore flip-flops on a Tuesday—Mom would never allow open-toe in the office.

I step out the door without slowing. Out of habit, I scan the yard and see the usual sights. Mom's sprawling flower gardens are fully awake this time of year, coneflowers rising above the beds to catch the morning sun. Their pink and purple petals droop slightly, which, I think, only adds to their character. Tucked among them, lavender and sage sprinkle in silvery touches to contrast the roses. As much as I make fun of these gardens—because my mom lies about them—I do love them. I love this whole place, and I'll miss it when I leave.

My eyes bulge when I spot the goat pen gate *wide open*!

And not a goat in sight!

Not wide open like the goats pushed it open, but wide open like someone had neatly propped it that way. Frantically, I scan the field for the goats—and for my dad. He's the only one who would take them out, but it's never been at this hour before.

I glance toward the barn.

No goats.

The hills.

No goats.

The porch, where they aren't supposed to be. I pray they are just being naughty.

No goats.

My heart ramps up as my gaze cuts to the road. We aren't near a main highway, so I don't have to worry about them getting into traffic, but they can still get lost. "Cinnamon!" I cry, because she's usually the best behaved and the most likely to come running.

Nothing.

"Toast!"

Nothing.

"Crunch!" On any other day I'd have to giggle I'm screaming for cereal, but today I sprint up the large hill. By the time I scramble to the top, I'm out of breath but I need a better view of the area.

Nothing.

My goats are gone.

And oddly, so is everyone else.

This isn't an accident.

This was revenge.

My mom hates those goats, but she knows how dear they are to me. This has her hand all over it. In desperation, I race to the far end of the fence, scanning the tree line and neighboring fields. My chest tightens with every second that passes without movement. They get out all the time, but never through a propped-open gate. Plus, they don't wander far. They usually come to the porch to show off their escape.

My hands shake as I pull out my phone and call my dad. He answers on the third ring. "Hey, Lottie."

"The goats are gone." My words tumble over each other. "All of them, and the gate is open like someone left it open. Did you move them?"

"What? No," he says immediately. "I ran into town early for an appointment to get new tires. Everything looked normal when I left at six."

My pulse roars in my ears. "Are you sure you didn't let them out to play and maybe forgot?"

"Like I said, everything was normal when I left. I didn't have time to let them out." He sighs, like he already knows something's wrong. "We both know this is the game they play."

"This isn't them breaking out. Gates don't just magically prop open. Someone let my goats out on purpose."

"Don't go accusing your mom just because you two had a falling out at work."

The words feel like a slap. "I didn't even say her name," I snap, even though I absolutely was thinking it.

"You were about to," he says, "and that's not fair. I bet if you look, you'd see her car gone too."

I do a visual sweep of the driveway, where only my Land Rover is parked. "You're right. Nobody is here now, but someone opened the gate."

"I'm just saying—"

"I have to go," I cut in and end the call before he can finish.

My hands shake harder as I go back to my recent calls and press Ty's name.

"Hey, Queen," he greets me.

"Did you just call me Queen?" I gasp, my breath hitching at the swooniest thing I've ever heard. But I'm dizzy with worry for my missing goats, and I can't think straight.

"I guess I did. Is that okay?"

"No, I mean... yes. But not now. I don't have time to flirt, because my goats are gone. The gate got left open, and no one is here. I'm panicking."

"Did you check the flower gardens?" he asks. "They like to get in there. Or—"

"I already checked, and they aren't there!" I hate that I'm losing patience for small talk, but I'm struggling to breathe with my racing heart, and I'm sucking air as I jog along the fence line. "They bust out of their pen all the time, but they never leave, and the fence wasn't broken. It was perfectly intact. Someone opened it. I just, I don't understand why my mom would—"

"Wait," he says too slowly for my rising panic. "Why would your mom want your goats gone?"

"I don't know." My voice shakes as I hold in my fears. "But she hates them. She hates that they're mine. And she hates I—" I stop, breathless, bracing a hand on my fear-weakened knees to pant. "I don't know. I don't know. I just know they're gone."

This can't be happening.

Any second they could be getting run over.

I need to find them before they die!

"Okay," he says calmly. "Take a breath. I have to finish up my exit interview today, but I'll let them know I have an emergency and come as soon as I can."

We hang up, but I don't hang up my search. I race through the tall grass, my flip-flops sliding in fresh mud as I cut across the field. My lungs burn, but I don't slow, remembering one time the goats got out—I found them down by the creek. It was fine then; the water was low. But it's not low now. The creek is much fuller now, and I'm not sure they can swim. Panic propels me to run as hard as my heart will allow until I skid to a stop at the field's edge.

They're there!

Splashing like idiots, they butt each other playfully near the water's edge. Toast is eating something I can't identify, but they all look unbothered and *alive.*

My knees give out.

I collapse into the grass, half sobbing, half laughing. My hands press into the earth as my chest caves under relief and tears cascade down my cheeks.

Hot tears.

The kind my mother calls weak. Out of habit, I press my face into my hands to stop them, but they pour out—relief so sharp it hurts. This goes deeper than the goats. It's years of pent-up emotions I've blocked, and the dam has finally been breached. It's fear I didn't let myself feel, and anger I've swallowed for decades.

And guilt.

Because I assumed my mom did this. It made sense—she's the type to take something I love and call it a lesson.

I swipe at my face, and I smile at my incredibly naughty goats. There's something wrong in not trusting my own mother. The fact I instantly assumed this was her doing tells me more about the choices I need to make ahead than anything else. Overwhelming relief floods me, and I sink to the ground, cross-legged, letting the tears fall freely. My face is hot and wet. I don't wipe the tears away, because I don't want to stop. I don't want to be told to stop.

I don't know how long it lasts, but I'm no longer crying when I hear footsteps behind me. I don't flinch because I'm numb. Then weight settles beside me. I glance sideways and see Ty's sneakers, mud-splattered at the toes. He plops down beside me, close enough our arms touch. After a second, his hand finds mine.

We stay like that, watching the goats wander farther down the creek. I have to scoot forward a few feet to keep them in view. Ty scoots too and eventually breaks the silence. "You were crying."

My voice comes out wrecked but honest. "Yeah. And it felt good." I'm surprised by the truth.

"You probably need to cry." His thumb rubs a slow circle on my hand. "You had a lot of stress these past couple weeks. Not to mention being let go from your job." He pulls back enough to look at me. "Not to rush you, but we should maybe get them back in the pen before they go too far down the creek," he says gently. "The creek looks pretty deep down there."

I look past him, at the house in the distance. The weight of all the unhappy years that linger inside those walls crashes over me, and I'm relieved I've run out of tears. All I have left is a shake of my head. "No. I'm not putting them back in the pen. I'm loading them in their trailer."

"Okay," he says. "Do you know where you're going?"

"Away." I stand, shoulders squared, ready to do what I must.

With Ty on my heels, I storm up to my room, and I fling open the closet doors, grabbing my old duffel bag. I'm half surprised all my clothes are still hanging neatly like I left them, and my mom didn't use the opportunity to publicly donate my stuff to Goodwill for PR. I can't even laugh at the ridiculous thoughts flying through my head as I tug the zipper a bit harder than necessary.

"Lottie, what in the world is going on?" My mom stands in the doorway, arms crossed, mouth thin. "You're being awfully loud."

I don't look at her. In one sweep, I scoop all my T-shirts from the closet and dump them into the open bag, hangers and all. Ty steps forward quietly, tugging at the hangers to help the shirts fit better. Neither of us looks at my mom, but I grunt, "What are you doing home in the middle of the day?"

"I came when your father texted me the goats were lost. Ham and I both did, but when we pulled up, we saw them on their leashes and tied to the porch. Did they not want to go back in their pen?"

I give her a side-eye. Like she cares about my goats enough to come home midday. She's clearly concerned about something else. "I didn't put them in their pen because I'm going to load them up and take them with me. I'm moving."

Her head tips to the side. "What are you talking about?"

"Just what I said." I open my sock drawer, decide I need everything, and dump the entire drawer into my bag before sliding it back. Her eyes widen as she watches. "I can't be here anymore."

Her head tilts away from me, as if she wishes to add physical distance. She plants her hands on her hips, exactly how she always does before taking control of a conversation. "Lottie, where do you think you will go with three goats?"

"I'll figure it out." Refusing to cower, I level my gaze with hers, and widen my stance, stamping determination on my face. We enter a silent stare down.

It's quiet for a long beat before Ty steps forward. "Hey." His voice is soft. "I'll help you move, but not like this."

My mom lets out a humorless laugh and brushes off his words with a flick of her wrist. "How noble of you, Ty."

He remains loose, seemingly unaffected by her insults. "I don't want her leaving hurt."

"You don't want?" my mom snaps. "This isn't about what *you* want. You've already caused enough damage. I had everything planned for Lottie with Bodan. If it weren't for you butting in, she'd be on her way to the Senate in a few years. Now she can't even take care of herself without a job. Let alone those goats. She'll be lucky to find a job bagging groceries after the scandal you two created. What a joke."

Tension coils through me before I cough out, "Mom—"

Before I can yell about all the ways she has damaged me, Ty steps in front of me—not blocking me but inserting himself into the conversation. "You can be angry," he says evenly. "I get that. But you don't get to speak to Lottie like that."

As much as I want to avoid eye contact with my mom, I have to see her expression. No one has ever spoken up for me like that, and she's not going to take it lightly. My mom blinks several times while her body stiffens. "Excuse me? Is that how you talk to a senator?"

"Look," Ty continues, "Lottie's allowed to make her own decisions, even if they aren't what you want. She's put up with your demands for far too long."

I go numb.

Ty is really doing this.

He's standing up to my mom, who I turn to, bracing for smoke to shoot from her ears as she goes ballistic. Her eyes narrow, and she snaps back in a mocking tone, "You think you're going to be Lottie's savior?"

"No, she doesn't need a savior. This isn't about that." He reaches back and touches my hand. "I care about her deeply, but I also care about your family. I've known you all for years. That's why I don't want her running away while things are unresolved—but that doesn't mean I'm standing back and letting you bully her."

My heart melts. I didn't know shy Ty, the boy I've known since I was in grade school, had it in him to stand up to my mom. He stays fixed on her, going off without wavering, "And while I'm at it, I want to address the hockey comments you've made. I've worked hard to get where I am. I'm good at what I do, and I make a great living. Thousands of guys would die to be in my position. I won't apologize for anything. I know you look down on me because I don't have some corporate, bow tie-wearing job. I don't care what you think."

He steps back, positioning himself next to me. "If you want to salvage any relationship you have left with your daughter, you need to get over yourself," Ty continues. "Because from now on, anyone who disrespects her answers to me."

And ... my jaw drops.

Heavy silence presses in.

A frown sags on my mother's lips, and I brace for the lecture to end all lectures. The world is likely to tilt off its axis from the explosion she's about to have. Ty has no clue what he's set into motion. I cringe and wait.

"You remind me of someone." She zeroes in on Ty. She's not yelling, but shockingly calm. "Or I should say you remind me of someone who promised me the world and left me standing in the wreckage when it fell apart."

I hold my breath, unsure where she's going with this sob story. She's not screaming yet, but it must be coming ...

Ty nods once. "I'm sorry that happened to you, but I'm not that person."

My mom stares at the floor, and I start to doubt she'll explode. Her expression is completely foreign to me and heavy. "Lottie, I was only trying to protect you," she says with a hitch in her voice.

I tuck in my chin and peer at her. "Protect me from what?"

Her hard expression softens, sadness lurking behind her eyes. "I don't need to go into all the details now. Just know I was young once too."

I've never felt sorry for my mom, but a tinge of sympathy rises in me. Whatever happened to her definitely had an impact. She looks at Ty. "I don't like this. I know your type, and you're clearly going to break her heart and ruin her life."

"I won't promise not to hurt her," he says calmly. "Promises like that are easy to say and easy to break."

Mom's mouth tightens, and my heart sinks.

What is he even saying?

"But I will promise this," he continues, not breaking eye contact with her. "I will never make her earn my love. I will never walk away when things get hard. And if she decides tomorrow she doesn't want me anymore, I'll let her go—because all I want is for her to be happy."

He breaks eye contact with my mom and turns to me. My heart nearly stops when he adds, "That's how I won't break her heart. By treating her like her happiness matters more than my own."

A bomb could explode in the room, and no one would flinch. I desperately want to fling my arms around Ty and kiss him, but my mom glares like we're two teens in over our heads. I'm not sure she'll ever accept I'm living my own life. Her lips roll in slowly, and she nods several times, as if the bobbing motion soothes her. After a beat, she simply says, "Okay."

"Okay?" I repeat, unsure what she's okay with.

"Yes, okay." She nods faster. "You're an adult, as you so rudely pointed out, so I'm getting out of the way." She wags her finger at Ty and back to me. "But let's be real here for a moment. You won't find anywhere to take those goats. Why don't you leave them here until you find a place? It's their home too."

I crinkle my nose. "Since when do you care about the goats?"

"I don't care about them. I just know the trouble they cause. I can imagine if you try to board them somewhere, they'll get into trouble, and it's all over social media—"

"Ah!" I cut her off but then stop. She's worried the goats will bring public drama. Shaking my head, I bite my tongue while Ty smiles at me, as if to help me stay quiet. My mom will never change. That doesn't mean I can't change how I react to her and how I let her arrogance affect me. Today, I'm choosing to stay unbothered. "Okay, Mom, deal. I'll leave the goats here. I guess it doesn't hurt to stay in the guest cabin until I have a new place, but it's going to be sooner than you think."

"Fine." Her voice ticks up, like she's taking control of the conversation again. "I have meetings tonight and have to leave again, so make sure you get them back in the pen." She starts walking away but pauses at my doorway. Without looking back, she says, "If you need a reference for work, I'm happy to help with..." her voice trails off, and she murmurs, "Just give Brett a call, and he'll get you what you need."

"Sure." My voice is so quiet I doubt she hears it. She's never been generous with her time and has already turned on her heel and headed down the hall. Once her footfalls hit the steps, the tension finally drains from my body, and I sag onto the edge of my bed with an exaggerated groan.

Plopping down next to me, Ty pulls me into him. I don't resist, practically crashing into his chest. "Are you okay?"

I nod against his chest. "Thank you for not letting me run away with my goats like a crazy person. I was so stressed out."

"It's what I'm here for." His lazy smile is back, as if assuring me our lives will be smooth from here on out.

"That was emotionally exhausting. I didn't expect her to speak to you like that—or you to her. You were amazing. She was terrifying."

"Ah, she was easy. She didn't even throw anything."

"Yet."

He laughs as he hooks a finger under my chin. I grin as his eyes soften in the way that pulls me to him, and I lean until our lips press together. Despite the stress of the day, the kiss is light and playful, and I can feel him smile. When we pull back, he locks eyes with me. "I didn't mean to take over. Are you sure you're okay staying here?"

"Yeah," I say softly. "Mom and I are good at faking nice to each other, and you said if she's rude to me, you'll take care of her. I guess I will just call you if anything happens."

"You know," he says, looking down at me, his eyes dancing, "you're welcome to stay with me at the Four Seasons. I'm here for a few more days. I can sleep on the floor."

I wrinkle my nose. "Absolutely not. I don't like the idea of leaving my goats because they're so naughty. I need to be here." I crash back onto my bed, and he stretches out beside me, his arm wrapping behind my shoulders like it's always belonged there.

"So," I say with a sigh, "what do you want to do now?"

"This." He smiles down at me as he wraps his other arm around me, and I snuggle closer. Outside, the goats are probably eating chunks of the porch for lunch, but I don't care because I'm wrapped up in the moment.

I smile from the inside out. I stood up to my mom. Ty and I are together. And I'm finally making my own decisions. Good or bad doesn't matter—only that they're mine. I glance up at Ty, the best decision I've ever made.

"Yeah, let's do this."

Thirty-Seven

Tyson

A week later

THE U-HAUL IS PACKED tighter than I thought possible, especially for someone who has never had her own place. Man, Lottie has stuff; boxes in every size and shape, labeled in her loopy handwriting, are stacked neatly in every inch of the trailer.

Ham hauls the last box up the ramp while I wrestle with a bag of feed that apparently weighs a lot more than I thought. All three goats circle the trailer like they're trying to solve the mystery of what's going on. Once Crunch realizes I'm carrying a bag of his food, he runs straight for me. I extend my leg, putting a foot between us. "Don't even think about it."

My stern warning doesn't deter him, and he swerves around my foot, and butts his head into the sack like he's trying to break it open with his sharp horns. "Stop it," I yell.

Lottie giggles. "You have to speak their language." Before I can ask what that means, she drops to her knees in the dirt and cups her hands around Crunch's tiny face. Then she proceeds to do the most ludicrous thing I've ever seen her do.

She bleats.

And not just a little one.

But she's fully committed and in perfect pitch. It's absolute insanity, and she's clearly lost her mind. Somehow it works. Crunch turns to her, seeming to forget about the bag of food long enough for me to scurry up the ramp and place it out of reach. It's like she's flipped a switch, and they trot toward her, their tails flicking.

I lose it. This woman is kneeling in the dirt, making goat noises without a shred of self-consciousness, and I've never loved anyone more in my life.

The thought hits me so hard I have to act on it.

I grab her wrist and tug her to me before I can overthink it. She stumbles into my chest and gapes at me with surprised eyes. "What—" she starts.

"I love whatever is wrong with you."

"Wow," she murmurs. Her smile turns slow and dangerous. "Did you just seriously say the L word?"

Jolting my head back, I realize I did. I mean, I didn't mean to blurt it out. It slipped into that sentence, but I don't regret it. I lower my face to level my gaze with hers, pulling deep eye contact. "I guess I did, and I do. I love you."

"I love you too." She leans in, brushing her nose against mine. I'm about to go in for a kiss when the moment is broken.

"Okay," Ham says loudly, leaning against the trailer. "As touching as that was, I'm still a little lost about everything. Where exactly are you two disappearing to?"

Lottie turns toward Ham. I don't want to let her go, so I hook my thumb through the loop on the back of her jeans. She smiles, glancing back at me, then looks to Ham again.

"Mapleton," she says. "Dad offered to let me stay at the lake house rent-free, since no one's there to keep an eye on it anyway. The second he offered, I knew it was right. It's home—more than DC ever was."

He nods, thoughtful. "And are you going to live off a money tree?"

"I haven't the slightest idea." She shrugs a little too whimsically for a conversation about finances. "I have lots of savings since I saved so much living at home. That will buy me time to figure something out. Whatever it is, I know it's going to be something normal, so I blend in. I'm so tired of being the senator's daughter."

"And you?" Ham turns to me next. "Your tournament is over. You play in Minnesota. How are you planning to make this work?"

I lift one shoulder in a shrug that's carefully casual. "I don't have a plan, but I know it's going to work. It has to."

I don't say more. I press my bottom lip in, sealing off any more details. I have something I'm working on in secret but don't want to risk ruining everything. My attention shifts to Lottie as she coaxes Toast toward the horse trailer, and I can't help but smile.

"Help me get these goats in the trailer." She looks back at me, the fading sunlight catching the side of her face in a way that leaves me breathless. "We should probably hit the road soon if we want to beat rush hour."

"Do you need to say goodbye to your parents?" I step forward, falling into pace beside her as we scramble to herd the goats toward the ramp. I've got some unfinished business with Crunch, so I square up to him like I know what I'm doing—which is my first mistake. He spots the trailer immediately and drops to the ground like he'd rather die than get in it.

"I said goodbye this morning. Don't worry, it was amicable." She nabs Toast by his collar and leads him into the trailer without any problems. "Besides, I'll see my mom in about a month when she comes to Mapleton. I guess that's one of the good things about choosing Mapleton. I get to move away from my parents, but since that's also their home, I'll see them enough."

"And since my parents still live there," I chime in, "I can visit a lot too." Stepping forward, I grab Crunch's collar, and try to pull him up, but, surprise, he won't budge. "Look," I say as I widen my stance and prepare to carry a heavy load. "You don't scare me." I lean forward. Since he's anchoring himself to the ground, it makes it easy for me to scoop him up, all two hundred pounds, and waddle my way to the trailer. With a grunt and a huff, I get him in there, with Cinnamon trotting along after. She must have seen the others leave and decided she didn't want to get left behind. I back out of the trailer and shut the door, panting like I just finished working out.

"All right." I turn back to Lottie, wiping my hands on my pants. "I'm ready when you are."

Lottie turns to Ham. "Are you sure you're okay driving the goats all by yourself?"

"Please, it will feel like a vacation driving alone. I'm looking forward to it."

"Okay." Lottie looks to me, then back at Ham. "Let's do this." Ham turns and climbs into his truck, already hitched to the goat trailer, while Lottie and I head for the U-Haul. I slide into the driver's seat and take a minute to adjust the mirror and buckle my seat belt. When I start the engine, I notice she's staring at me. "What?"

"Are you sure you can drive this?"

"I just won a national hockey tournament against the best guys in the country. I'm pretty sure I can handle a U-Haul, even if it's pulling your Land Rover." Of course, I fail to mention that I've never driven anything bigger than a standard SUV, but she doesn't need to know that.

"Okay, then." She relaxes into her seat, and I wait for Ham to pull out first, clearing the way. Then I shift into gear and ease forward. I'm quiet as I concentrate on getting a feel for the road, and Lottie pulls out her phone. "Oh, Brett sent me a message. Wonder what he wants?"

"Bow Tie Brett?" I struggle not to sound jealous. She doesn't work for her mom anymore. He doesn't need to be messaging her personal phone. "What does he want?"

"It looks like a video." She clicks on it as her eyes widen. "Oh, great, it's a video of my mom's press conference from this morning. I can just imagine—" Her voice trails off as her mom's voice starts to play, and I'll admit I hold my breath so I can hear it better. The woman scares me.

"Senator Halloway, you've previously expressed disdain for the hockey players, but it turns out Tyson Lane, one of the players who is originally from one of your voting districts, led his team to winning the tournament. Have you changed your opinion of him at all?"

My jaw drops as I grip the steering wheel until my knuckles turn white.

"Thank you for the question. I would like to address this issue. As you said, Tyson Lane is from Mapleton, but he's more than that—He's a fine young man, who's dating my daughter. He's my future son-in-law. I couldn't be prouder of him."

I slam my gaze to Lottie's. My ears have finally lost all function, because it sounded like she said she was proud of me, and I know that can't be right. There's no way I actually earned her respect. "What did she say?"

"I need to hear that again too." She presses the back button and replays the video. We listen in silence, making sure we heard what we thought we heard. When it's over, Lottie places her phone in her lap and sighs. "Now that you're a national hero this week, she's using you for votes. I'm so sorry."

I smile and drop a hand from the wheel, feeling more confident driving the U-Haul now. "I'm not sorry, and remember, you aren't apologizing for her anymore."

Silence lingers, both of us seemingly lost in thought at Lottie's Mom's declaration.

Lottie shifts in her seat and takes a drink from her water bottle. "It doesn't bother you," she says, breaking the silence, "that she basically lied and said we were engaged? We aren't. Oh—wait. Brett just texted. Look at that. My mom's rumors are already getting out of hand. He wants me to confirm if I'm your fiancée or not. What the—can you believe my mom is at it again?"

I don't answer right away, still focused on getting a feel for driving this thing. Can't show weakness. The road stretches out in front of us, fields on either side. It's not lost on me that this was Lottie's home, and she's leaving it all behind.

"Tell him I'm not your fiancé...yet." I sneak a look at her to tease her, but she stares back with wide eyes and a pouty grin that undoes me. I can't believe how lucky I am. "But you are my queen." The word queen lands softly, not heavy like I've been practicing it for an entire decade.

She smiles, her eyelids lowering sweetly. "No one's ever said something like that to me without wanting something in return."

"Well, you better get used to it, because from here on out, it's you and me—and you're all I see." I take a left onto the highway and head off into our next chapter.

Epilogue

The Following July

THE OLD DOCK CREAKS in the familiar way that welcomes us, but that's not important. What's important is the lake looks exactly how it's supposed to. Like July. Wearing Ty's holey hockey jersey with pride, I lean back, my bare feet dangling inches above the surface. I hardly take the jersey off when I'm at the house, except for washing it, but it's by far my favorite thing to lounge in.

"Do you remember," Ty says, tipping his head back as he relaxes and gazes at the blue sky above, "that time you were wearing Ham's big flip-flops and you lost your balance and tripped while you were running down this dock, and you dumped your ice water all over me?"

"I did not dump it," I say, laughing. "I shared it lovingly with you."

"Oh, is that what you are calling it?"

"Yes, I was being thoughtful." I grin at the memory. "I remember you laughed so hard, because I fell in the water."

"I remember thinking"—he glances at me, his eyes soft— "that I was actually a little glad it happened, because you grabbed a towel and tried to help wipe my arm off. I was so shy, I could barely speak. You touching me was too much."

"Yeah, right." I tease back. "That was, like, so many years ago. You didn't like me then. That was the summer you brought that girlfriend here."

He blinks. "What girlfriend?"

I turn onto my side, propping my head on my hand. "Oh, come on. What was her name? Brinley or was it Brenna? Talk about flip-flops—her high-heel wedges clomped the ground when she walked. Talk about annoying."

"You're making this up." He shakes his head. "She was not my girlfriend."

"Am not." I gesture with my hands as I go on, "She had this smile—kind of upside down, only showing her bottom teeth. I couldn't make that face if I tried."

He laughs, shaking his head. "I don't remember her at all."

"Please, now you're lying, because you know she was annoying! There is no way you could forget the way she clung to you like you were her pet."

"I genuinely have no idea who you're talking about," he says. "But apparently you wrote her autobiography. What's up with that?"

I shrug, smiling at the lake. "I might have been jealous."

"Interesting." He nods. "Maybe I brought her here for that reason."

"Wait. What?" I whip my head toward him. "So you do remember her! You're lying. Was she actually your girlfriend?"

He just smiles—the maddening, lazy grin that gives nothing away. "I might have had my own fake-date situation going on—for my very own important reasons."

"Stop! You did not." I narrow my eyes as I dip my toes in the water and splash water at him.

He doesn't even flinch when a generous splash washes over his legs. "I don't remember exactly anymore, but she's not important." He reaches out, brushing the edge of my jersey. "You know," he says casually, "I wish you wouldn't wear my name all the time."

"What does that mean?" I frown. "You gave me this jersey. Are you embarrassed?"

Sighing, he leans forward and grabs something from the cooler at his side. It's rolled up tight, and he holds it out. "Put this on."

"I don't need a towel," I say automatically.

"It's not a towel." He pushes it forward. "This one doesn't have a hole in it either."

I stare as my heart sinks. "I love wearing your holey jersey. Why would I want to wear that?"

"Just take it. A friend gave me this one; you should wear it. I'm tired of seeing my name on you."

"What do you mean tired of your name on me?" Half mad, I snatch the jersey and hold it up. As it unrolls, a box lands in my lap—a tiny velvet jewelry box. My lips part in awe as I can't tear my gaze from it. "Ty, what is that?"

"You know exactly what that is." He watches me like this is the exact reaction he hoped for. "Open it."

"I don't think I can. My hands are frozen."

Retrieving the box, he opens it and holds it so I can see. My brain tells me the sun is glinting, or something is playing a trick on my eyes, but I stare so long I can't deny it. It's a ring.

A thin band set with a single stone—simple, not flashy, but more than enough. My breath rushes out of me in a whisper. "Oh." I look back at him, and memories hit me all at once: scraped knees on this dock, every July we've spent here, almosts and what-ifs, and the way he looked that night in the Land Rover when we almost kissed.

"So, ah," he says, "I think it's time we give you the same name as me. Then, when you're wearing my jersey, it's both our names. What do you think?"

I laugh once at his casual proposal. "You hid a ring in a jersey."

He shrugs. "Does that surprise you?"

"I need to see the full presentation," I tease. "Like, you're going to have to get on a knee for this one."

He exhales but doesn't hesitate. One knee hits the dock, and he reaches for my hand, sliding the ring onto my finger. It fits perfectly. "Lottie, will you marry me?"

Tears well, blurring him and the lake as I hyperfocus on him. "Yes," I whisper, letting the tears flow freely down my face.

His lazy grin slants on his lips. One hand frames my face; the other swipes at a tear from beneath my eye. The tenderness steals my breath before our lips even touch. His mouth finds mine in a kiss that asks and answers all at once. When we pull back, he motions toward the jersey again. "Put it on."

"What?" Confused, I grab the purple jersey and hold it up. "Are there earrings in here too?"

"No." He chuckles, holding out the shirt so I can see it. It's not anything close to his Minnesota Jersey. Now, I'm confused as to why I'd want a random jersey. I read it once, then again.

"Where'd you even get this jersey?" I ask.

"I told you, a friend gave it to me." A sly smile spreads on his lips. "Remember Bill Baker? I used to play for him here in Mapleton."

"Yeah, didn't he lose the team over some scandal?"

"Yeah, well, his stepson owns it now. Bill still has his hands in it, but he's starting an NHL expansion team here in Vermont, and I'm on it."

"Say what?" I swear I see tears glistening in Ty's eyes as his smile grows wider than ever.

"Yeah, I started hearing rumors when I was in DC, but I wasn't sure what I wanted to do—because you were still in DC. When everything with your mom went down and you chose to come here, I knew what I wanted. Bill wasn't ready to sign players yet; he had to pass a character test, and the NHL wasn't sure they wanted to take a risk on him. After months of league meetings and board approvals, he finally got the green light and called me last week." He gestures to the jersey. "So … what do you say? You put this on, and we make Mapleton our forever home? We buy this place from your parents, and we make July last for ollways."

For a second, I can't speak. This dock, this house—they've been the beginning and the breaking of so many things in my life. I look down at the jersey in my hands, then at the ring catching the light, then sweep my gaze back to him. My throat tightens, but I push through it. "I say," I manage, smiling through tears, "I like the sound of that. Ollways July."

He lets out a breath that turns into a laugh as I pull the jersey over my head. I barely get it straight before his hands find my waist, and he leans in for another kiss. From the other side of this dock, and in their pen, Crunch bleats. I can't help laughing into Ty's mouth, and he chuckles against my lips like he wouldn't trade this moment for anything in the world.

Stars, Stripes, and Hockey Nights

Stars, Stripes, and Hockey Nights: A sweet hockey romantic comedy series where hockey isn't just a game—it's an American tradition. This summer, celebrate our nation's 250th birthday with the swooniest hockey all-stars as they take the ice in a festive exhibition tournament.

When USA's top NHL stars arrive in Washington, DC, they're competing for more than a championship title. Between face-offs and slap shots, these all-American heroes find themselves taking their biggest risk yet—falling in love. Expect prank wars, locker room banter, fireworks—on and off the ice—and sparks that light up more than the scoreboard.

Each book in this closed door romcom series is a complete standalone, featuring a different hockey hero taking his shot at forever. Because love isn't just won in the arena—it's written in the stars and stripes of the heart.

Available titles in this series:

Oh Say Can You See by **J.P. Sterling**

By the Dawn's Early Light by **Tia Marlee**

What so Proudly We Hail by **Marion De Ré**

At the Twilight's Last Gleaming by **Ellie Hall**

Stripes & Bright Stars by **Faith Carter**

Through the Perilous Fight by **Elana Johnson**

O'er the Ramparts We Watched by **Larrissa Hommes**

So Gallantly Streaming by **Dulcie Dameron**

Rocket's Red Glare by **Kerry Evelyn**

The Bombs Bursting in Air by **Dineen Miller**

Gave Proof through the Night by **Gigi Blume**

Our Flag Was Still There by **Leah Busboom**

Home of the Brave by **Brittney Mulliner**

Binge the series: https://www.amazon.com/dp/B0GDY2T6S4

And something amazing! Did you know we have a limited-edition, custom-made coloring book and reading log to go with this series! It comes with a full-sized sticker sheet and available now.

Grab your coloring book

here: https://authorelanajohnson.com/products/stars-stripes-an

d-hockey-nights-coloring-book-and-reading-journal

Take your love of sweet hockey romance to the next level with this pre-signed limited-edition coloring book and reading journal. Color your way through the 13-book *Stars, Stripes, and Hockey Nights* series, rate each story, discover new authors, and celebrate the series one page at a time.

Character Cast

Lottie Halloway: brother is Ham, mom is a senator, Lottie Dah (nickname from Ty)

Tyson Lane: in love with Lottie for years, best friend is Ham, hockey defensemen

Hamilton/Ham Halloway: best friend is Tyson, sister is Lottie, mom is a senator, head of security for his mom

Brett/Bow Tie: works for Senator Halloway's campaign

Senator Halloway: Lottie and Ham's mom.

Dad Halloway: retired professor

Bodan Bowey: Lottie's fake date, works at the Smithsonian

Coach Badaszek: head coach for the U.S. Stars team.

Taz Houlihan: Tyson's friend who plays in the NHL and on the Stripes team

Maddie: Long time friend who used to date Taz Houlihan

Bryce Chambers: left defense hockey player from Denver on the Stars team

Hartman: hockey player on the Stars team

Stone: hockey player on the Stars team

Kingston: hockey player on the Stars team

Leniecker: hockey player on the Stars team

Jeremiah Precio: hockey player on the Stars team

Baptiste Marchand: hockey player on the Stripes team

DiFranco: hockey player on the Stars team

Stagmeire: hockey player on the Stripes team

Jake Twiles: hockey player on the Stars team

Ted Powell: hockey player on the Stars team

Blake Davis: hockey player on the Stripes team

Beau Tucker: an oil tycoon billionaire, married to Clover

Trey Micheals: tech billionaire

Chase Sullivan: hockey player on the Stripes team

Reeves: hockey player on the Stripes team

Hank Bowey: Bodan's grandfather. Pulitzer Prize winning author

Jayce: hockey player on the Stripes team

Dashiell DiFranco: hockey player on the Stripes team

Levi: hockey player on the Stars team

Dante: hockey player on the Stripes team

Animals:

Cinnamon: Lottie's female goat, doesn't get into trouble unless the others pressure her

Toast: Lottie's goat, who responds only to Lotti

Crunch: Lottie's goat, the instigator

Introducing Dreamers Hockey

Some of you guessed it—and trust me, it's even better than you imagined.

It's three brothers on the same team!!!

Bill Baker is back and causing problems (as usual), teaming up with rival-turned-bestie Blake Anton and pulling his three sons straight into the NHL spotlight. Preston, Peyton and Paul are chasing their dreams on the ice... but off the ice?

That's where things get dangerous.

Because dreams are easy.

Love? Not so much.

The Dreamers: Where chasing the dream is easy... falling in love is not.

The first book is coming this September! *Mug Shot* is a flirty neighbors-to-kisses romcom about a hockey captain who lives by the rules and the girl next door who keeps rewriting them. A feel-good story about discovering that home might be the person across the hall.

Preorder available now: https://www.amazon.com/dp/B0H2N2G5Q5

Acknowledgements

I am so incredibly excited—and grateful—to finally take a moment to thank everyone who cheered on this project.

Kerry and Elana, thank you for all the things. I can't begin to list all the ways you contributed. This project simply wouldn't exist without you. It has been such a gift to work alongside you both, and I hope you love this series as much as I do.

To all the authors in this lineup, it has been an absolute pleasure working with each of you. Thank you for trusting the process and jumping in with us on this wonderfully crazy dream.

To my editing team—Rebecca, Karen, and Sara—thank you for your time. And to my ARC readers, while I can't name you all, I want to give a special thank you to Jane, Debbie, and Bernadette for always being so generous with their time and sending me those sneaky little typos.

To our scream team—your support means more than you know. Heather, you are such an incredible champion for the book community. And Kim, Valarie, Louise, and so many others—seeing you all support these books is truly humbling.

To the readers!!!!!!! We know a hockey + Fourth of July mashup might not be the most expected combination but you embraced it, and that means everything.

And Rebecca, our amazing designer, you've been with me through four shared worlds now, and your creativity, patience, and talent continue to bring these stories to life in the best ways. These series wouldn't be what they are without you.

To my narrator team, Kasey and Kyle. You both are an absolute gift to voice acting.

To my family, who lovingly puts up with me living in fictional worlds half the day.

God, my Father in Heaven. No explanation needed.

I know I've missed people, and I'm so sorry if I did but please know how deeply grateful I am.

Free Gift

Driving Miss Crazy is a fun novella to introduce you to Mapleton's newest AHL hockey team, Granite Ice. You'll get a glimpse of the world in this sweet read that's meant to be consumed in two-three hours. It has no cliffhangers, a guaranteed HEA, all the swoons, but no explicit scenes. If you love this book, then you'll want to continue with my Sweet Hockey Romcom series already in Kindle Unlimited and ready for you to binge.

Grab your free gift here! https://bookhip.com/SCSWDRP

About J.P. Sterling

J.P. Sterling grew up watching old reruns of Lucille Ball and Mary Tyler Moore and fell in love with wholesome entertainment and slapstick comedy. She loves leaning into the over-the-top humor and full circle moments, especially if it means the underdog gets to shine.

Aside from writing, she's also a wife, homeschooling mom, a holistic dietitian, a former college professor, and lover of all-things dark chocolate.

*No swears. Just kisses. No Blasphemies. *

Let's get social!

Hey, you amazing reader! You are invited to join my private reader group for all-things clean books and friends. Enter the group here: https://www.facebook.com/groups/150085076408 1965

Other places to follow me:

Instagram: https://www.instagram.com/stories/authorjpsterli ng/

Facebook: https://www.facebook.com/jpsterlingauthor/

Amazon: https://www.amazon.com/stores/author/B01N9TJ XJN/about

Also by J.P. Sterling

<u>Dreamers Hockey</u>

Mug shot (Coming September 2026)

<u>Stars, Stripes, and Hockey Nights (All Standalones)</u>

Oh, Say Can You See

<u>Sweet Hockey RomCom (All Standalones)</u>

The Pucker-Up Pact

Shot Through the Heart

All I Need is my Glove

Till Sudden Death Do Us Part

<u>Sweet Hockey RomCom Adjacent (Standalone)</u>

Driving Miss Crazy

<u>Rivalry Rewritten (Duet)</u>

An Icicle Made for Two

Some Guys Get All the Pucks

<u>Timeless Christmas Tails (All Standalone)</u>

Have Yourself a Legendary Christmas

<u>Christmas Shenanigans (All Standalone)</u>

Mingle All the Way

Tis the Season to Get Married

Let's Not and Sleigh We Did

Hark! The Hot Santa Sings

<u>The Coffee Loft Series (All Standalones)</u>

Pardon My French Press

No More Mr. Chia Guy

Truely, Madly, Steeply Brew

<u>A Modern Fairy Tale Series (All Standalones)</u>

Royally Rugged

<u>Bosses and Billionaires Series (All Standalones)</u>

Maid for my Billionaire Boss

Knock! Knock! It's Your Enemy Boss

Kissed by My Billionaire Boss

Marooned with My Celebrity Boss

<u>A Heart that Dances Series</u>

Dancing on Broken Ankles

The Stars We See

A Heart that Dances

A Heart that Loves

<u>Water and Stone Duet</u>

Ruby in the Water

Lily in the Stone